I0690310

SPEAK OF THE DEVIL

VEGAS SLAYERS - BOOK 1

CHRISTINE POPE

This is a work of fiction. Names, characters, places, and incidents are either the product of the author's imagination or are used fictitiously. Any resemblance to actual events, places, organizations, or persons, whether living or dead, is entirely coincidental.

SPEAK OF THE DEVIL

Copyright © 2025 by Christine Pope

ISBN: 978-1-946435-82-8

Published by Dark Valentine Press

Cover design by Indie Author Services

Ebook formatting by Indie Author Services

All rights reserved. No part of this book may be reproduced in any form or by any electronic or mechanical means, including information storage and retrieval systems—except in the case of brief quotations embodied in critical articles or reviews—without permission in writing from its publisher, Dark Valentine Press.

Chapter One

—·«⟨ɢ·◉·ɞ⟩»·—

ONE CHANCE.

That was all he had, and Caleb Lockwood knew he needed to seize it...or be stuck in Hell forever.

As soon as he saw the red-haired woman stab her slender blade into Belial's black heart, there was only a second when Caleb could act.

When he and the other demon-kind had begun to swim their way up from Hell, he'd caught a glimpse of two other red-haired women lying dead on the floor of the huge candlelit room he'd seen just beyond the huge gates the demon lord had summoned, women he guessed must have given their lives to provide the enormous power necessary to unlock a portal to the underworld. Once fully open, those gates would have allowed the denizens of the netherworld to escape their prison permanently and begin new lives on Earth.

Until then, though, they were vulnerable.

No one nearby in the cavernous chamber—not the redhead with the sword, not the group of people huddled on the floor a few yards past her, people he couldn't see clearly because of the dimness of the room, not Belial himself—had been paying any particular attention to the pair of dead bodies...or to Caleb.

Why would they? He and his kind were considered the lowest of the low in the underworld's hierarchy, those who'd had the misfortune to have their demon blood mixed with that of humans.

And that meant he didn't owe the demons swarming in the Stygian blackness behind him a damn thing. They could stay in Hell and rot.

Just as the hellgate fell to nothing around him as Belial drew his last, unlamented breath, Caleb made the leap into the body of the nearest woman. Maybe he was only a quarter-demon, but he could still possess a human being. Not for days or months or even years the way some of Hell's citizens could if they were sufficiently motivated, but he didn't need nearly that long.

Just an hour or so.

It was horribly confining in there, though, giving him the sensation of being trapped in a room with the walls closing in from all sides. He'd never possessed a dead person before, and the feeling of the woman's body shutting down cell by cell made him feel as if he couldn't quite breathe.

Don't panic, he told himself. *You'll be out of here soon enough.*

Which he was. Because he couldn't open the dead woman's eyes, he was unable to see what exactly had happened in the aftermath of the confrontation with Belial. A confusion of voices, some that were brisk and official, obviously police and paramedics and anyone else who'd appeared to clean up a scene that even Caleb had to admit must have been a colossal mess.

He was placed on a gurney—well, the woman's body was, anyway—and wheeled out to an ambulance, then roughly loaded inside. It wasn't as if they had to worry about jarring their patient, not when she was already dead.

No sirens, either, no frenzied rush to the hospital to try to save her. She'd been dead for at least ten or fifteen minutes when Caleb leaped into her body, far past any need for heroic efforts.

But then he got what he wanted, which was to have her moved off the gurney and into a locker at the morgue so they could perform an autopsy at their leisure.

No sound that anyone else was working right then, either. He really hadn't expected anyone to be, not when he could tell it was the middle of the night—or rather, the very early morning, maybe around three or four.

Time to get out of there.

He let his consciousness flow away from the woman's body and take form outside the storage locker, then paused to gulp in some air. Before now, he'd never had any reason to possess someone, much preferring to use his demonic shapeshifting abilities to further his goals—well, to be fair, those had been his father's goals, and he'd only been an unwilling pawn in his schemes—and he thought he'd do whatever he could to avoid possessing a person in the future.

It had been way too cramped in there.

No clothes except the tattered pants he'd worn in Hell, and it was goddamn freezing in here. That was all right, though.

He knew exactly where he needed to go.

The room hadn't changed a bit since he'd lived here, which would be going on ten years now. Caleb wished that he hadn't been able to detect the passage of time while he was in Hell, but part of the torture was knowing exactly how many years and months and days...and minutes and seconds...he'd been trapped there.

Two years, two weeks, and one day, plus a couple of hours.

But who was counting?

Anyway, he'd moved out of the house where he'd grown up as soon as he turned twenty and had bought a place of his own, but his mother didn't seem to have touched a single thing in his former bedroom. Same dark blue-gray paint on the walls, same modern metal and glass furniture. God, she'd hated it when he redecorated the room on his eighteenth birthday, even though his parents had told him he could do whatever he liked with the space.

She probably hadn't believed that he would choose something so jarringly at odds with the Ethan Allen aesthetic of the rest of the house... which was exactly why Caleb had picked out the decor in the first place. Brooke Lockwood never had wanted to acknowledge that the world might not always go her way.

How had she fared these past two years, with both her husband and her only son presumed dead?

Most likely, she'd sailed on serenely as she always had. She'd never been the type to lean toward introspection.

But because she hadn't touched anything, Caleb figured the clothes he'd left behind would still be here as well. He was under no illusions that the loft where he'd been living ever since he moved out had been just as untouched, mainly because Brooke had never approved of the space and thought he should have bought a nice house the way the other quarter-demons of his generation had done.

Not that she'd known they had demon blood running through their veins. No, those guys were only his friends, part of the popular, well-off group that had dominated their high school and then DePauw, the liberal arts college they'd all attended, mostly because it hadn't been considered safe for them to leave Greencastle to get their degrees.

Or maybe that was what Caleb and his friends had been told because it was easier for them to stay where the older generation could keep an eye on them.

After all, those diplomas had just been for show. They'd all known they would get work from either their half-demon fathers or their fathers' half-demon buddies, and wouldn't ever have to worry about making ends meet.

Expression darkening, Caleb went to the dresser and got out some jeans and underwear, a T-shirt, and a pullover hoodie. He'd left these clothes behind when he moved into his loft because they'd been a little too small, but after being trapped in Hell for two years, he'd lost enough weight that they fit him just fine.

He'd need to do something to get that muscle

back on his body. Luckily, the demonic blood in his veins would allow him to build it up without too much work.

The clock on the bedside table told him it was a little past five in the morning. While he briefly considered going to wake up his mother now, he knew she wouldn't appreciate being roused before her usual time for getting out of bed, which had always been eight-thirty for as long as he could remember. When he was younger, they'd had a live-in nanny who drove him to school and made sure he had breakfast, and once he was old enough, his parents both told him he was responsible for getting to school on time.

Nurturing they were not.

Rather than put on one of the old pairs of sneakers he found in the closet, he went over to the bed and climbed on top, even though he didn't bother to pull up the covers. No, he'd just wait here and rest his eyes for a bit, and soon enough, it would be eight-thirty, and he could go downstairs and reveal that he wasn't quite as dead as everyone had thought.

He must have been more tired than he wanted to admit, because when Caleb opened his eyes again, it was now past nine o'clock, much later than he'd wanted to sleep.

Well, Hell could definitely suck the strength right out of you.

Those few hours of sleep had helped, though. He already felt stronger and more awake.

And was that the scent of coffee seeping under the closed bedroom door?

No, he was probably imagining it. Not because he didn't remember that his mother always made coffee as soon as she came downstairs, but just because the house was too big for any smells like that to find their way up to his room on the second floor.

Sunlight slipped past the blinds, and after he got out of bed and tied on his tennis shoes, he went to the window so he could look outside. The sky was half covered in clouds, and all the trees were now bare, the lawn yellow from frost, but Caleb thought the bleak, late autumn landscape was still the most beautiful sight he'd ever seen.

He took a quick detour into the bathroom to splash some water on his face and run damp fingers through his hair. Even though he did his best not to look in the mirror, he couldn't quite avoid catching a glimpse of his face anyway—cheekbones sharper than he remembered, dark eyes shadowed despite those hours of sleep he'd just enjoyed, sandy blond hair a mess.

Hell could definitely do a number on a person.

Scowling a little, he left the bathroom and headed downstairs to the kitchen. Because his father and the rest of that generation had known they might disappear at any time if Belial decided to call them all back to Hell, they'd cooked up several different cover stories to explain such a mass vanishing. The problem was, Caleb didn't know which one Daniel might have left in place with his attorney to cover such a contingency, so he'd have to play this by ear. Even so, he had a feeling there wasn't much he could say to adequately explain where he'd been for the past two years—or where his father had disappeared to.

Unlike his son, Daniel Lockwood appeared to be stuck in Hell permanently.

Good riddance.

Down here, Caleb could definitely smell coffee, although there were no other scents of food being prepared, no eggs or bacon or pancakes or even toast. Brooke Lockwood ate half a grapefruit every damn morning no matter what, and rarely if ever allowed a complex carb or a piece of red meat to pass her lips.

Too bad, because he was damn hungry.

When he entered the kitchen, he saw that she stood with her back to him as she sipped from a china coffee cup and stared out into their backyard, where the pool was covered for the winter and everything looked bare and dead.

No big mugs for her, that was for sure. He recalled the time when he was in third grade and still trying to pretend his family was normal, and he'd bought her a pretty coffee mug painted with roses.

Maybe she'd said thank you. But that mug had disappeared into the cupboard, never to be used a single time.

"Hi, Mom," he said.

Brooke Lockwood turned and stared at him. Some women might have dropped the cup they held out of pure shock, but she was far too disciplined for that.

Very slowly, she set the cup down on the table in the nook.

"You've come back."

Against all odds. However, as much as Caleb might have liked to up-end her carefully ordered world, he knew this wasn't the time for the truth. He'd come here to get what he needed and then disappear again.

"Sort of," he allowed. "I need your help, Mom."

Her mouth thinned. It looked fuller than he remembered, but, considering how much time— and money—she'd spent at medi-spas and had done whatever she could to hold back the march of time, he supposed it wasn't so strange that she might have gotten some more fillers and other work over the past two years.

Still not overdone, though. Brooke Lockwood would never be one of those women with horribly exaggerated lips and brows raised almost to her hairline. No, she looked like herself, albeit a self a good ten or fifteen years younger than her current fifty-five.

"I thought you were dead," she said, ignoring his previous comment. "Where's your father?"

Rotting in Hell where he should be passed through Caleb's mind, although he knew better than to utter those words to his mother. She needed to continue to live in safe ignorance; Daniel Lockwood had never told her the truth about himself or his compatriots, and Caleb saw no reason to tell her the real story now.

Honestly, he didn't think she deserved it.

"Gone," he said briefly. The less he said, the better, since she hadn't revealed what made-up tale had been in play to explain his disappearance. "And he won't be coming back. I assume he left everything in order, though."

Because although the Greencastle demons had been living the high life here on Earth, they'd all known that their tenure in the mortal realm might come to an abrupt end at any time, and therefore they'd been careful to have iron-clad wills set up to ensure that those they left behind would have access to the wealth their families had accumulated over the last several generations. His father had been first among equals, president of the local bank and a millionaire many times over.

Caleb knew his mother wouldn't have been hurting financially these past two years. Whether she'd grieved over the apparent loss of her husband and son was an entirely different matter.

If she had, she showed no sign of it now. Then again, he didn't know why he should have expected anything else from her.

"Of course he made sure everything was taken care of," she said, and her eyes—the same dark brown as his own—narrowed for a moment. "But you still haven't told me where you've been. How is it that you survived the sinking of the boat but stayed away for two years?"

Ah, so that was the story his father had used. A group expedition to go fishing in the Gulf of Mexico, a tragic shipwreck with all hands lost. Very neat, very clean...and no pesky dead bodies to worry about.

"It's better if I don't talk about that," he replied, mostly because he hadn't completely figured out his personal cover story.

For a moment, Brooke only looked at him. Then she said, "You need money, is that it?"

"I do," he replied simply. "I can't stay here. It isn't safe."

Whether that was strictly true, he couldn't say for sure. However, he had to believe that the authorities would have investigated the supposed shipwreck and the disappearance of all the other half- and quarter-demons who'd made Greencastle their home base. Reappearing after so much time had elapsed would only stir up the sort of questions he really didn't want to answer.

For a moment, Brooke was silent. Then she reached for her cup of coffee and took a sip.

She hadn't offered him any, which didn't surprise Caleb too much. Because she wouldn't have been expecting to entertain guests this morning, she would have prepared just enough for herself and no one else.

He made himself wait, knowing this was just another of the endless games she'd played throughout his entire life. Yes, he supposed he could have used his demonic powers to lay hands on the safe he knew was hidden in his parents' bedroom closet and unlock it himself, and yet he still preferred to ask for the money rather than take it without permission.

It would be nice to see if his mother could manage one selfless act.

If not, then he'd empty the safe and disappear

before she even had a chance to figure out what had happened.

"How much?" she asked at length.

Caleb wouldn't allow himself to relax, although he did permit himself an inner sigh of relief. "How much do you have on hand?"

Her mouth compressed again. "Around fifty thousand, give or take. If you want any more than that, then we'll have to wait until the bank opens."

Which was the last thing he wanted to do. Although he knew he could stay hidden at the house while she went to the bank and made the withdrawal, he couldn't help thinking that the sooner he was away from here, the better.

"Fifty grand is fine," he said. "That'll be enough to get me started."

Her dark eyes searched his face. "Get you started where?"

It was a topic he'd already begun to ponder, knowing that returning to Greencastle permanently wasn't an option. Too many explanations he'd have to make...too many questions he wouldn't want to answer. He'd really enjoyed living in L.A., but going back to Southern California also wasn't feasible, not when he knew the *Project Demon Hunters* gang still lived there and might be able to sniff him out. Maybe some might say all was well that ended well, considering the way they'd joined forces and sent the entire Greencastle contingent to Hell along with their master Belial, and yet Caleb had to believe they still carried a grudge.

Better to go someplace where he had no connections...and where presumably they didn't, either.

Hell, contrary to most beliefs, wasn't a place of eternal fire and unending heat. No, it was a world of cold, bitter winds and no shelter, of emptiness and grief and gnawing loneliness.

Caleb needed the exact opposite of that—a place teeming with life around the clock, a place where he could disappear among the crowds and the tourists and the frenetic activity.

"I don't think I can tell you that," he said after a pause.

Brooke regarded him for a moment before she put down her coffee cup once again. "Give me a few minutes."

She left the kitchen while Caleb made himself stay in the spot where he was standing. It would have been way too easy to head over to the cupboard, get out a mug—maybe the rose-painted one she'd scorned so many years ago, just as a little fuck-you—and pour out the rest of the coffee waiting in the carafe of the fancy Breville machine sitting on the counter, but he wasn't going to sink to her level.

No, he'd just get the money and bail, and know that he'd never have to come back here after today.

It wasn't as though she was going to miss that $50K. That much was only pin money to her, and he had no doubt that she'd go to the bank and get what she needed to replace it almost as soon as he was gone.

A few minutes later, Brooke returned, now holding a black briefcase that Caleb recognized as one of his father's.

"I didn't count it," she said as she handed him the briefcase. "But it should be somewhere between forty-five and forty-eight thousand."

More than enough to get started—and he already had a good idea about how to build that nest egg into something much bigger.

"Thanks," he replied. "I appreciate it."

For a second or two, she only looked at him, expression almost blank. "Do you, Caleb?"

He met her gaze, and she blinked and then glanced away. "It'll help," he said easily before pausing as a thought crossed his mind.

Maybe he shouldn't ask, and yet....

"What happened to my loft?"

Brooke waited to reply until she had her coffee cup back in hand and had taken another sip. "You were gone more than a year. I paid the property taxes the first year, but then Larry said I should really sell it."

Larry Moore, the family attorney. He wasn't a part-demon, but his instincts were cutthroat enough that he might as well have been.

And Caleb had always gotten the impression that Larry was interested in Brooke, although he'd known the lawyer was way too smart to show any real signs of his attraction when Daniel Lockwood was still around.

With Daniel out of the way, Caleb supposed it had only been a matter of time before the shark started looking for chum.

"How much?"

His mother didn't pretend to misunderstand the question. "Obviously, much more than what I just gave you. It's not like I keep that kind of money on hand, you know."

True enough. All the same, Caleb wanted the real number, just so he could keep his mental accounts straight.

"How much?" he pressed.

"A little over two hundred," she said. "We got a fair price."

He supposed she would. Property values in Greencastle weren't anywhere close to what they were in Los Angeles, so a bit more than two hundred thousand for a loft—even one that had been completely updated—without any land was still pretty good.

When he didn't reply right away, Brooke said,

"If you'll tell me where you're going, then I can send you a cashier's check for that amount. I never intended to keep the money from the sale of the loft."

It was tempting...but Caleb knew it was better for everyone concerned if she had no idea of where he planned to end up.

"No, I'm good," he replied.

For the first time, real worry flickered in her eyes. "So...what? You come back after being gone for more than two years and won't give me a single word of explanation as to where you've been all this time or how you survived when no one else did, and you won't give even a hint of where you plan to go after this?"

He hesitated. A shadow outside the kitchen window caught his eye, and he watched for a few seconds as a crow landed on the dry grass in the backyard and began pecking in the dirt for seeds. Something about the black bird silhouetted against the yellowed grass and surrounded by bare trees made a shiver run down his spine.

Too cold here. After two years in Hell, he never wanted to be cold again.

"You want to know where I'm going?" he asked, and Brooke gave a very small nod.

Maybe the tiniest hint couldn't hurt.

"Someplace warm, Mom," he replied.

"Someplace *very* warm."

Chapter Two

—··《《·◎·》》··—

"IS IT HAUNTED?" THE WOMAN IN HER TOO-loud polyester shirt and overly tight jeans asked, and Delia Dunne had to force herself not to roll her eyes.

Kinda can't tell for sure until we're inside, ran through her mind, although she kept the snarky words to herself. Snark generally didn't help when you were dealing with antsy clients.

"Let's go in and find out, shall we?" she replied, knowing she was over-compensating and now sounded way too perky.

But her client—Marti Fields, a recent divorcée who was parlaying some of her settlement into buying a new house—didn't seem to notice anything off about her tone. "All right."

Marti's lack of enthusiasm was obvious...even though she was the one who'd been insistent on this quickie showing...but Delia pushed any doubts aside. After all, it was pretty normal to feel nervous about walking into a house that might or might not be haunted.

She already had the code to the lockbox, so she entered it, pulled out the keys, and then opened the front door. A waft of cool air drifted out to meet her, telling her that someone had forgotten to turn off the air conditioning. Wasteful, especially since temperatures on this early January day were floating around in the upper sixties and there wasn't any need for the A/C. Either the house cleaners or the people who'd come in to clean the carpets had forgotten to shut it off.

Well, she'd turn it off once they were done here and then let her mother know, since it was her listing and she'd need to tell the cleaners to be more careful next time.

Delia was at the house in more of an adjunct capacity.

Technically, the state of Nevada didn't require sellers or listing agents to disclose when someone had died on a property, but a lot of them did anyway, figuring it was better to be open about such things. And even when people tried to be tight-lipped, the information often got out there anyway, thanks to several websites where all you had to do was enter an address to discover whether there had been a death in a house.

In this particular case, the home was a cute one-story in Sunrise Manor where the previous owner's troubled son had overdosed in the spare bedroom. She'd put the house on the market almost immediately following the funeral, telling Linda Dunne—Delia's mother and the listing agent—that she couldn't stay there another moment.

"I want to believe Troy has moved on," the woman had said during a tearful meeting with mother and daughter agents. "But I keep hearing strange noises, and I don't know. I just don't know."

Privately, Delia thought the source of those noises was probably packrats or other rodents, since the house backed up to a golf course and the neighborhood was already known to have a critter problem, but she'd dutifully agreed to check it out. However, houses in that development were going like the proverbial hotcakes, and she hadn't had a chance to come by and scope the place out on her own before Marti called the real estate office and asked for a showing.

Linda had explained the situation, but Marti was insistent, so Delia agreed to be the one to do the showing...and check for any ghosts who might have decided to take up residence in the modest Spanish-style home.

She had to admit that her first impression was

of a place that was very neutral and didn't have the slightest whiff of anything supernatural about it. Then again, a 1990s-vintage tract home in suburban Las Vegas was the sort of setting that didn't exactly lend itself to the spooky or arcane.

"Everything seems fine so far," she told Marti, who had followed her inside but was also hanging back, obviously ready to let Delia take the full force of any ghostly attacks that might occur. "Why don't you take a look at the kitchen and the great room, and I'll check out the bedrooms and bathrooms before you go back there?"

"That's a very good idea," Marti replied at once, clearly relieved. She had bleached hair with obvious roots and wore way too much mascara, but she had a friendly smile. "And maybe I'll take a look at the backyard, too."

In Delia's opinion, there wasn't much to look at—the previous owner hadn't bothered with anything in terms of landscaping, so there were a couple of palm trees in desperate need of trimming, a bunch of gravel, and not much else—but possibly Marti wanted to see if there was enough room for a pool or something.

"Sure," she said. "I'll be just down the hall if you need me."

The other woman nodded but turned away almost at once, intent on taking a look at the amount of storage the kitchen offered. Delia thought that seemed like the perfect opportunity to head toward the bedrooms and make a quick assessment.

Even though she knew the overdose had happened in the larger of the two secondary bedrooms, she headed for the main suite anyway. Ghosts didn't always stay in the exact spot where they'd died, and besides, this was her first chance to get a good look at the property. Although their mother-daughter team shared responsibilities equally and Delia often handled listings that didn't have anything supernatural going on at all, Linda normally would have passed this one on to her daughter, thanks to the death that had occurred in the house. However, Delia had been out doing a showing when the owner of the Sunrise Manor house came in to get it listed, so her mother had taken care of the paperwork.

Not much to see in the master suite, that was for sure. As far as Delia could tell, the only thing really wrong with this place was that it was stuck in the late '90s and desperately in need of an update. The white tile in the bath and beige carpet in the bedroom had probably been installed when the house was built, along with the garden tub that took up too much space in the bathroom and the cramped fiberglass shower surround that, while clean, had some stains that even the most dedicated scrubbing couldn't get out.

Dutifully, she stood in the middle of the bedroom and closed her eyes, even as she held her hands at her sides, palms facing slightly upward. She couldn't say exactly why, but that position always seemed to work best when she was trying to determine whether a house was inhabited by spirits who didn't know it was time to move on.

Nothing at all here, though...at least, not in the main suite.

While she didn't exactly sigh, she did allow herself a breath before she headed over to the secondary bedroom where the boy had died. He'd only been nineteen, and Delia wondered if someone who had so much life remaining might have left more psychic residue than a person who'd departed this plane after a long and happy existence.

Impossible to tell whether the boy had put his personal stamp on the small, square room when he lived here, because now it wasn't much more than a white box with beige carpet. Once again, she paused in the middle of the space and allowed her mind to be still so she could see if she was able to pick up on any ripples in the energy of the bedroom, anything to show that he lingered here.

And...bupkis. Delia didn't pretend to be infallible, but she'd been doing this for more than ten years now, ever since she was eighteen and had walked into a condo her mother was about to put on the market and had sensed the presence of something she couldn't see, and she couldn't feel a single thing in the house.

Which was good, right? If she couldn't get even the slightest hint that the boy's spirit remained in the home, then that meant he'd moved on and there was no reason in the world why Marti Fields couldn't put in an offer, secure a short escrow since she was preapproved and had twenty percent to put down on the place, and start a new life in her new house.

Even though Delia doubted she'd sense anything, she went into the smallest bedroom as well, a spot barely ten feet by ten feet. She couldn't imagine actually trying to fit a bed in there, but she supposed it would work fairly well as an office.

Just as she began to close her eyes and reach out for any ghostly vibes, a terrified shriek came from the kitchen, followed by the unmistakable grinding sound of the garbage disposal.

"Help! *Help!*"

Delia bolted out of the bedroom and ran to the kitchen, where Marti's head had been smashed against the counter by invisible hands—and it looked as if those same hands were trying to drag her into the sink, where the garbage disposal whirred away.

Holy shit.

She smashed the switch that activated the

damn thing, but it kept going. So much for that idea.

Instead, she grabbed Marti by the shoulders and pulled her away from the sink. For just a moment, Delia could sense some kind of resistance, as if whatever had caught hold of the other woman had no intention of letting her go.

But then it disappeared, and she stumbled backward, sent off balance by the sudden release of pressure. Gasping, Marti put her hands on the Formica countertop and straightened before looking around her with wide, staring eyes, eyes made even paler and frantic by the black mascara that had been smudged all around them.

"You couldn't pay me to live here!" she spluttered, and, hanging on to her purse's shoulder strap as if it was some sort of lifeline, she ran from the room.

Seeming to sense she was gone, the garbage disposal abruptly shut off.

Delia planted her hands on her hips. She knew what she needed to do next...and wasn't looking forward to it.

"The ghost attacked Ms. Fields?" her mother asked, sounding shocked, and Delia nodded as best she could with her iPhone wedged under one ear.

"Sure looked like it to me," she replied, fishing around in her purse for what she privately thought of as her ghostly first aid kit.

Except in her particular case, it was more about getting ghosts to move on rather than fixing what was wrong with them. She wasn't the ghost-whisperer, just someone with a real estate license who used her weird talent to sense spirits and then encourage them to try a new plane of existence so she could sell the property they'd been haunting.

Although she couldn't see her mother right then, Delia had to believe she was shaking her head. "We've never had a ghost get violent like that."

No, they hadn't. Oh, sure, there had been spirits that knocked on the walls or turned the water on and off, or that picked up random objects and moved them from one room to another. In all those cases, though, it had felt much more as if the ghosts were just messing with people rather than trying to cause any real harm.

Whereas she was pretty sure the ghost in this house would have been just fine with turning Marti Fields' face into hamburger.

Delia tried her best to banish that horrible image from her mind.

"It's kind of unusual," she said, fingers closing around what had used to be a purse-sized first aid kit and which now held the kind of small, white candles usually employed in those Swedish angel chimes people used to decorate at Christmas, a tiny vial of holy water, a chunk of palo santo wood for cleansing the air, and a small glass ashtray she'd stolen from Caesar's Palace years earlier while still going through her rebellious stage. "And I think we lost the sale."

Her mother released a breath. "Well, I'm not happy to hear that, but I suppose it's understandable. Just get the place cleared as best you can, and we'll have to hope the next showing has a better outcome. It's a good thing that houses in Sunrise Manor are moving quickly right now—I'm sure we'll find another buyer soon enough."

From some people, that might have been optimism without any real foundation in reality. Coming from Linda Dunne, it was pretty much a certainty. Delia knew she might have been a little biased, but although Las Vegas boasted plenty of first-class real estate agents, she had yet to meet anyone who scrutinized the town's sales trends and housing data the way her mother did.

"Oh, sure," she said, then shifted her phone to her other ear, since it was starting to grind the backings of her multiple piercings into her skull. She'd gotten all those earrings back when she was the lead singer for Final Girl, the band she and some friends had played in during their senior year of high school and the first couple of years of college, and had never bothered to get rid of the rows of little garnet studs even though she dressed a lot more conservatively now that she was selling houses.

"But I have a showing at four," her mother went on, "so I need to get out of the office. Are you going to be all right there by yourself?"

A very good question. The ghost didn't seem to have directed any of its ire toward her so far, but Delia knew better than to allow herself a false sense of security. Spirits could be capricious.

"I'm fine," she said. "I'm just about to get everything set up, and then I'll see if I can convince this guy that it's time to move on to the next world."

"I'll call to check in after my showing," her mother told her, and Delia allowed herself a small roll of her eyes since she knew Linda couldn't see her.

Maybe one of these days, she'd realize her daughter was a grown woman of twenty-eight and had been doing this sort of thing for almost a decade.

"Okay," she replied. "But I'll probably be done by then."

"Even better," her mother said. "Because I just got another message about the Sunrise Manor house, so the sooner it's cleaned up, the better."

"It'll be done before you know it," Delia promised, and hoped she wasn't blowing too much sunshine on the subject. While she'd sent dozens of spirits on by that point, she'd never encountered one as violent as the ghost that appeared to be inhabiting this house.

"Good luck!"

Her mother ended the call there, and Delia gratefully plucked the phone out from under her ear and tossed it into her purse. Then she reached in the inner pocket and pulled out the Zippo lighter she'd bought at a smoke shop years earlier before she kicked the clove cigarette habit she'd picked up while playing with her band, then lit the little stick of palo santo.

Cleansing light, cleansing energy, she thought. The smoke from the piece of sacred wood began to drift upward, and although she didn't breathe it in, she still allowed herself to stand there and smell its acrid yet somehow also aromatic scent, knowing how much it helped to clear the air, so to speak.

Once she knew it was well and truly kindled, she set the piece of palo santo down on the ashtray and then lit a white chime candle and set it next to the piece of palo santo. She'd already rubbed the bottom of the candle with some sticky paste that would allow it to stand upright in the ashtray, since she didn't want to have to carry around a candlestick in addition to all the other junk she already had in her ghost-banishing arsenal.

Something shimmered at the edge of her vision, and she turned to see the ghostly outline of a gawky male figure hovering in the air a few feet on the other side of the kitchen island where she'd set up the candle and palo santo.

It sent her an inquisitive look, and Delia did her best to smile.

"Hi, there," she said. Most of the time, the ghosts she sensed never appeared at all, were only a whisper of a presence, but every once in a while, they materialized enough so she could see them. Clearly, this spirit was a strong one...but she already knew that. Otherwise, it would never have been able to manipulate matter in such a way that it could flip the switch for the garbage disposal, let alone force Marti Fields' head into the sink.

However, it wasn't making any threatening movements toward her, so Delia decided it was probably safe to proceed.

"Was this your house?" she asked, and the ghostly figure dipped its head. Sure, she'd already guessed that was the case, but she figured it would be easier to start with an innocuous question and proceed from there. One other time, she'd communicated with a spirit in the same way, with her doing all the talking and it only nodding or shaking its head, but the experience was still a little jarring.

And since this ghost seemed to understand what she was saying, she knew she needed to get to the bottom of its behavior...while at the same time convincing it that there was no reason for it to remain on this earthly plane any longer.

"Why did you do that to Marti?" she asked next, frankly curious. The attack had seemed deeply personal, but Delia knew the other woman had never set foot in the house before. A sudden thought prompted her to add, "Did she remind you of someone?"

The spirit faded in and out and then nodded again, even as it mimicked the motion of a person rocking a baby in their arms.

Oh, boy. They were moving into dangerous territory a lot more quickly than she'd anticipated.

"Did Marti remind you of your mother?"

Again, the spirit seemed to flicker, like an incandescent bulb that was about to breathe its last.

The lights in the kitchen flicked on and off, and the garbage disposal growled. Delia made herself hold her ground, even though she'd never encountered phenomena like this before and wasn't sure what she should do next.

What she really wanted to do was grab her purse and bolt out the door, but professional pride made her stay where she was. No way was she going to run out of here like a scared little kinder-gartner.

"And you were angry with your mother for some reason?"

Before Delia could even begin to react, the spirit moved toward her with blinding speed.

Moved *through* her.

It went through her mind's eye with a flash—a woman with unnaturally blonde hair that looked very similar to Marti's drunkenly laughing with a man who helped her onto the sofa, where they kissed and fondled one another until she passed out.

The man...who looked like he was probably in his early forties, with thinning brown hair and a goatee...leaving the comatose woman on the couch so he could go down the hallway to the bedroom where her fourteen-year-old boy slept....

Delia closed her eyes, and the horrible visions abruptly ceased. But in that moment, she knew everything—how the boy had been abused and gathered the courage to go to his mother with his terrible secret...how she'd insisted he was lying.

How he'd buried his pain and his shame with drugs and alcohol, finally succumbing in that very same room only two days after his nineteenth birthday.

"I'm so sorry," she whispered. "I'm so sorry no one listened to you."

The spirit had reappeared by that point, and now floated in the air only a few feet away from her. He seemed more solid now, solid enough that she could see his eyes had been blue, almost the same clear, azure shade as the cool January skies outside.

"I believe you," she said. "I saw what happened. But your mother isn't here. She put the house on the market and moved out after what happened."

The ghost's mouth moved, forming a single word. *Where?*

"I don't know," Delia replied, even as she wondered whether she would have told him if she actually knew his mother's current address. It had to be somewhere in the listing paperwork, but Linda was the one who'd set all that up.

Honestly, considering the way the woman had ignored her son's pleas for help, she deserved to be haunted by his vengeful spirit for all eternity.

But Delia knew that wasn't why she was here. No, she'd come to the house to ascertain whether there was a ghost at all—which there certainly was —and help it...help *him*...move on.

"She's paying for what happened," she said clearly. "Paying every day, knowing she should have listened and didn't. And her blindness made her lose her only son. That's her own hell, and she's living in it. You, on the other hand—you told me your story. I see you, and I believe you. Now, though...now it's time to let this place go. It's time for you to go on to the next phase of your existence."

The spirit cocked its head to one side, now looking confused.

"It's okay," Delia said, doing her best to sound confident and encouraging at the same time. "I've done this with lots of people. They get a little confused sometimes about where they need to go, but I know they go to a better place than this one."

Well, that was what she wanted to tell herself. A self-described agnostic, she'd never believed in Heaven and Hell or any sort of biblical interpretation of the afterlife. Lots of reading on the subject —and talking to the mediums in town who were the real deal and not just fakes trying to bilk unsuspecting tourists out of their hard-earned dollars— told her that something waited on the other side, even if she couldn't say for sure exactly what it might be.

A new life with new lessons to be learned, if the mediums were correct.

For a long moment, the spirit continued to float there, those blue eyes—the only thing about the apparition that had any real color—fixed on her face. However, Delia guessed something must have gotten through to it, because it lifted one hand, possibly in farewell, and then disappeared.

She continued to stand next to the island, though, partly because she'd had one or two instances where she thought a ghost had taken itself off, only to be startled when the phenomenon she was investigating started right back up again... and partly because she knew she still was a little off-balance from what the boy's spirit had shown her.

Some things weren't meant to be seen.

But after a minute or two passed, she realized it truly was gone.

Thank God.

Businesslike now, she snuffed the small white chime candle by lifting it and pressing the wick against the ashtray—a psychic had told her never to blow out candles used in rituals, since doing so would blow away any good juju she might have summoned—and turned on the water in the sink so she could safely douse the stick of palo santo.

"Peace be on this place," she said simply. A while back, she'd started saying that after she was done cleaning a house, and although she didn't know for sure whether it made any difference at all, she thought the words made a nice end cap for her rituals.

Just as she was returning her cleansing kit to her purse, her phone rang from somewhere inside. She scrabbled for it, fingers closing around the wallet case as the iPhone rang a third time.

"Delia Dunne, Dunne and Dunne Realty," she said.

"Hello, Ms. Dunne." It was a man's voice, deep and friendly, although she didn't think she'd ever heard it before. "A friend gave me your number. I heard that you handle certain... supernatural...problems?"

Well, she supposed that was one way of looking at it. No point in denying what he'd just said, not when her services were some of the Las Vegas real estate community's worst-kept secrets.

"I do," she said briskly. "Are you concerned about a particular property you're interested in buying?"

"Not exactly," the man replied. He hesitated, as if deciding how he should proceed, and then added, "Tell me—what do you know about demons?"

Chapter Three

—·‹‹‹·◎·›››·—

THE SOUND OF SLOT MACHINES AND chattering voices surrounded him, but Caleb ignored it, instead focusing on the cards he currently held in his hand. After doing this for almost two months, he'd gotten pretty good at keeping his focus fixed on the here and now.

In this case, it was the casino at the Golden Gate, a small hotel off the Strip that he hadn't yet visited. Ever since coming to Las Vegas immediately after he left Greencastle, he'd done his best to move from casino to casino, never winning too much at any one place, even as he took care to change his appearance every time.

Tonight he wore the face of a man he'd seen at Caesar's Palace a few weeks back, a tourist in his late forties with thinning fair hair and the kind of tan that indicated he might be getting a visit from the melanoma fairy in the not-too-distant future. He preferred to use the appearances of other men, just because, while his demon blood allowed him to shapeshift, it was still much easier to copy the faces and bodies of those who were close to him in height and build. At almost six foot two and around 185 pounds—all this eating at casino buffets over the past couple of months had helped him gain back the mass he'd lost in Hell—he knew there weren't too many women who shared his physique.

The seed money his mother had given him was parlayed into more than ten times that amount within only a few days of his arrival in Las Vegas, allowing him to buy a house for cash and settle into this new life. His demonic powers gave him the ability to create a new identity complete with driver's license and Social Security number, and because he liked his name but knew that "Caleb Lockwood" might have thrown up some red flags, he was now Caleb Lowe, a name he knew he'd answer to but was still enough different from the one he'd been born with that he didn't think it would cause any problems.

Fifty grand here, forty there...maybe a hundred grand if he was feeling flush on a particular night and didn't plan on returning to that casino any time soon. It was so easy to make the dice flip the way he needed, or to ensure that a dealer would only cause him to go bust in a game of blackjack when he wanted them to. Of course he needed to lose now and again, just so he wouldn't rouse too much suspicion.

But he won more than he lost. Far, far more.

Right now, he had almost two million bucks stashed in various banks around town. Caleb honestly wasn't sure what he planned to do with all of it, only that he felt much better having that much of a cushion. His home—which apparently had once been featured on some basic cable house-flipping show—he'd gotten for below asking because it had been on the market for a while, so that was one expense he didn't need to worry about any longer. He'd also bought a big black Range Rover, a much better vehicle than the old Nissan pickup he'd driven in Los Angeles when he was pretending to be a lowly assistant in the television industry, but he didn't even drive his new ride that much.

No, it just seemed safer to take taxis and Ubers and Lyfts, so that any cameras keeping watch outside the casinos wouldn't see him driving away in the same vehicle over and over again.

Right now, he was holding a straight flush, while he knew that the woman to his left—blonde and Botoxed within an inch of her life—only had two of a kind. The man to his right was the real problem. He wasn't some tourist here to play a few games of poker before he headed off to a show, but someone Caleb recognized, a man he'd seen around town and knew was very good at what he did. Under normal circumstances, Caleb doubted he would have been able to beat him.

These weren't normal circumstances, though... not when his demon powers were involved.

It was so very easy to ensure the correct cards gravitated to his hand. Not in any way that could be traced or even arouse suspicion, but still, he knew when he sat down to play, he was going to win.

Unless, of course, he wanted to lose so his winning streaks wouldn't arouse suspicion.

He'd lost the last hand, though, so there was no way he would let this one go, not when there was almost ten grand in chips sitting in the middle of the table.

"I'll raise one thousand," he said, pushing a small stack of chips toward the others.

The blonde's eyes widened, but she picked up her rum and Coke and took a sip before announcing, "And I'll see you."

Bad move, although Caleb wouldn't bother to tell her that. While not exactly drunk, she clearly wasn't operating with all her regular faculties, either.

Then again, someone who had that many rocks on her fingers—and around her neck and hanging from her ears—could probably lose much more than the current pot and still not bat an eye. Thanks to his attuned demonic senses, he knew those diamonds were genuine.

No partner in evidence, so he couldn't be sure whether she'd gotten lucky in a divorce or was a self-made woman.

It didn't matter to him one way or another. He wasn't here to worry about her personal life, but to liberate her of some funds she obviously would never miss.

"Call," said the other man, the one Caleb had guessed was a professional. He looked vaguely annoyed, as if he wished he was playing against people more worthy of his mettle.

Well, the joke was on him.

"Straight flush," he said as he placed his cards on the table.

"Oh, shit," the woman sighed, laying down her two eights.

The professional sent Caleb a steely look. "Three aces."

Which should have been enough. But with a straight flush running from an eight to a queen, Caleb had emerged victorious this round.

"Good game," he said, keeping his tone utterly neutral.

Then he pulled the chips toward him and placed them in the chip rack he had sitting next to his elbow. He'd already won a grand, but that was peanuts compared to the eleven thousand and some change his straight flush had earned him.

He tilted his head toward his erstwhile poker partners and headed toward the cashier. It wasn't very late—just a little past ten o'clock—but he thought he'd won enough tonight. As it was, he'd probably need to start looking for another bank to deposit his winnings. Four were already maxed out to their FDIC limits, and the one remaining was getting there. Sure, he also had some more cash hidden away in safe deposit boxes, but getting to it wasn't as easy as simply using a Visa debit card.

Anyway, the more places he stashed his money, the less chance of anyone being able to track down where everything was hidden.

The cashier took the chips, checked his fake I.D.—he always made sure to use his powers to alter it so it matched his shapeshifted identity—and handed over his cash in neat bundles, which he slipped into the messenger bag he always carried with him when he went on these gaming forays. He liked the bag because he could slip it over his neck and forget about it, while his father's old briefcase would have required a lot more tending.

Caleb already had his phone out as he stepped away from the cashier's cage so he could summon a Lyft to come pick him up. Although he alternated between ride services, he never had them take him to his house, but rather to a neutral location like a strip mall or a bus stop just distant enough that it would be difficult to trace him to his home base. From there, he would simply find a shadowy spot he could teleport from and get home that way.

Maybe no one was watching him at all, and these maneuvers were nothing more than his way of making himself feel more important than he really was. As far as he could tell, even when he went around wearing his real face—which was most of the time, actually, whether going to the bank or the grocery store or the gym—no one seemed to pay any particular attention to him.

Why would they? According to the world, Caleb Lockwood had been dead for two years...and he'd never hung out in Vegas. In fact, the first time he'd even left Indiana had been when his father sent him to California to try to track down the *Project Demon Hunters* footage so the hometown demons could make sure they were able to release it to further their own ends...namely, to create confusion and disbelief in the general population, to make people realize Hell was real and that the foundation their shallow lives were built on amounted to very little.

In the end, though, it had turned out to be little more than an internet phenomenon, with thousands of talking heads on YouTube explaining how the footage had been faked and that of course

Hell—and the demons who dwelled there—didn't exist.

But even though those plans had turned out to be a lot of sound and fury and not much more, the situation had still been an utter shitshow. Sure, he'd done as he was told and had found the hard drive containing the files, but still, the last thing he'd expected was to fall hard for the very woman he'd been trying to con.

Rosemary McGuire.

He still found himself thinking about her way too much. It would have been easy to say the not-quite obsession had everything to do with a bruised ego and nothing more—she'd dumped him before she'd even found out he was part demon and had taken up with a frigging Episcopalian priest, of all people—but Caleb wasn't so sure about that. In the beginning when they'd been working together to find the footage, he'd realized he enjoyed being around her way more than he should have, and was all too glad to spend time with someone who seemed all right with taking him at face value.

Well, until the angelic blood she'd inherited from her father asserted itself and made it clear there weren't going to be any dalliances with men who had demon blood running in their veins.

All the same, he hadn't quite been able to let it go, had still searched online for mentions of her once he was safely back in the mortal realm...even though he knew all he was doing was frustrating himself that much more.

Had it been stupid to send her a wedding gift after he learned she was getting married around Christmas?

Probably.

Then again, she'd thought he was safely banished to Hell. Most likely, all he'd done was create a mystery she couldn't solve as she tried to figure out who could have sent her the butterfly pendant with its dancing complement of diamonds.

The Lyft driver who picked him up didn't seem inclined toward conversation, and Caleb was just fine with that. No, he'd go home, put his winnings in a safe, and then do some research to see which banks or credit unions would be the most likely candidates for opening a new account. Luckily, most institutions here in Las Vegas were used to people depositing large sums of cash after a lucrative night at the casinos.

Tonight, he had the driver take him to a shopping center about a mile away from his house, one with a Safeway that was open twenty-four hours. After adding a sizable tip in the app, he thanked the guy and headed into the grocery store.

However, picking up some late-night snacks wasn't Caleb's intention. He went straight to the pet food aisle, one that just happened to be ignored by the store's security cameras, and sent a quick glance around him. The aisle was utterly deserted, and no one seemed to be coming this way.

A shift in intention, and he was standing in the living room of the house that had been his home for the past two months. He'd bought it fully furnished, so all he'd needed to do was show up with a toothbrush and some clothes.

At first, he'd toyed with the idea of redoing parts of the house, since some of it was a little too Vegas and over-the-top for him, but he had to admit the place was starting to grow on him, even the glowing neon "PLAY" sign that hung on one wall in the family room, which was dominated by a big black pool table.

Or maybe he simply enjoyed being here because he knew his mother would absolutely hate the place, right down to the crystal chandelier that dangled over the standalone tub in the main bathroom.

He rarely drank when he was gambling—even though he knew a couple of cocktails wouldn't come anywhere close to affecting his demon-enhanced constitution—but when he got home, he almost always poured himself something, whether that was a few fingers of bourbon or a Scotch and soda.

Tonight, bourbon seemed easier, so he got down a glass and fixed himself a drink before heading into the living room. One of the reasons he'd bought the house was the dark blue paint that made the space moody and inviting, reminding him a little of the color he'd painted his boyhood room at home.

Then again, maybe that hadn't been such a great idea. He tried to think of Greencastle as little as possible these days.

Out of all of them—half-demons and quarter-demons alike—he'd been the only one to escape.

Sheer dumb luck, probably. Getting around in Hell was never easy, since it wasn't as if there were nice paved roads and street signs and phones with GPS to get you where you were going. He'd wandered for what felt like eons but eventually had returned to the dead forest where the demon lord Belial liked to hold court. Not because he had any wish to listen to that big bastard's pontificating, but mainly because even a grove of dead trees felt more like home than the trackless, stony wastelands that made up the rest of the place.

And that was why Caleb had seen the portal opening into the firelit room where the dead redheads had lain...had watched as another red-haired woman—like enough to the other two that he thought they might have been sisters—and Belial had fought...had taken the leap of faith that had brought him back to the real world.

No one else from the Greencastle contingent

had been anywhere near the grove of dead trees or the portal the demon lord had opened there, so they were now trapped in Hell forever. Unlike regular demons, they couldn't be summoned, so once they were banished, that was it.

While he had to admit that having the half-demons remain there was no great loss—like his father, they were a bunch of greedy, officious assholes—he didn't think it was fair for the quarter-demons of his own generation to have suffered the same fate. They had far more human blood than not, and were mostly victims of circumstance.

But because he couldn't do a damn thing about their situation, he knew he probably shouldn't waste too much brain space on it.

He flicked the switch to turn on the gas fireplace and sat down. What he hadn't been expecting was to find how cool Las Vegas actually was in December and January—nothing like his hometown of Greencastle, of course, but still chilly enough that he didn't feel entirely stupid about using the fireplace. It would have been better to have arrived in the dead of summer when he could have allowed the hundred-plus temperatures to bake the last icy cold of Hell out of his bones, but beggars couldn't be choosers. To be honest, he would have been all right with landing in Buffalo in midwinter as long as it meant he wouldn't have to spend another moment in the underworld.

The bourbon was warm against his throat, though, and he had to admit that he could have done a lot worse. Now he had a home base and an easy way of making sure the money continued to flow in, and all he had to do was maintain the status quo and he'd be home free.

Sure, this new existence was a little lonely, but he had only himself to blame for that. He'd hooked up with a couple of women right after arriving in Las Vegas, before he'd even bought this house and was bouncing from hotel room to hotel room, but that had only been an exercise in relieving the biological backpressure that had built up during his tenure in Hell.

Actually allowing someone into his life, let alone telling them the truth about his origins?

Caleb doubted that would ever happen.

Chapter Four

DEMONS?

Seriously?

But Delia had made herself listen to the pitch from the man on the phone, which was mainly that demons were just as real as the ghosts she banished from haunted tract homes, and that he'd like to meet her to discuss the matter further.

Despite her inner misgivings, she'd agreed to the meeting, saying she'd see him at Mothership Coffee Roasters downtown at ten o'clock, and that had seemed to be the end of that.

Except now she sat in her living room, nursing a glass of red wine as she watched the flames in her gas fireplace dance behind the glass enclosure, and wondered if she might have lost her damn mind.

It's only a meeting, she reminded herself, and sipped some more pinot noir.

True, except she could have easily turned the man—Robert Hendricks—down and said that sorry, demons weren't her field of expertise.

He hadn't sounded crazy on the phone...but then, they rarely did.

And although he hadn't mentioned any exact numbers, she'd gotten the impression that he was ready to lay a substantial amount on the line if he thought she could help him. Money wasn't a problem anymore, not when she sold at least a house every month and also received ten percent of the commission whenever her mother sold a home that Delia had cleansed, but despite that, she wasn't about to look an unexpected windfall in the mouth.

But still...demons?

There had been that crazy flap on the internet a few years ago, when footage from a show that had never aired—*Project Demon Hunters?*—flooded YouTube and other social media channels, but the hubbub had died down after a bunch of rumors circulated that the images of those horrible demonic creatures had been doctored somehow and the whole thing was a fake. In fact, she thought she remembered reading a story that said the footage had been leaked by the show's creators in retaliation for the cable channel that had funded the show going in and adding special effects without their permission.

Anyway, she'd assumed it had all been a bunch of sound and fury that signified absolutely nothing at all.

But...what if it hadn't been?

Although the room was warm enough, a shiver still inched its way down Delia's spine. Maybe she should text Robert Hendricks and tell him sorry, she'd just checked her calendar and had a conflict and would need to cancel.

That was the coward's way out, though. No, she'd agreed to this meeting, and she would see him tomorrow morning as they'd planned. If it turned out he was stark raving mad, well, that was the reason for setting up their meeting in such a public place.

And if he sounded plausible?

That, Delia reflected, might be even worse.

By ten o'clock, a lot of the early morning rush had already subsided, but Mothership was still busy enough that she was glad she'd arrived a few minutes early so she could grab a venti Americano and a relatively quiet table off to one side. The place had a great outdoor patio area, but on this particular January morning, it was still just a little too nippy to sit outside for any length of time.

However, the interior of the coffee shop was

light and bright, with high ceilings and lots of windows and mid-toned wood, just about the opposite of the sort of location that would seem conducive to discussions about demons. Delia settled down at the table she'd found and blew on the surface of her coffee while she waited.

Which wasn't for very long, because less than five minutes after she'd seated herself, a tall man with graying dark hair and wearing a gray sportcoat and jeans and loafers entered the shop and came immediately over to her table.

"Delia Dunne?" he asked, and she nodded. It wasn't too surprising that he'd recognized her, considering how her photo was prominently displayed on the Dunne & Dunne website.

"Mr. Hendricks?" she responded.

He shook his head, smiling as he extended a hand. "Robert, please. Do you mind waiting a few more minutes while I get some coffee?"

"Not at all," she said. "Take your time."

"Thank you."

The line at the counter was pretty much nonexistent by then, so he was able to place his order and come back to join her, coffee in hand, in only a couple of minutes. By that point, Delia's Americano had cooled enough that she was able to take a sip, glad of the happy tingle of caffeine hitting her veins. Sure, she'd already had a cup at home earlier that morning, but she figured it was probably a good idea to get some extra coffee in her before they got into the whole demon thing.

"Thanks again for meeting me," Robert told her as he sat down in the chair opposite hers. Up close, he looked like he was probably closer to fifty than forty, with laugh lines around his eyes and skin the warm tone of someone who was outside a lot.

And he definitely didn't look like a crackpot who believed in demons. No, he seemed much more like someone who would approach her looking to buy a vacation home on a golf course.

She glanced around them, but neither of the two closest tables was occupied.

Might as well dive right into it.

"So, what makes you interested in demons?" she asked, hoping she sounded neutral and not at all judgey.

The laugh lines around Robert Hendricks' eyes deepened as he smiled again. "Put like that, I suppose it does sound kind of crazy."

"Well, I clean haunted houses," she said. "So I probably have a different definition of 'crazy' than most people."

Still looking amused, he picked up his cup of coffee—plain old black, as far as she could tell— and took a sip. "I suppose you have a point there. Anyway, I'm a member of a group of casino managers and owners, and lately we've been noticing some suspicious activity."

"'Suspicious'?" she echoed, wondering exactly where he was going with this. Surely if there were some sort of shenanigans going on at the local casinos, it would be a matter for their in-house security to handle, or maybe even the police if they thought some kind of actual fraud was occurring.

Robert Hendricks paused there, and Delia noticed how he also sent a quick look around them, as though to ascertain no one was close enough to be listening to their conversation.

Rather than answer her question directly, he said, "What do you know about demons?"

"Not a lot," she replied, deciding it was better to be honest and allow him to determine whether he'd made a mistake in contacting her. "My specialty is earthbound spirits."

A sip of coffee, and he asked, "You've never gone into a house where you could tell something was wrong but also somehow felt it wasn't an ordinary ghost you were dealing with?"

Delia drank some of her coffee as well, mostly because she knew she could use another hit of caffeine before responding. "Once," she said, and Robert nodded.

"What did it feel like?"

That experience had happened almost five years ago now, and she'd done her best to put it out of her mind—especially since she'd never had a repeat of that awful feeling of wrongness in the pit of her stomach, a sensation that told her something much worse than a simple disgruntled ghost had taken up residence in the gorgeous mid-century home in Paradise Palms, a listing her mother hadn't wanted to let go because the place was selling for almost a million and a half.

Problem was, something awful had lived in that house, something that had sent her back to the days of her childhood when she'd played Bloody Mary in the Mirror with her friends during sleep-overs and had run screaming from the bathroom. And sure, she'd retained enough presence of mind not to do the same thing when she walked into the foyer of the house, with its rock waterfall on one side and rock-surrounded planter on the other, but the deeper she'd gotten into the place, the worse she felt, finally turning back after she reached the kitchen and thought she might throw up.

Afterward, she'd told her mother something was horribly wrong with the house, and Linda, not one to be thrown off-balance by pretty much anything, had apparently made a few discreet calls, and not long afterward, someone else had come out and cleansed the place. Delia hadn't asked who their savior was when it became clear her mother didn't want to talk about it, and she'd done whatever she could to forget about the place.

"Just wrong," she said, then added frankly, "Like it was going to make me vomit if I stayed in there for too much longer."

"A common reaction, or so I've heard," Robert replied. "Demon infestations can have a profound effect on people, especially if they're already sensitive—which you must be, or you wouldn't be in your line of work."

Delia supposed he had a point there. Then again, she'd never tried to call herself an empath or a light-worker or any of the other phrases that got bandied around in New Age and spiritual circles. Maybe she had an interesting gift, but that was as far as she was willing to go when describing her talents.

"I suppose so," she said, not wanting to say much more than that.

Her dubious tone didn't seem to put off her companion, because he went on, "Anyway, demons are able to shapeshift, to put on faces that aren't theirs in an attempt to hide their identities. They can also manipulate matter in a variety of ways... including making sure they win at the casinos."

Delia didn't bother to stop her eyebrows from lifting in disbelief. "What...demons come up from Hell just to play the slot machines?"

Robert gave her a gentle smile, one that seemed to acknowledge her reaction without agreeing with it. "Well, to be fair, we haven't noticed much manipulation of the slot machines—probably not enough profit in it, unless you're playing the really big ones. And when someone wins a high enough amount on one of those machines, then lights and sirens go off and it attracts a lot of attention. Someone manipulating a poker hand here and a throw of the dice there is going to be a lot more difficult to track down."

All right, maybe he had a point. Still....

"So, you think a demon has come to Las Vegas and is messing with the cards and the dice so he can win a million and take it back to Hell with him?"

Another of those small smiles. "You can't take money to Hell. But that doesn't mean he can't be banking it here in order to afford himself some creature comforts while he's on Earth."

"And when he's done, he'll just go back?"

Now Robert's expression turned serious again, and he reached for his cup of coffee and had another sip. "That's the problem. We just don't know. The people we've consulted have told us that sometimes demons only come to this plane for a short time—to slum it, more or less—while others decide they're comfortable here and do whatever they can to stay away from Hell for as long as is feasible."

Since everything Delia had read about Hell made it sound like the sort of place where you'd want to spend as little time as possible, she could see why a demon might want to come to this plane and do a little partying...and then hang around rather than return to the proverbial pit of despair.

On the other hand, this all sounded like a big ball of crazy.

"Why a demon?" she asked, leaning against the back of her chair. "I mean, doesn't it make more sense that a regular human is doing all this supposed cheating?"

Robert sipped some more coffee. "Of course it makes more sense. And our security teams analyzed all the security footage and couldn't see any outright evidence of cheating. That doesn't change our reality, which is that we've had many more big winners the past two months than usual. One of the other casino owners brought in a psychic to check out his place, and she said she sensed something dark and left almost immediately. Two more tried the same thing, with similar results."

"So you came to me because I'm the only person in town with a reputation for getting rid of ghosts," I said, and he nodded.

"I—we—realized that this must be something of a jump for you. But no one else in the psychic community has been able to help us at all."

Delia really didn't like being lumped in with the rest of the town's psychics, since it wasn't like she read people's palms or threw Tarot cards to tell someone's future. Like it or not, though, she had some kind of special sixth sense when it came to this sort of thing, which she assumed was why Robert had reached out in the first place.

And yet....

"Why not contact the demon-hunter guy from that *Project Demon Hunters* thingy?" she asked next. "Michael...."

She let the words trail off there because she honestly couldn't remember his last name. Still, it would have been easy enough to look up.

"Michael Covenant," Robert said smoothly. "And yes, we tried reaching out to him, but he told us that he wasn't traveling to handle cases of infestation or possession while his wife was finishing up her doctorate in Tucson."

"If that's even what's going on here," Delia replied. "It doesn't sound as if the demon you're worried about has taken up residence anywhere in particular, so this wouldn't be an infestation."

"I suppose that's true enough," Robert said, looking unfazed. "But our problematic friend is still causing a good deal of trouble for the casinos, and we'd like it stopped sooner rather than later."

Delia wasn't sure exactly how she was supposed to accomplish that. Sure, she could send ghosts on to their next reward without too much trouble, but a demon? Would they expect her to fling holy water around and say things like, *I cast you out, demon!*

Somehow, the mental image made her want to

chuckle, even as she guessed that Robert wouldn't be too happy to hear she was somewhat amused by the situation.

"I'm not sure," she said, each word slowed by reluctance. "This really sounds like something a priest should handle."

"We plan to ask for the church's intervention at some point if necessary," Robert replied, clearly not put off by her comment. "But we don't want to do that until we're sure of what we're dealing with. That's where you come in. Once you can tell us definitively that you've sensed a demon's presence in one or more of our casinos, then we'll go to a priest for help."

Well, that sounded a little better. It didn't seem as if Robert and the other casino owners had any intention of putting her in harm's way, only wanted her to use her talents to give them some confirmation that their current problem was much more than a single grifter who'd figured out how to cheat at both dice and cards. Once she'd ID'd the problem, then she could step aside and let the real experts handle it, much like a house inspector who might call out issues with the wiring and the plumbing but who would then have actual contractors come in to fix the problem.

"I can't promise anything—" she began.

"I don't expect you to," Robert cut in, his tone friendly enough that the interruption didn't feel rude. "I know this isn't an exact science. But to show you that we're serious...."

He reached into the inner pocket of his sport-coat and pulled out an envelope, then set it on the tabletop and pushed it toward her.

Almost of its own accord, her hand reached for the envelope and she looked inside, expecting a cashier's check or maybe even a check drawn on the casino Robert represented.

But no, the envelope contained several stacks of bills held in place with rubber bands.

"That's ten thousand," he said. "If you're able to find traces of demonic activity in our casinos and we're eventually able to catch our culprit, we'll double it. But no matter what happens, you can keep the deposit."

Ten grand, just for walking into a casino and taking a psychic sniff.

And let's not forget the possibility of earning twice that amount.

Delia reached for her Americano. "Well, Mr. Hendricks," she said. "It looks like you've hired yourself a demon whisperer."

Chapter Five

—·‹‹‹‹·☾·›››·—

THIS PARTICULAR NIGHT, CALEB DIDN'T plan on winning anything substantial. Although he hadn't sensed anything obviously amiss, his sixth sense told him that it was better to lie low for a while, even if he had no intention of stopping these casino visits altogether.

They were the closest thing he had to a social life.

So he played craps and blackjack and Texas Hold 'Em, won a hundred bucks here, lost fifty there, and did his best to give off the aura of someone who was in Las Vegas to have a good time but definitely wasn't serious about gambling. Tonight he wore the face of someone close to his age, a Hispanic man around thirty, and drank a couple of cocktails and flirted with the waitress, all while he wondered just what the hell—no pun intended—he was doing here.

Sure, he wasn't buried in snowdrifts, and sure, no one in Las Vegas knew who Caleb Lockwood even was, but still, deep down he realized he couldn't hang out in casinos forever, even if doing so helped pad his bottom line.

With the new identity he'd invented for himself, he could have done anything he liked.

Well, almost anything. Part of the reason he'd been okay with following his father's orders and going to L.A. to find the missing *Project Demon Hunters* footage was that he'd gotten to work in the television industry while there, had gotten just a taste of the one thing he'd actually wanted, which was to go to film school and make directing or producing or something along those lines his career. His father had put his foot down, of course, because Caleb's role in life had been to do whatever Daniel Lockwood said...and to eventually take over as bank president once his father's tenure on Earth was over and he needed to return to Hell.

Being trapped in Hell was almost preferable to staring at spreadsheets all day.

None of that had come to pass, of course, thanks to the way the half-demons and their sons had been banished from this plane, and even though he was now free of his father, Caleb knew he didn't dare go near Southern California, not when he was worried that Rosemary or someone else in the *Project Demon Hunters* gang might somehow be able to sniff out his presence there.

So, Las Vegas it was. But maybe he could pad his resume to get himself a job in local TV news, something like that. It would have to be behind the scenes, since he'd never had any desire to be on camera—and doing so probably wouldn't have been the safest thing in the world anyhow, considering the way he was trying to maintain a low profile—and yet he knew he needed to find something to occupy his time.

Meanwhile, though, he'd gamble and go to the shows, or hang out in the updated Brady Bunch house he'd bought and do his best to act as though everything in his life was just hunky-dory.

As he went to cash in his winnings, though, a woman with long red hair walked past him, and he found himself stopping so he could stare after her.

Not because she was pretty, even though she was, and not because her nearly waist-length copper locks were so unusual—he honestly wasn't all that into redheads, although he knew he'd be eternally grateful to the unknown woman who'd driven that slim blade right into Belial's black heart —but because of the power that shimmered around her, visible to his part-demon senses even though he knew no one else would be able to detect it.

She was definitely all human, and yet different at the same time, the aura she gave off not anything like what he'd sensed in Rosemary McGuire after her angelic powers had awakened. No, this reminded him more of what he'd felt from Glynis, Rosemary's mother, who was completely human but still possessed her own psychic gifts.

Caleb doubted the redhead could be related to any of them—the McGuire women all had curly brown hair—but he supposed those sorts of talents cropped up in the general population from time to time.

And because the red-haired woman was definitely the most interesting person he'd encountered tonight, he wanted to do what he could to follow her without being too obvious.

She seemed out of place in the casino, and that wasn't only because she wore a professional-looking knee-length skirt and a silk blouse in a smoky teal color that beautifully complemented her fiery hair rather than the jeans and T-shirts—or the odd cocktail dress or blazer—sported by the other denizens of the casino. No, she kept looking from side to side as she made her way across the floor, almost as if she was on the hunt for something...or someone.

Casino security? She didn't really give off that vibe, and she didn't feel like a cop, either.

Maybe she'd come here to meet someone and was having a hard time finding them.

Something about that explanation didn't seem right, though, which only piqued his interest that much more.

As much as she was looking around her, she didn't seem to have noticed him following a few yards behind, pausing from time to time to inspect a slot machine as though weighing whether it was worth taking the time to feed a dollar bill into the thing, but never allowing so much distance to open up between them that he couldn't keep track of where she was going.

Once or twice, she did pause and glance over her shoulder, but her gaze didn't linger enough for him to think he'd aroused her suspicions.

The woman made an entire circuit of the casino floor, and eventually stopped near the door that opened onto the baccarat rooms. So far, Caleb hadn't played any baccarat, mostly because that tended to be a game for high rollers and one that might send increased scrutiny his way, even though he never wore the same face twice.

Was she going inside?

Apparently not, because after standing there for a moment, she shook her head and then continued on her way.

Whatever she was searching for, it didn't seem to be here. She frowned a little, looking uncertain, and then walked away from the baccarat rooms and toward the entrance to the casino. Lacking anything better to do, Caleb followed her, still taking care to hang back so she wouldn't notice him.

Sure enough, she went outside, although rather than pausing at the valet station, she strode purposefully down the sidewalk, seeming to head for the next casino, which was located about a block away. Just as he went through the automatic sliding doors, he let his appearance shift again, this time to a balding man in his forties dressed in a button-up shirt and jeans, the sort of person he doubted she would look at twice, making sure to time the change perfectly so the movement of the doors would blur any footage the casino's CCTV cameras might catch.

The ploy seemed to have worked, because she didn't throw any of those wary glances over her shoulder, almost as if she knew that whoever she was looking for, she wouldn't find them out here on the street.

Which, on that particular Friday night, was plenty crowded, so he didn't have a problem continuing to tail her, letting the other people on the sidewalk ebb and flow around him, creating an effective shield.

Then she entered the Palace Station, the flashing lights over the entrance painting her hair almost magenta before she disappeared into the dim interior.

Caleb quickened his pace so he wouldn't lose the woman, and slipped into the casino only a few yards behind her. Honestly, he couldn't even say why it felt so important to follow the redhead and see what she was up to, except that his life had already fallen into a sort of humdrum routine, and encountering someone with her kind of powers was like dropping a zesty slice of lemon into an otherwise blah glass of water.

And that was without even knowing the reason for the mission she was apparently on.

This casino was smaller and shabbier, but her behavior was pretty much the same—she made a circuit of the floor, zigzagging past the slot machines so she could walk by the poker and black-jack tables before she paused for a moment to watch a couple of craps games in the process.

Was she a gambler trying to suss out the competition?

He would have said she didn't give off that vibe, either, except that his time here in Las Vegas had taught him that professional gamblers came in all shapes and sizes and styles of dress, so it was difficult to pin them down just by looking at them.

And she wasn't a hooker, that was for sure. Although he thought she had on some makeup, it was fairly subdued, and while she wasn't wearing a suit, that slimly tailored skirt and silk blouse were still more suited for a boardroom than a casino floor.

Even if that skirt showed off a nicely sculpted ass and a seriously fine pair of long legs.

No, he wasn't going to ogle her...even if he had to admit she was fairly ogle-able.

Instead, he paused at a slot machine and fed it a dollar bill, then pulled the handle. It would have been so easy to make it come up all cherries, but the last thing he wanted was to get a jackpot while she was standing only a few feet away and possibly draw her attention.

No, scratch that. He wanted her to look at him —at *him,* Caleb Lockwood, and not the middle-aged loser he'd disguised himself to be. Although she wore that faint frown again and had her hands on her hips, indicating she wasn't entirely happy with her life right now, she looked both beautiful and smart, the kind of person he'd been thinking he needed to find.

Yeah, he thought. *Because your last try at getting romantic with a psychic turned out so well.*

Actually, it had been an unmitigated disaster, but he still didn't think that was really his fault. He hadn't been able to detect Rosemary's angelic nature, had thought she was nothing more than a beautiful woman with some serious psychic gifts.

But her angel blood had sure smelled his

demon blood as soon as things looked as if they might get really physical. After that, she couldn't get away from him fast enough.

History probably wouldn't repeat itself, even though he didn't think the red-haired woman was anything other than a regular mortal with some psychic ability. They existed in the human population and had for thousands of years—if not more.

No, probably better that he continue his solitary existence for a while longer, if for no other reason than he was still getting his bearings and introducing anything new into his life here wouldn't be a very smart idea.

Then the woman shook her head and moved toward the exit, the one that led to the casino's parking garage.

Was she leaving?

It sure looked that way. He wanted to swear, knowing it would be a lot more difficult to continue the pursuit with his own vehicle still sitting in the garage over at the Bellagio.

For now, though, about the only thing he could do was keep to the shadows and hope he'd be able to catch a glimpse of her car as she drove past. If he got her license plate number, then it shouldn't be too hard to track her down.

And now Caleb enters the crazy stalker phase of his exile went through his mind, and he couldn't quite keep himself from grinning. Anyone watching would have thought for sure that he'd lost it.

He hadn't, though. This was just a way to amuse himself and waste a little time. Besides, the longer he stayed out, the more he could delay going back to his empty house.

Yes, there she went, driving past in a little white Hyundai Kona hybrid. The make and model of the vehicle weren't important, though. No, what was important—even more than her license plate, which he quickly consigned to memory—was the magnetic sign affixed to the passenger-side door.

Dunne & Dunne, Las Vegas Real Estate Experts.

Ah, she was a realtor. That at least explained why she'd been dressed the way she was, although he had to admit that he'd also met plenty of real estate agents who weren't nearly so formal.

Now he knew where she worked...and that would allow him to learn a whole lot more.

Much more than he'd been expecting, actually. Sure, he went immediately to the Dunne & Dunne website after he got home—well, once he'd ordered some DoorDash and poured himself a beer—and confirmed that the red-haired woman was Delia Dunne, junior partner in the agency, which appeared to be run by her mother Linda. The older woman resembled her daughter a great deal, except for the red hair. Was Delia's father the redhead, or had a couple of recessive genes popped up from somewhere?

It happened.

The truly interesting stuff, however, he found through Googling Delia's name, since the agency website didn't offer much beyond the bios of its two agents and a listing of all the properties they were currently representing. Well, and an enigmatic "additional services" tab, which sent you to a web form to fill out, along with a phone number you could call.

Exactly why people would feel the need to explore that "additional services" tab became clear soon enough. Delia was a cleaner, although not the sort the mob called in to mop up after a particularly bloody hit.

No, she was someone who could sense if a house was haunted and then perform the necessary rituals to send the resident spirits on to the next plane of existence.

Well, that explained why he'd sensed such a powerful psychic aura around her. But what the hell had she been doing roaming around those casinos? Were they haunted?

He didn't think so. Although ghost-hunting wasn't his field of expertise, his demon blood still allowed him to sense if any other entities were lurking around a place, and he hadn't detected a single thing as he walked through the casino floors.

Well, nothing except a lot of desperation, greed, and bad choices.

The doorbell rang, so he set his laptop down on the coffee table and went to greet the DoorDash driver and collect his bag of Thai takeout. Once the transaction was handled, he headed back into the living room and fished out the box of spring rolls, figuring he'd munch on those first before he moved on to the entrees and rice.

Now that he was back at fighting weight, he didn't need to worry about how many calories he consumed or how much grease or fat or sugar might be contained in any of his food. Just another benefit of the demon blood that flowed in his veins.

With his free hand, he opened up his laptop again and stared at Delia Dunne's photo for a long moment. There was something very no-nonsense about the set of her pretty mouth and the way her hazel-green eyes met the camera, as though challenging the photographer to say something about her admittedly offbeat side hustle.

He wanted to know why she'd been exploring those casinos with so much purpose today, even as he tried to figure out the best way to approach her without arousing too much suspicion. If he hadn't just bought a completely updated and remodeled house, he could have posed as a prospective client looking for a new home here in Las Vegas.

No, he needed to think of something else. She was the most interesting thing he'd come across in his new life, and he wasn't about to let this go.

Frowning a little, he wiped his fingers on one of the napkins tucked into the bag of takeout and picked up the container of cashew chicken he'd ordered, then absently fed himself a few bites as he considered the problem.

Even though he already owned a house, that didn't mean he might not be interested in purchasing a second property for rental income or finding a fixer-upper he could flip. He certainly had enough ready cash on hand to buy a distressed property. Hell, his new identity had awesome credit and he could probably qualify for something pretty impressive, although the last thing he wanted was to get bogged down in the mortgage process.

No, much better to look for something he could buy for cash. Besides, presenting himself as an investor with that kind of ready capital would probably make him that much more attractive as a client.

Speaking of which....

He set down the container of cashew chicken, then reached up to run a hand through his hair. Here at home, he always looked like himself, mostly because he knew his neighbors might get suspicious if it seemed as though a parade of strange men was coming and going from the house.

And he knew he wanted to meet Delia Dunne while wearing his own face. A calculated risk, he supposed, but there was no reason for her to know him from Adam, not when he'd looked entirely different when he was tailing her at the casinos earlier today.

A quick perusal of the properties Dunne and Dunne were representing told him there were several that might work. Or, even better, he could hint to her that he was all right with buying a property other people had been avoiding due to a pesky resident ghost.

He couldn't wait to see her in action.

Chapter Six

THE REQUEST FOR A MEETING HAD COME through the agency's website, so Delia didn't know quite what to expect from this Caleb Lowe. He was looking for an investment property of some sort and had hinted that it might be a cash transaction, so she was expecting someone maybe in their fifties or sixties, a man who'd already paid off his mortgage but still wanted to participate in the real estate market rather than socking his cash away in a mutual fund or a money market account.

Those expectations couldn't have been more wrong.

He was maybe a year or two older than she was, with thick, messy dark blond hair, piercing brown eyes, and the face of a male model who spent most of his time in Europe but had decided to come slumming in Las Vegas, for whatever reason. Black leather jacket with a simple gray T-shirt underneath, faded jeans and black boots...a watch strapped to his wrist that looked unobtrusive enough but she knew must have cost at least five figures.

"Thanks for meeting with me," he said as he reached out to shake her hand. He had a nice voice, too, one that was warm and mellow but not overly deep, and his handshake was firm without feeling as though it was going to crush her fingers.

"It's no problem," she replied. "Thank you for reaching out to Dunne and Dunne. Would you like to take a seat?"

She inclined her head toward one of the two chairs that faced her desk, and Caleb sat down while she resumed her perch in the leather office chair where she'd been sitting before he knocked.

"So," she continued, "you're looking for some kind of income property?"

"Yes," he answered at once. "I've come into some money, and since I'm not interested in playing the stock market, I thought real estate might be the answer to making that money work for me."

"Well," Delia said with a professional smile, one she hoped wouldn't reveal how much she'd love to sell this guy a house, "property is always a good investment. We've had some ups and downs, thanks to low inventory and then high interest rates, but the market has begun to correct itself over the past six months, so I think we'll be able to find something that fits your needs and budget."

As long as his needs weren't too crazy and his budget wasn't too low. Even Las Vegas's expansive real estate market had its limits.

Leaning forward in his chair, Caleb replied, "I was hoping to get a deal on a distressed property, a place that doesn't have anyone interested in it because of its...issues."

For some reason, she had a feeling he wasn't talking about foundation cracks or galvanized plumbing that needed to be replaced. "What kind of issues, Mr. Lowe?"

A glint entered his dark eyes. "You can call me Caleb. No point in being formal, right?"

Most of the time, her clients preferred to be on a first-name basis, but she never presumed. Then again, her first look at him had already told her that he didn't seem to be the type to stand on ceremony.

"Sure, Caleb," she said easily. "Did you want to stay within the Las Vegas city limits, or are you all right with looking in Henderson or Summerlin, places like that?"

"I'd like to stick with Las Vegas if possible," he replied. "But I'm open to other options if we find the right property outside town."

Well, that was something. Not that there

wasn't plenty of inventory in Las Vegas itself, but the broader the parameters, the better the chance of finding a house that would be the right fit.

"But it sounds as if you're okay with a fixer-upper."

He grinned. "Sure. I was kind of hoping to find a house that other buyers have avoided because of... well, let's call it supernatural involvement."

There it was. Then again, it wasn't as if Delia had ever done much to hide her particular area of specialty, or otherwise her clients would have had a much harder time tracking her down. Heck, *Las Vegas* magazine had published a piece on her about eighteen months earlier.

"It looks like you've done your homework, Caleb."

He settled back in his chair and crossed one leg over his knee. The black motorcycle boots he wore were scuffed, the jeans faded. If it weren't for the Patek Philippe watch casually strapped to one wrist, he probably wouldn't have looked like the sort of person who could afford to buy a house for cash.

But appearances...especially in the real estate business...were often misleading. In fact, Delia's experiences had led her to believe that the worse off a person looked, the greater the chance that they had some serious cash on hand.

"I like to know who I'm working with," he

said, then shot her another of those disarming grins. "And sure, I'd be lying if I didn't say that I've probably watched too many episodes of *Ghost Hunter Adventures*. It just sounded like it would be interesting to try purchasing a property that other people have avoided because it has a couple of ghosts who've decided to take up residence."

She could disabuse him of that notion at least. "Most of the houses here in Las Vegas that have been proven to be haunted have only one ghost. It's probably because there isn't a lot here that's more than fifty or sixty years old, so it's not as if we have properties where multiple people have passed away on the premises."

"But there are haunted ones."

The note in his voice was almost pleading, sort of like a kid asking his parents to reassure him that Santa Claus was real.

"Oh, yes," she replied. "More than you might think. Las Vegas is a big town, so it's going to have its share of murders and suicides and overdoses."

"So...ghosts only haunt a house if they've died violently?"

He looked genuinely interested, and Delia found herself smiling again.

Damn, he was cute.

"Not always," she said. "There've been cases where one spouse has passed away and the other was still alive, and a spirit lingers because it doesn't want to move on without their partner. And some-times—sometimes they stay for reasons we can't begin to guess."

Like the ghost of the elderly woman who didn't want to leave the condo that had been her home for forty years. She never did anything malicious, but if the new residents tried to set up the furniture in arrangements she didn't like or hung pictures in places she didn't approve of, everything ended up in a big pile in the middle of the living room.

Needless to say, that particular condo had buyers shuttling in and out until someone finally contacted Delia to help the woman move on. She'd been a stubborn ghost, refusing to listen to any of Delia's persuasive arguments...until she finally explained that the home wasn't hers anymore and that what the ghost was doing was next door to trespassing. The woman must have been the extremely law-abiding sort when she was alive, because as soon as she heard that interpretation of the situation, she promptly disappeared, never to be seen again.

"You can handle any of that, though, right?" Caleb asked. "I mean, what's your success rate?"

"One hundred percent," Delia said proudly, even as she thought, *So far.* "That doesn't mean it's not harder to dislodge some spirits than others, but eventually, they all realize that they're not meant to stay here and vacate the property."

"Sounds good to me," he said. "So, what've you got in inventory right now?"

"None of the properties Dunne & Dunne are handling are haunted," she replied.

Her mother had told her when she came in this morning that the Sunrise Manor house already had three offers on it...and besides, the ghost of the owner's troubled son had obviously moved on, so Delia knew it didn't fit Caleb's parameters. And since she'd run into plenty of kooky requests—including a house with a basement for a dominatrix who wanted to work from home and several clients who insisted on specific house numbers because they were lucky—she wasn't going to worry too much about someone who wanted a haunted house.

As his expression began to fall, though, she added, "But that doesn't mean there aren't a few here in Las Vegas. Let me get my folder on that."

She turned away from him so she could lean down and open the file cabinet next to her desk. Maybe it would have been smarter to keep all this information online, but she liked having physical printouts of the various listings so she could hand them over to a client to look at more closely.

Inventory was always low after the holidays, but now, two weeks into the new year, things were beginning to pick back up a bit. Still, she only had two houses that she knew for sure were haunted, and two others that had sounded promising but which she hadn't had a chance to personally investigate yet.

"I have these four," she said, sliding the folder toward him. "All of them are single-family residences, which I assume is what you're looking for?"

"I'd prefer it," Caleb replied, dark eyes scanning each listing as he shuffled his way through the papers she'd provided. Then he paused and pushed one back toward her. "This place looks like it might work."

He had a good eye, that was for sure. Located in Paradise Palms, the house was a mid-century gem—or at least, it would have been if it hadn't been partially gutted, the flip unfinished.

"What's the story?" he added. "Ghosts chase off the contractors before they could get the job done?"

Delia allowed herself a smile. "Something like that. The house was tied up in probate for a long time because the owner didn't have a will. The heirs—the man's niece and nephew, since he didn't have any children of his own—finally sold it to some house flippers, but they only got partway through the reno before they abandoned the project, claiming that tools and supplies kept getting moved or hidden, and that work they'd done would be torn apart when they came back to the job site the next day. I guess once you've retiled the same bathroom three times, you're ready to throw in the towel."

"I can see that," Caleb said, dark eyes glinting with amusement. "Have you tried to work with this particular ghost?"

She hadn't, mostly because the listing agent, one Paige Loomis, thought that Delia's ghost-cleaning side business was nothing more than an elaborate fraud.

Joke was on her, Delia supposed, considering the place had now been on the market for almost a year and the flippers who'd bought it were climbing the walls despite lowering the price multiple times. All it would have taken was Paige giving her a call—well, and paying a modest fee— and Delia could have taken care of the problem in an afternoon.

However, while Paige Loomis might not have approved of Delia's methods, the other agent couldn't prevent her from showing the property. If Caleb liked what he saw and decided to buy the place, then she'd come in, take care of whatever spirit had taken up residence in the house, and call it a day.

"No," she said. "But that won't stop us from taking a look." She paused there, deciding she'd better be clear about what Caleb was getting himself into. "There's a lot of value to be had in the place—once it's fixed up, it'll easily fetch at least a million, probably more. But it needs a ton of work. Have you ever flipped a house?"

"No," Caleb said, looking cheerful. "Have you?"

"A few," Delia replied. That was going on five years ago now, when it had been easier to purchase distressed properties, make some judicious improvements, and then earn a decent return on your investment. She and her mother had both decided, once inventory began to shrink and interest rates started to inch up, that it was better to get out of the flipping business and concentrate on just selling houses.

But even though the experiment hadn't turned into a permanent sideline, it had still earned them a tidy chunk of change, and Delia knew she was much more familiar with the process than a lot of other real estate agents out there.

"Then you'll be able to provide any advice I might need," Caleb said, still appearing utterly unfazed.

She thought he might change his tune once he took a look at the place and realized he was going to have to drop at least another hundred grand just to get it put back together, but he was the client. That was his decision to make.

"All right," she said, and scooped up the listings

for the other three houses so she could return them to their folder. "Let's go take a look."

From the outside, the house didn't appear too bad. Yes, the lawn was a dry yellow mess, the palm trees planted to one side desperately needed to be trimmed, and the tree to the right of the front walk had been neglected for so long that it was now more an enormous bush than anything else, but the house itself seemed all right, except for needing a new roof and some paint.

Inside, though...well, that was an entirely different matter.

"You weren't joking," Caleb said after she'd retrieved the key from the lockbox and let them inside. "It looks like they've been testing missiles in here."

Immediately past the large double doors was a wilderness of exposed two-by-fours, stacks of drywall, and pallets of tile and flooring. The new stainless-steel appliances sat in the middle of the living room, looking forlorn.

"I'm not much for sugarcoating things," Delia replied. No, she'd much rather a client knew the worst and made a decision based on all the available information rather than think they were inheriting a turnkey home.

Not that the best iPhone filters in the world could have made this place look like anything except the construction zone it truly was.

"Still...."

Caleb stood in the middle of the space, hands on his hips, and didn't seem too daunted by what he saw. The flotsam and jetsam everywhere couldn't hide the way the light streamed into the room from a pair of oversized sliders that opened onto the yard—a yard that backed up to a golf course, providing lots of green, relaxing views from every window at the rear of the house.

Nodding as he went, as if ticking off every project he detected, he headed toward the kitchen, which was another huge, empty space except for a refrigerator big enough to be used in a commercial kitchen, as well as a few pipes sticking out of the floor.

"Is that where the island is supposed to go?" he asked, pointing at the exposed plumbing, and Delia nodded.

"Yes. The plumbing and electrical have been roughed in and passed inspection, so at least you won't have to deal with that. However, all the other rooms have been just as gutted and need to be rebuilt from the ground up."

He was silent for a moment, dark eyes surveying the space. Once it was all put back together, it would be spectacular, thanks to the second set of sliding doors that opened from the breakfast nook and let even more light pour into the space.

"How much?" he asked, and Delia blinked at him.

"Well, they're asking five-fifty, but I think we can talk them down, considering how long the place has been on the market."

Caleb sent her a smile that was almost but not quite indulgent. "No, I meant to finish all the renovations."

A bit of color touched her cheek, even as she told herself it had been an honest mistake. "Probably a hundred grand at least. A lot more if you want the place to be as authentic as possible."

"A restoration versus a renovation?"

Delia nodded, feeling a bit more sure of herself now. "Right. The floors have all been pulled up, but you can see in the corners where it used to be terrazzo. It went out of fashion for a while, but now people who're restoring these mid-century homes like to install the real deal if it's in their budget. But even if you only did the ground floor and put in wood or luxury vinyl plank upstairs and down in the lower level, it would still probably double the flooring budget."

A lot of people would have blinked or showed some sort of reaction at the thought of paying close to fifty grand for flooring, but Caleb only nodded, looking thoughtful. "How would that affect the resale?"

"Hard to say," Delia replied. "Putting in terrazzo isn't the same thing as adding a bathroom or a bedroom. A lot of the time, it comes down to what the buyer is looking for. But I'd probably recommend going with wood floors throughout, just because it'll still look spectacular while appealing to a larger group of prospective buyers."

He seemed content with that answer, because he only nodded again and then asked to see the upstairs.

So she showed him the rest of the house, which, as she'd already warned, was just as torn apart as the kitchen and the living room. However, he seemed impressed with the size of the place, which included four bedrooms and four bathrooms, along with that huge bonus room—or man cave, or kids hangout—on the lower level next to the garage.

"I can see the potential," he said once they'd come back up to the main level. "It doesn't feel very haunted, though."

No, it didn't. The whole time they'd been exploring the property, she'd allowed that sixth sense—or whatever you wanted to call it—to range outward a bit, trying to see if she could detect even the slightest wisp of a ghostly presence.

She hadn't felt a damn thing.

That was the problem with ghosts, though. They didn't always manifest when you wanted them to, and a place that could be absolutely rife with spirit activity for one family or group of people could be silent as the grave...pardon the expression...for another.

"Well, we're just walking around," she said lightly. "So the spirit might not consider us disruptive or a threat. I'll bet if we started putting up drywall, we might experience something."

The corners of Caleb's dark eyes crinkled in amusement. "I'll keep that in mind."

"Let's take a look at the backyard," she suggested. "There's a pool, but, like the rest of the house, it needs a lot of work."

"But not as much work as digging a whole new one," he replied, and she allowed herself a smile.

"No."

They went outside through the slider in the living room, into a backyard that also needed a whole lot of love, from the dead grass to the shaggy palm trees.

But the yard was oversized in a way that yards rarely were these days, and with the property backing onto the golf course, whoever lived here would never have to worry about rear neighbors.

A stray golf ball every once in a while?

Probably.

Caleb had given the yellowed lawn only a brief

glance before he headed over to the pool, which was located off to one side rather than directly behind the house. Delia wasn't sure why the original builders had put it there, since these days most people liked to have the pool where they could see it from the main living space, but she doubted her client would want to spend the money to relocate it, not when he was considering the house as an income property and not his primary residence.

Now he'd paused near the edge of the empty pool, dark eyes keen as he surveyed the cracked plaster and the extremely dated blue-patterned tile that marked the perimeter.

"And those cracks aren't a big problem?"

"They look worse than they are," Delia replied as she walked over to stand next to him. "Get a decent team in here to resurface the pool and—"

She'd been about to say, "It'll be good as new," but even as her lips parted, something behind her —something that felt like a pair of large, heavy hands—planted itself in the center of her back and pushed.

For one hideous moment, she thought she was going to tumble right into the deep end of the empty pool. But then Caleb's hand wrapped around her bicep, hanging on tightly and yanking her away from the edge, back to the relative safety of the concrete surround.

An odd frisson moved up her arm at his touch,

a sensation that wasn't exactly unpleasant but was still unexpected enough that she took a step backward.

At once, he released her. "Didn't mean to startle you," he said. "I just figured you wouldn't want to fall in there headfirst."

"Probably not," she replied, a little surprised by how much her voice shook.

"Did you lose your balance?" he asked.

That would have been the easy reply. Then again, he'd specifically chosen this house because he was looking for a property whose troubles were at least partially supernatural in origin.

"No," she said, glad that she now sounded a bit steadier.

Caleb's head tilted in question, and she gathered her breath.

"Something pushed me."

Chapter Seven

CALEB HADN'T SENSED ANYTHING OFF, BUT he'd seen with his own eyes the way Delia had almost taken a header into the empty swimming pool. And since she had way more experience with haunted houses than he did, he knew he needed to take her words at face value.

Still, whatever spirit was lurking here, it must be in extreme stealth mode, because normally his demon blood would have signaled him that something wasn't quite right about the property.

"Are you okay?" he asked, and Delia nodded.

"I'm fine. Thanks for the save."

He glanced over at the swimming pool. Since they'd been standing near the deep end, she would have fallen about nine feet.

She could have broken her neck.

Which he guessed was exactly what the ghost had intended, and rage boiled in him.

That cowardly piece of shit needed to be banished to the next dimension, stat.

"I guess it's annoyed that someone came to look at the property," she went on. "From what I've heard, it hasn't even been shown for at least a month. The ghost probably thought it had gotten rid of all of us annoying mortals."

A corner of her mouth quirked as she spoke, and Caleb couldn't help being impressed by the way she'd taken the supernatural attack in stride.

Then again, she probably had plenty of experience dealing with this sort of thing.

"So...now what?" he asked.

She hefted the big black purse she'd been carrying a little farther up her shoulder. "Now I try to get it out of here."

This was what he'd been waiting for. The attack had come out of nowhere, but his demon-tuned reflexes had prevented their outing from ending in tragedy.

Now he wanted to see how Delia Dunne handled the obnoxious spirit who clearly wanted her gone.

"Need any help?" he asked, doing his best to sound casual.

"No," she said at once. "It's generally better if I

do this kind of thing alone. Having someone else around can mess up the vibrations."

Because Caleb had halfway expected that sort of response, he didn't allow himself to be too disappointed. However, if Delia thought he was just going to let it go, she was in for a big surprise.

"There's no way I'm leaving you alone here after what just happened."

She looked up at him, one thumb still looped in the strap of her oversized purse. "I'll be fine."

"Will you?" he countered. "What if this thing decides to throw a pallet of flooring at you or something? If it almost pushed you into the pool, then it obviously can interact with physical objects in some way."

Now her expression turned doubtful, and he could almost see her ticking over her counter-arguments and trying to decide whether working alone was worth the risk.

"All right," she said at last, then surprised him by smiling. "I suppose it would be taking too much of a risk to be here by myself. Just...try to watch and not say anything, okay? This can be delicate work."

"Don't worry—I'll shut up."

Her hazel eyes flickered with amusement. "Let's go into the pantry. It's the only place in the house that has anything resembling a tabletop."

He'd noticed it when they entered the kitchen, a walk-in space that would probably be an awesome addition to the place once it was finished, but now still had the Formica counters and screamingly loud mustard and white wallpaper that once had probably adorned the entire room. Why anyone would choose that color in a space that was intended to whet your appetite, he had no idea.

Thank God that kind of thing was just as out of fashion now as a pair of go-go boots.

Delia went into the pantry, set down her purse, and pulled out a tin that contained a stick of what he thought was palo santo wood, a little bottle of holy water, a small white candle, and an ashtray from Caesar's Palace.

Sacred and profane ran through Caleb's head, and he just barely stopped himself from smiling.

"Can you stand at the entrance?" she asked as she rooted around in her purse again, this time pulling out a Zippo lighter adorned with a skull and crossbones, something that would have seemed more appropriate for a night out at a metal club than performing a cleansing in an empty mid-century house. "That way, you're not right next to me while I'm working, but you're close enough to help if anything goes sideways."

"Sure," he said, and took a few steps back so he was standing just outside the pantry.

Being part-demon, he wasn't too scared of the holy water, since it only worked on full-blood denizens of Hell, but he was still happy to put some distance between him and the little white plastic vial that waited on the chipped countertop.

Because he couldn't quite forget that one time when he and his father and the rest of the Greencastle demons had confronted Rosemary and her minister boyfriend and the rest of Rosemary's family, and the holy water they'd flung had raised welts on the part-demons. However, Caleb had always chalked up the unusual damage to their power combining and working together.

Delia, on the other hand, was obviously working alone...and since she thought he was just an ordinary guy, she'd have no reason in the world to throw holy water at him.

He wanted to ask her what she knew about the ghost that resided in this house, but since she'd told him to stay quiet, any questions would have to wait until she was done and the spirit had been banished. Besides, he had to believe if she'd had any real information to give him on that topic, she would have relayed it already. This wasn't her listing, so she probably didn't know anything more than he did.

She lit the little white chime candle, followed by the stick of palo santo. The acrid scent reached

Caleb's nostrils soon enough, but he didn't flinch. While he wasn't entirely of this earth, the sacred wood didn't really affect him...except for maybe making him feel like he'd cough his head off if he inhaled too much of it.

But while he had no problem with the tools Delia was using to get the spirit to move on, he could tell the ghost had a different opinion on the subject. When they'd first walked through the house, he hadn't sensed it at all, and neither had he felt anything when they went outside. The attack that had almost broken her neck had been a surprise to them both.

Now, though...now he could feel it, sort of like the first thunderheads that began to build up on a hot summer afternoon, not a threat so far, but something that could change at a moment's notice.

Well, not a threat to him, anyway. The ghost might not have known exactly what he was, but it seemed to understand he wasn't quite like the woman who stood a few feet away, now with the palo santo stick in one hand so she could wave it around and let the smoke purify and cleanse their immediate surroundings.

"I know you're here," she said, and her voice now was soft, almost pleading, very different from the brisk, businesslike tone she'd employed ever since Caleb first walked into her office. "And I know change can be difficult. But there's no reason for you to linger here. There is so much waiting for you, so many opportunities that don't exist for you on this plane. It's time for you to move on."

A wave of cold hit his body, and he realized the spirit had passed right through him, heading toward Delia.

In that moment, Caleb knew far more about the home's resident ghost than he'd ever wanted to.

And he understood exactly why it had lingered here rather than moving on to the next phase of its existence. While Delia's motivations were pure, and he was sure she only thought she was helping these earthbound spirits relinquish their former lives so they could ascend to the next plane, in some cases, they remained behind simply because they didn't want to go to Hell.

Having spent a few years there, he could sympathize...but that didn't mean he wanted this murderous bastard hanging out in a property he wanted to buy.

Although she no longer stood at the edge of an empty pool, Caleb knew Delia was still in danger.

A word of warning would only let her know that her new client was a little bit more than he claimed.

Better to handle this himself.

Because although he couldn't be banished like a regular demon might, that didn't mean he couldn't attempt a banishing of his own.

No words spoken, no cajoling to get the ghost to relinquish its grip on this house. After that brush-by with the spirit, Caleb had seen everything...and now knew that the lower-level bonus room he'd already imagined turning into a man cave hid its own terrible secret.

The bodies of the five women the ghost had lured here during his lifetime, strangled and then buried.

He'd have to do something about that once the house was his.

In the meantime, this was all about brute psychic strength.

Flaming fingers grasped the ghost by its neck. For one horrible second, the spirit glared into Caleb's eyes, all its hatred burning as bright as the fire that even now began to envelop him.

Go to Hell, you bastard!

The intention, the thought, was all he needed to employ. Shrieking, the spirit vanished, sucked down into the water-stained subfloor...heading much deeper than that.

Delia's eyes widened for a second, and then she looked around, the confusion in her pretty features shifting into something like relief.

"I think it's gone," she said.

Oh, the spirit was definitely gone. Maybe it could take Caleb's former spot in Hell.

He sure didn't need it anymore.

"How can you tell?" he asked, doing his best to act as if he had no idea of what had just transpired.

She looked around them, then picked up the piece of palo santo from where it rested in the ashtray and gently blew it out, followed by the white chime candle, although she extinguished the candle by stubbing it against the ashtray rather than blowing on it.

"It's hard to explain...a sort of lightness, I guess. Something in the atmosphere of the house has shifted."

"That's good," Caleb said. "So, it's safe now?"

A pause, and then she stepped out of the pantry so she could stand in the middle of the kitchen, arms outspread. With her coppery hair falling loose over her shoulders, she looked like some kind of pagan priestess.

Well, except for the gray suit and black pumps she wore.

"I think so," she replied.

"Perfect," he said. "Because I want to make an offer."

They went back to the office so Delia could put together the paperwork. On the drive over, she'd suggested an offer of $475,000, which sounded fine to Caleb. If the current owners were desperate enough, they'd take it. Otherwise, he was fine with some back and forth.

"And now we wait," she said after the files had been sent off to the listing agent. "It's late on a Friday afternoon, though, so we might not hear back for a bit."

He was okay with that. After all, he'd mostly manufactured this quest to buy an income property to get closer to Delia Dunne and learn a little bit more about what made her tick, so waiting to hear whether the offer had been accepted was no big deal. True, he'd had to step in to protect her during the banishing, but he had no doubt that if they'd been dealing with an ordinary spirit and not a sex-crazed serial killer, then she could have managed on her own just fine.

"That's all right," he replied, then paused. This was the time when he should thank her for her help, say goodbye, and head home.

But it was Friday night, and he didn't want to sit in his house by himself yet again. Sure, he could have headed to the casinos, but he thought a much more interesting challenge stood in front of him now.

"How about I take you to dinner to celebrate?" he asked.

A flicker of doubt showed in her eyes. Then she smiled and said, "Don't you think we should hold off on the celebrating until we know whether the sellers have accepted your offer?"

Caleb only shrugged. "Let's just say I have a good feeling."

Delia's lips parted—possibly to tell him it was a little early to have a good feeling about anything—but then her phone, which was sitting on her desk, let out a soft *bing* to let her know she had a new text message.

She scooped it up, looked down at the screen, and offered him a smile of her own. "You must be psychic. That was the listing agent letting me know the sellers have accepted our offer. Their only stipulation is that it has to be an as-is sale with no inspections, but I assume you're all right with that?"

More than all right. Honestly, Caleb didn't see how a home inspector could have even done much with the place, considering its current condition.

"That's fine," he said, and she gave him a nod before sending off a quick text. A moment later, her phone *binged* again.

"They'll sign off on the offer tomorrow morning," she told him. "On Monday, you'll need to get proof of funds from your bank, but I assume that won't be a problem?"

"None at all," he assured her. Probably the biggest issue would be deciding which accounts he wanted to empty, but he had the weekend to figure that out.

And to collect some more winnings at the casinos to replace what he was spending on the house, although he wasn't about to mention that particular detail to her.

"So I guess we have something to celebrate after all," he added, and Delia's expression turned almost too neutral.

"That's very kind of you, Caleb, but—"

"But what?" he broke in. "It's getting toward dinnertime, and we should eat. Unless you have plans, of course," he added.

He didn't think she did, but he figured he should offer her that way to decline his invitation, just in case.

For a second or two, she didn't reply. Then she shook her head.

"No plans. Well, unless you count hanging out with the fish and nuking leftovers."

"'Fish'?" he repeated, and this time she smiled —an expression that looked completely genuine.

"With the hours I work, having a dog or a cat didn't seem like a very good idea. But the fish don't seem to mind that I'm gone most of the day, and when I'm home, at least it feels as if I have someone there to keep me company."

Her existence sounded almost as lonely as his. But no, she was on her home turf here, and presumably had family and friends she could spend time with when she wanted to. After a long day, though, she probably just wanted to head home and put her feet up most of the time.

"And the fish won't mind that you didn't go straight home after work?"

Now she grinned. "I think they'll survive."

Chapter Eight

—·‹‹‹·◎·›››·—

HE TOOK HER TO BATTISTA'S HOLE IN THE Wall, an Italian restaurant that Delia and her family had often visited when she was growing up but which she hadn't been to for a while. She was a little surprised that Caleb knew about the place, since it was kind of off the beaten track.

Then again, internet searches pretty much ensured that anyone could find even the most obscure dining spots.

Because it was still early—they arrived at Battista's at about a quarter after six—they were given a nice booth off in a corner. If this had been a date, Delia would have been glad of the privacy.

As it was....

Caleb didn't seem to notice anything fraught about the situation, though, and only asked if she'd been here before and, if so, whether she had any favorites.

"Their cannelloni is delicious," she said. "And I love the eggplant parmesan. But really, you can't go wrong with pretty much anything on the menu."

"Plus, no worries about ordering the wrong wine," he replied with a grin.

Not at Battista's, where house wine was included as part of your dinner. You could always order a cocktail instead, but she was just fine with having some chianti with her meal. After that encounter with the angry ghost by the swimming pool, she knew she needed some kind of muscle relaxant.

"They kind of took the guesswork out of that part," Delia said. Should she ask him about wine, and whether he knew much about it?

No, that seemed like too personal a question. So far, they were talking about surface-level stuff, and she wanted it to stay that way. Then she could tell herself this wasn't a date, just a business dinner provided by a grateful client.

Even if Caleb Lowe was by far the best-looking client she'd ever had. When they'd walked into the restaurant, several heads had turned, and Delia was pretty sure those patrons hadn't been looking at her.

Why would they, when her companion was a guy who looked like a male model?

Their waiter came by and took their orders—Caleb opted for steak, while Delia decided to indulge herself with the cannelloni, mostly because it had been so long since she'd had it that she thought she should revisit the dish to see if it was as good as she remembered.

Once their wine had been dropped off, Caleb said, "How soon do you think I can get started on the renovations?"

Another nice, safe topic. After all, it wasn't as if she thought they should talk openly about what had just happened at the house on Pueblo Street.

Not that Delia was still entirely certain about what had gone down an hour ago. Yes, she was pretty sure the ghost had been sent off to the next plane...but she also couldn't quite shake the feeling that the banishment had felt almost too easy, as if her own powers of persuasion weren't the whole reason why the spirit had decided to move on.

"Probably around a month," she replied. "Even without having to get financing, it still can take a few weeks to get the title transferred. Waiving the home inspection will speed things up a little, though, and I can make some inquiries with contractors I've worked with in the past to see if they're available."

This offer seemed to reassure Caleb, because he relaxed against the back of the booth, saying, "That would be a big help. I've heard horror stories about people who've hired the wrong general contractor and gotten into a world of hurt."

"Yes, there are plenty of those to go around," she said. "But I've got some good contacts, so we'll make sure the team who comes in to reno the place won't leave you stranded."

They chatted then about the house flips she'd done with her mother, the information appearing to reassure him that much further—not only because it proved she had experience with this sort of project, but also because she knew the right places to go for materials, and who was reliable and who wasn't.

As they talked, though, Delia couldn't help wondering just what she was getting herself into. Wasn't she supposed to walk away after the deal was done and let the buyer handle any renovations?

Most of the time, yes. But somehow she found herself all but promising that she'd hold Caleb Lowe's hand through the whole process.

Suckered in by a pretty face, she supposed... even while she couldn't help thinking it might be a little bit more than that.

However, the rest of their meal was uneventful enough, and once they were done, they got in their separate vehicles and headed for home. Yes, they'd meet on Monday so they could sign the offer, and Caleb could give Paige Loomis the bona fides from his bank to prove he had sufficient funds for the transaction, but at least Delia would have a little decompression time to try to analyze everything that had happened over the past few hours.

Her neighborhood was about twenty minutes from Battista's, so she got to the house a little past seven-thirty. She set her purse down on the dining room table and headed over to the sideboard where the fish tank rested, then sprinkled some food into the water.

"Chow time," she said cheerfully as the tetras and cichlids surged toward the surface to get their nibbles.

That duty handled, she went into the kitchen and poured herself some water from the pitcher in the fridge. Although she'd only had one glass of wine with dinner, she was thirstier than she'd expected and drank almost the whole tumbler, then refilled it.

Most of the time when she'd found a house for a client, she was relaxed and happy afterward—and not only because of the big commission coming her way. No, she was always glad to help people find their forever homes...and that included the ghosts she sent on to the next plane.

Something about this situation felt almost surreal, though, and she didn't think it was just because of the way the ghost had attacked her.

Caleb's hand on her arm, sending a shiver

through her body that she didn't think was only because she had been shocked and afraid.

Two violent ghosts in a row. Did that mean anything, or was she just having a run of bad luck?

She took the glass of water with her into the living room and sat down on the couch. The night was chilly enough that she could have turned on the fireplace, but for the moment, she was all right with merely resting on the leather sofa she'd bought a few months earlier and thinking over everything that had happened today.

Was it weird that a thirty-year-old man with no discernible career had this kind of cash to throw around?

In some towns, sure. In Las Vegas...not so much. He'd said he'd come into money but hadn't elaborated, so it could have been anything from an inheritance to a few weeks of really good luck at the blackjack tables. While the casinos always came out on top, that didn't mean there weren't plenty of people who won millions anyway.

Caleb Lowe could have just been one of those lucky ones.

Still....

Delia set her glass of water down on a coaster, then got up from the couch and headed into the extra bedroom she used as an office so she could fetch her laptop.

A couple of quick searches didn't pull up

anything about Caleb Lowe—or rather, she found plenty of individuals with that same name, but none of them were the man she knew. No social media, no newspaper mentions of winning big poker tournaments or anything like that.

So what? Plenty of people managed to keep a low profile and didn't waste their time on Facebook or TikTok or whatever.

But her instincts kept telling her something else was going on here.

Luckily, she had someone who could help.

Prudence Nelson had been the bassist in Final Girl, and after the group broke up, the members still kept in touch. Sarah, the drummer, had moved to L.A., so Delia's contact with her was mostly through social media, and Toni, the lead guitarist, had gotten married not too long after the band split and started a family...but Pru had decided to get her private investigator's license and be her own boss.

Delia had only asked for Pru's help a couple of times, mostly because she hadn't wanted to seem if she was taking advantage of her friend's unique access to information. Every once in a while, though, she came across a client who got her spider sense tingling, and that was when she felt as if she needed to reach out.

Right now, her spider-sense was going kind of crazy.

And she knew Pru would probably be home, just because she hated crowds and did all her socializing on the quieter nights of the week. No way would she be fighting the Friday night throngs when she could stay safely in her house.

Sure enough, she picked up on the second ring. "Hey, Delia. Who do you want me to snoop on now?"

Since that was just Pru being Pru, Delia didn't take offense. "My new client. On the surface, he seems okay, but..."

"...but you're getting the sense that something isn't on the up and up," Pru finished for her. "What's his name?"

"Caleb Lowe," Delia replied. "He's around thirty or thirty-one, I think."

"Does he live in Vegas?"

"Yes. Fairly new to town, though. He bought a house here about a month and a half ago, but I'm not sure whether the information would be on the county recorder's site yet. They're pretty backed up."

"I should still be able to find something. Give me a sec."

A faint clunk of a sound, probably Pru setting down her phone so she could use both hands to type on her keyboard. Delia had been over to her townhouse plenty of times, so she knew her friend used one of the spare bedrooms as an office and had a big iMac on one desk and a PC with multiple screens on the other. Maybe she had a laptop, too, but Delia had never seen it.

Only a couple of minutes passed before Pru picked up her phone again.

"His driver's license was issued in late November. And yeah, found his house, too—2642 Saguaro Court."

So the assessor's office had cleared some of their backlog. Well, home sales always slowed down around the holidays.

Something about the address seemed vaguely familiar to her, but she put that aside for now, figuring she could look it up herself once she was done talking to Prudence.

"This is weird, though," Pru went on, and Delia found herself sitting up a little straighter on the sofa.

"What's weird?"

"I can't find a single thing about this guy before he got that driver's license. I mean, he has a Social Security number and a credit score, but his credit report is awfully blank for someone who's rattling around in the low 800s."

That was strange. Delia knew that part of having a high credit score was having responsibly held credit for multiple years, and not just having credit card bills or car or house payments that had been made on time. It should have been impossible to have such a high score without any evidence of the credit that had been used to build it.

"Witness protection program?" she suggested, only half joking.

Pru chuckled. "That makes as much sense as anything else I can think of. I'll poke around some more, though—this is just surface-level stuff." She paused there before adding, "Did you sell him a house?"

"We're in the process," Delia said. "He's paying cash...he told me he'd just come into some money."

"Well, that's easy to do in Vegas," Pru replied. "But usually you don't see people in the WPP having that kind of money to throw around."

Delia didn't pretend to be an expert on the subject, but yes, that didn't feel quite right. It seemed to her that people were generally given new identities and jobs and a place to live, not hundreds of thousands of dollars—maybe more—to invest in whatever income property caught their fancy.

"You think he might be on the run?" she asked, and now Prudence laughed outright.

"I suppose it might be a possibility," she said. "But if he was really trying to hide out, he wouldn't be buying property. Even when you pay cash, there's still a paper trail."

A very big one. Also, Caleb seemed fine with a remodel that would involve him interacting with a bunch of contractors...and sticking around for the six months or more that all the work would require.

That didn't feel to her like someone trying to maintain a low profile.

"Anyway," Pru added, "it's not like you have to keep working with him after the sale is final, right?"

Well....

"I sort of volunteered to help him with finishing the reno," Delia said. "It's a massive project."

"Since when are you a general contractor?"

"I'm not," she replied. "Mostly what I'm going to do is set him up with the right people. But still, it's not like this is going to be over once he signs the final paperwork."

Although Delia couldn't see her friend, she had to believe her expression turned sly.

"I suppose there are worse things in life than having to work with a hottie like this guy."

No point in asking how Pru had known that, not when she'd pulled up Caleb's driver's license online and therefore knew what he looked like.

"He's just a client," Delia said, knowing she sounded a bit too severe.

"Uh-huh. When was the last time you went on a date?"

"Look who's talking, Ms. 'I'm sitting at home with my computers on a Friday night.'"

"Going out on the weekend is highly overrated," Pru replied serenely. "Anyway, we weren't talking about me. We were talking about you."

"And I'm telling you that Caleb Lowe is a client and nothing more."

Was she protesting too much?

Maybe. If forced, she would admit that she found Caleb attractive. But there was also something about him that didn't feel right, even if she couldn't quite put her finger on what it might be.

"Well, he won't be a client forever," Pru said, her voice way too cheerful. "Then we'll see how you really feel about Mr. Hottie McHotterson."

"He could be gay," Delia said.

Not that she got that vibe from him, despite the perfectly coiffed hair and the expensive watch.

"He could," Pru agreed. "But you don't think so."

"No. Anyway, none of this is super-urgent. I just thought it would be a good idea to find out a little more about the guy in case there's something weird here that I need to be careful about."

Of course, if she was really trying to be careful, she would have turned down his offer of dinner...or maybe even told him that she didn't think she could help him with his house-hunting quest and that he should find another agent.

But it wasn't until they'd gone to the house on Pueblo Street together that she'd even started to sense there might be more about Caleb Lowe than met the eye, way too late to tell him he should work with a different realtor.

"I'll keep poking at it," Pru said. "If I find anything, I'll let you know. Maybe we can get together for margaritas on Sunday night?"

Technically, Sunday was still the weekend, but most of the rabid partygoers wouldn't be out and about when they had to get up and go to work the next day. And although Delia knew she'd be meeting with Caleb and Paige Loomis to sign the paperwork and get the ball rolling, that wouldn't be until late morning at the earliest.

Plenty of time to recover from a pitcher of margaritas.

"Sounds good," she replied. "Seven o'clock at Ghost Donkey?"

"It's a date."

They ended the call there, and Delia put her phone down on the coffee table. It still felt a little weird to reach out to Pru like this, even though she knew she was just keeping her bases covered. Ignoring her instincts was never a good idea, and besides, it wasn't as if she was asking her friend to dig up every single piece of information she could find about Caleb Lowe, right down to the name of his pets when he was back in grade school. No, she just wanted some kind of an idea about where he'd come from...and the source of his money.

After all, the last thing she needed was to be

working with someone who'd stolen from drug dealers or the mob or whatever.

Life was complicated enough without getting dragged into that kind of drama.

Having reassured herself that her motives were pure, Delia got up from the sofa and went down the hallway to her bedroom. An hour or so of watching TV in bed sounded like the best way to wind down what had turned out to be a much more hectic day than she'd planned.

And then she'd sleep and hope she wouldn't dream about the nightmarish sensation of those two angry hands pushing against her back...or about the strength of Caleb Lowe's fingers as they grabbed her by the arm and saved her from serious injury, if not worse.

The way his dark eyes had met hers across the table at Battista's.

Damn it.

You will not get involved with a client, she told herself. *You will* not.

She just wished she believed herself.

Chapter Nine

—·((·◎·))·—

CALEB HAD DRIVEN HOME AFTER HIS dinner with Delia Dunne, but a restless fifteen minutes or so of puttering around the house told him he wasn't going to be content with hanging out and watching some TV.

Maybe he should get a dog.

The idea had occurred to him more than once after he'd bought the place—it had a big yard, and he could certainly adjust his schedule to be around more to play with the pup. When he was a kid, he'd had a dog, a scary-smart German shepherd who'd been his constant companion. As he grew older, he realized the dog hadn't been much more than a prop to make the Lockwoods look as much like the typical all-American family as possible, but the boy he'd been hadn't cared.

No, he'd loved Riley and had mourned when

the dog passed at the ripe old age of thirteen, about the maximum expected from that breed. By that point, Caleb was almost twenty and already thinking about moving out, and losing Riley had seemed to be a sign that it was time to go.

But eight o'clock on a Friday night wasn't exactly prime time to visit an animal shelter, so it wasn't as if he could just run out and grab himself a new canine companion.

Instead, he got into his Range Rover and drove downtown, figuring he might as well start racking up some more wins to replace the money he was about to spend on the house on Pueblo Street.

And to pay for all the massive renovations it would require to make it remotely habitable.

Although things were supposed to slow down in Vegas after the first of the year before they ramped up again around spring break, Caleb didn't see much sign of that as he hunted for a space in one of the casino parking garages. He finally was able to snag one at the Strat, which seemed to be a signal that he should start his night of gambling there. Because he hadn't played at that casino yet, he figured it was ripe for the picking.

The darkness of the garage helped conceal him as he shifted his appearance, this time taking on the face and build of an Asian man in his forties. So far, he'd never deployed the same identity twice, using as inspiration people he'd seen on the street or at the grocery store or on the evening news, or failing that, using AI to cook up some useful faces. Once he saw a person, their features were permanently engraved on his memory, making it easy enough to shuffle through all their various visages and decide which one would be right for a particular occasion.

And when he went inside, the stray thought passed through his mind that, although the design elements might change from venue to venue, all casinos were still basically the same—noisy and dark and smelling of cigarette smoke.

In that way, he supposed they were a little like Hell.

He wanted to win, but he wasn't going to go crazy about it. Maybe 25K here, another 30K somewhere else, and he'd just hopscotch from casino to casino until he had another half million ready to be deposited in yet another bank. Eventually, he'd probably need to get a financial advisor who could help him guide it into T-bills or mutual funds or whatever, but for now, he kind of liked the idea of having millions stashed in the various banks and credit unions around town.

Blackjack first, followed by some time at the craps table. He went into the bathroom in between, making sure to change his appearance before he exited. While he supposed some people might be lucky enough to win big at both games, he thought it better to be careful and make the security team at the Strat—and their cameras—think that two entirely different people had won big tonight.

He got into the flow while playing craps, now wearing the face of a man around his own age, but with dark hair and hazel eyes and features that were entirely unlike his own. Roll after roll went his way, while crowds began to gather around the table and cheer him on.

Among the group were a couple of extremely attractive women, their interest piqued, he guessed, just as much by his appearance as the continued luck he displayed. One of them even leaned on him, rubbing her hip suggestively against his, and he knew she'd be just fine with him taking her home after he collected his winnings.

And would that be such a bad thing? It had been a while since he'd scratched that itch, and he had to admit the girl was pretty spectacular in that tight black dress with her blonde hair cascading down her back.

Out of nowhere, his mind conjured an image of Delia Dunne's face, of how shocked and pale she'd been after he caught hold of her and yanked her back from the edge of the empty pool.

Of how she'd gathered herself and gone inside and done her ritual anyway, when he guessed a lot of women would have run screaming for the door.

Suddenly, the blonde with her bleached hair and too-tight dress didn't seem nearly as appealing.

"Gotta cash out," he told her after he signaled the dealer that he was done and began to collect his chips.

The blonde sent him a lascivious smile. "That's okay," she said. "Maybe you can buy me a drink with all that money you just won."

It was a lot—almost sixty thousand, way more than he'd planned. But the rolls had kept going his way...of course they had...and he knew he'd allowed the game to string out longer than he'd intended because when he was watching the dice, he wasn't thinking about his dinner with Delia, the way her hazel-green eyes would light up with amusement at a comment he'd made or how her wide, friendly mouth would curve as she smiled.

Even in her business attire, she'd been a million times sexier than this fake blonde could ever be.

"Sorry," he mumbled. "I've got somewhere I need to go."

The woman's eyes—their color indistinguishable in the dark casino, and shadowed further by heavy fake lashes—narrowed.

"Asshole," she snapped, and flounced away from the craps table, presumably heading off to find more cooperative prey.

Well, he'd clearly dodged a bullet there.

He went and cashed out his winnings, which

were a little over eighty thousand between what he'd won at blackjack and craps. Although the woman working in the cage was professional enough, he could tell from her vaguely hostile air as she handed over the money that she wasn't too thrilled with him for making the casino take such a hit.

Time to move on.

From there, he drove over to the Bellagio, won another ten grand, and then wandered down the strip to Caesar's Palace, where he allowed himself a drink as he gambled, figuring this would be the last place he visited before heading home. By the time he was done, he knew he'd have won at least a hundred thousand, getting him to a place where he had begun to put a dent in the cost of his new house.

Except....

He'd gone to play roulette, thinking he might as well change things up a bit. This time, he wore the face and form of a chubby man with thinning hair who might have been in his late fifties or early sixties, not the sort of person who would attract hangers-on like the blonde at The Strat.

Well, unless he won another fifty or sixty thousand, something he wasn't planning on doing. No, he would pull in maybe a couple of thousand bucks at best, certainly nothing that would cause anyone to even lift an eyebrow.

And at first, it was fine. He'd win a spin and then lose one, knowing he could influence the wheel anytime he liked but was letting it roll on pure chance for the moment, hoping to lull the croupier into a false sense of security. The woman overseeing the spins looked like she might be around ten years older than he, with dark hair pulled back into a severe ponytail and her expression indicating that she could think of a whole lot of other places where she would prefer to be.

Although Caleb could sympathize—he didn't love hanging out in casinos, even as he understood they were the best way for him to put some quick money in his pocket—he also guessed that someone like her might not be paying as much attention to her work as she should.

Two spins in a row went his way, thanks to a subtle mental nudge, and the chips began to stack up in front of him.

Sounding bored, the dealer said, "Place your bets," and he pushed one of the stacks onto black seven.

Which of course was where the ball bounced a few seconds later.

Winning was a hell of a drug, though, and he let himself win the next three as well, only stopping because he realized he was inching toward another ten grand and that was over the limit he'd set for himself.

Another cashier's cage, another stack of bills pushed toward him. As always, he had his messenger bag secured around his neck and over one shoulder, and he shoved the money inside to join his winnings from earlier that night.

Definitely time to go home now. The people around him looked as though they planned to keep gambling and drinking until the wee hours, but he'd won more than expected and just wanted to get the hell out of there.

The first tingle of odd energy came as he was leaving Caesar's. While it was kind of a hike to get back to the parking garage at the Bellagio where he'd left his Range Rover, he hadn't felt like summoning an Uber or a taxi, figuring the streets were still plenty crowded and that he should be safe enough walking, despite the massive amount of money he carried in the messenger bag.

But something made the hair on the back of his neck stand up almost as soon as he was outside, and he looked all around him, wondering what the hell it was.

If he hadn't known better, he would have said he'd sensed another demon somewhere nearby.

Well, a full-on demon, since Caleb knew he was the only quarter-demon currently walking the face of the planet. Likewise for the cambions, the half-demons, his father among them. They were all stuck in Hell, thanks to not being quite nimble enough when the opportune moment came.

He sped up his pace, not enough to make anyone watching really notice a shift in his gait, but enough that he would probably shave a couple of precious minutes off his trek to the parking garage where his SUV waited. No point in trying to glance around again, not when he knew a demon could perfectly mimic a human appearance when it needed to.

But what the hell—pardon the expression— was a demon doing here in Las Vegas?

Even as the question surfaced in his mind, he thought he knew the answer well enough. Demons loved to feed on negative emotions, and there were certainly enough of those bubbling away in Sin City at any given time. Greed, lust, gluttony...a whole smorgasbord of the seven deadly sins was on offer here to an enterprising demon who decided to go slumming. They couldn't stay permanently, of course, but they could hang out long enough to do some damage.

There came that lifting of the hair at the back of his neck again, and he somehow knew the thing had come closer to him. Had it been able to sense his part-demon nature, just as he also knew it was somewhere close by?

Probably. Demons had their own super-attuned senses, and while they weren't exactly like his, they were definitely strong enough to make a formidable adversary.

If that was even what was going on here. For all he knew, the demon that had hidden itself in the Friday night crowds that filled the sidewalks along the Strip was only tailing him because it had sensed another of its kind in the immediate vicinity and wanted to come over and give him the demonic equivalent of a secret handshake.

Somehow he doubted that was the case, though. His time in Hell had taught him that every demon was out for itself, and he'd only been left alone because—despite being just one-quarter demon—he was more powerful than many of them, thanks to the way the demonic blood he'd inherited had come down from one of Belial's lieutenants, some of the strongest demons in existence.

But even though he thought he might be able to defeat whoever or whatever was following him, Caleb still wished he'd gone quietly into one of the public bathrooms in the Venetian and teleported himself back home. He could have come back to retrieve the Range Rover in the morning once the coast was clear.

He hadn't, though, which meant he needed to keep walking and pretend he hadn't noticed anything strange about one of the people in the crowd that surrounded him. At least he'd maintained the disguise of the mild-mannered, paunchy, middle-aged man he was pretending to be, so even if the demon decided to attack, it still wouldn't know what his true face looked like.

Past Flamingo Road, and then at last into the parking garage at the Bellagio. Once there, Caleb couldn't help sending a quick glance over his shoulder, but no one was anywhere nearby.

Had he been imagining things?

No, there had definitely been a demon. After spending two years surrounded by the infernal creatures, he knew all too well what the things smelled like, like someone who hadn't taken a shower in years finally deciding to have a dunk in a sulfurous hot spring.

It didn't seem to have come into the parking garage, so either it had decided he wasn't worthwhile prey after all, or it had hung back, waiting to see what he did.

His Range Rover was up on the third level. Caleb hesitated for a moment, trying to decide which way of getting there was more dangerous—stairs or elevator?

Both options had their own upsides and downsides, but after weighing them in his mind, he decided the stairwell was probably the better option. Worse come to worst, he could always teleport himself home and come back for the SUV, whereas if he was trapped in the elevator with any hapless humans who had the bad luck to be inside when his pursuer attacked, he'd have a lot fewer options.

It was never a good idea to show off your powers like that, not when doing so always led to a whole lot of unanswerable questions.

At least the stairs were well-lit and didn't offer many places for even a demon to lurk in the shadows. Caleb took the stairs two at a time, not caring if his actions contrasted sharply with the overweight man in his fifties he was pretending to be.

No one was around to see him anyway.

However, he slowed his pace when he emerged from the stairwell, pausing so he could send a wary look at his surroundings. Up here, there weren't nearly as many cars as there had been a few hours earlier, telling him that he wasn't the only one who'd decided to call it a night and head for home base.

Unless they'd only moved their partying operations to a different hotel.

Either way, it didn't matter to him. What mattered was that he appeared to be alone up here, and he didn't have that creepy-crawly sensation on the back of his neck, the one that down on the street had told him a demon was somewhere close.

Time to get the hell out of Dodge.

He reached into his pocket to touch the fob and unlock the Range Rover as he approached, walking quickly. A few more paces, and then he was there, pulling the messenger bag off his neck so he could toss it onto the passenger seat.

Before he could start to climb in behind the wheel, though, something dove off the roof of the SUV and plowed into him, knocking him to the ground.

Son of a bitch.

The demon was shorter than he, with grayish skin and red eyes and a bulging, bulbous head adorned by a pair of pointed ears. Because it was so small, it must have flattened itself against the roof of the Range Rover and hidden itself that way. Caleb had no idea what face it had worn while walking through the crowd, but it clearly had decided there was no need to disguise itself now, not when they were alone up here on the third floor of the parking structure.

"Take a hike," he said clearly, and the demon hissed at him.

"I want the bag," it said, and Caleb raised an eyebrow.

"To do what with? It's not like you need cash in Hell to cover the mortgage or pay for groceries."

Another hiss. "You're a cheat. You shouldn't have that money at all."

All right, he had to acknowledge that accusation was true enough. Still, he had to survive in the human world...and the demon didn't.

"A demon worried about right and wrong?" he countered. "That's rich."

The thing hissed again. "You're pretty full of yourself for someone who's only a quarter demon."

Caleb didn't bother to ask how it knew that. Demons could just tell.

"And you're asking for trouble," he replied. "Now, get out of here before I banish you."

Its reddish eyes narrowed. "You can't do that."

"Can't I? All that human blood in my veins lets me do a whole lot of shit that demons can't."

A second or two passed as the demon eyed him, clearly trying to weigh its chances of success. Caleb stood there and waited, knowing any shift in position on his part would only encourage it to attack.

And then it leaped into the air, clawed fingers reaching for him, reaching out to rip open his face—

Flames flared from his outstretched hands, and one fireball, followed by another, connected with the creature, knocking it back a good ten feet or so.

"I might be mostly human," Caleb said as he advanced on the demon. "But that doesn't mean I can't defend myself."

The creature bared its yellowed teeth. He'd encountered similar imps in Hell and knew they didn't possess his talent for summoning fire. No, they delighted in tormenting those weaker than themselves and were often employed by stronger demons and devils to carry out their dirty work.

In fact....

"Who do you work for?" he demanded, and the thing growled.

"I work for myself."

But something in the way those last two syllables squeaked past its jagged teeth told Caleb the demon was lying.

"You're not strong enough to make it topside on your own," he said. "Someone summoned you so they'd have a lackey. Who was it?"

Its reddish eyes widened in fear, and something about the way it glanced to one side told him the creature was about to bolt.

No way. Not when it would most likely go back and tell its master—whoever that was—that a quarter demon descended from one of Belial's lieutenants was now roaming the streets of Las Vegas, Nevada.

So much for the interrogation.

Caleb lifted his hands again, and this time, fire exploded from his hands and swirled all around, catching the imp-demon in its scorching embrace, holding the thing until it had shattered into ash.

Not a moment too soon, because in the next instant, the faint squeal of a set of tires from the direction of the ramp told him someone was approaching and he needed to get the hell out of there.

Doing his best to seem nonchalant...even as he summoned a small breeze to blow away the ashy remnants of the demon...he walked over to the Range Rover and climbed into the driver's seat. Just as he was fastening his seatbelt, the vehicle passed behind him.

It had the elegant script logo of the Bellagio painted on one door, with the word "Security" above it. Most likely, whoever was driving was just making their normal rounds, but to Caleb, its arrival was an additional signal that he needed to leave, and now. He always made sure to park carefully out of range of the nearest CCTV camera, and yet he also knew he shouldn't take any more chances.

Slowly, he backed the SUV out of its parking space and headed down to the lower level and the exit that opened onto Flamingo Road. The whole time, he'd made sure his disguise remained intact, but after he turned onto Las Vegas Boulevard and knew he was well away from the parking structure, he thought it was finally safe for him to let the illusion disappear.

As he drove, he couldn't stop himself from frowning.

Who had summoned that imp-demon... and why?

Chapter Ten

---·‹‹‹·☾·›››·---

EVEN THOUGH IT WAS THE WEEKEND AND Delia would have much rather taken a page out of her friend Pru's book and stayed home, she hadn't forgotten about her agreement with Robert Hendricks, and knew she needed to go and prowl a few more casinos to see if any demons were lurking there.

After her last experience, she was inclined to think that the only unusual individuals hanging out on the Strip were a few people with abnormally good luck, but if she wanted to earn that ten grand —and maybe more, on the off chance that she actually managed to detect something—then she needed to get her ass out there and do her job.

So that was why, once she was finished with her laundry and had done some general tidying-up around the house, she got out of her yoga pants and sweatshirt and into some jeans and low boots and her favorite dark green sweater, put on some mascara and lip gloss, and headed out to see if she could find anything of use.

It still felt strange to wander a casino floor and act as if it was perfectly normal for her to drift from one place to the next, doing her best to reach out with the same psychic sense that helped her make contact with ghosts to see if there was something else here, something not of this earth. A couple of times during this process, the security guards gave her the side-eye, and she paused and popped a couple of quarters into a slot machine so they wouldn't think she was there for an entirely different purpose.

Not that any of the "escorts" who tended to hang around the casinos and the clubs would let them be seen in public in such boring clothes or so little makeup.

But no matter where she went, she didn't detect a single thing...until she was in the parking garage at the Bellagio, of all places.

She'd moved her car there after exploring Caesar's Palace and the Hard Rock and the Venetian, and had to go all the way up to the third floor before she could find a space to park her Kona. Once she got out and began to walk toward the elevator, though, she found herself pausing, her spidey senses tingling all over the place.

Why this particular spot, she wasn't sure, because there certainly wasn't anyone or anything here of note except a few oil stains on the concrete and a discarded Starbucks cup.

And yet....

It was a little like walking into a room where someone had smoked a few hours earlier. Something about the smell still seemed to linger in the place, even though there wasn't anything about this particular location to signal why it might be important.

The sound of an engine came up the ramp, and she stepped out of the way so she wouldn't block the oncoming vehicle. It was a large Dodge Ram truck with a guy in a baseball cap behind the wheel, a man who didn't spare a second glance for her as he continued upward in search of a parking space.

Once he was gone, Delia moved back into the middle of the access lane, eyes narrowing. Look as hard as she could, she couldn't see a single thing to indicate there was anything unique or special about this spot.

Her psychic senses...or whatever you wanted to call them...told her a different story, however.

What had happened here?

She had no idea. The only thing she did know was that this didn't feel like a ghost.

Did that mean a demon had once been here?

Maybe. Or maybe she was imagining the whole

thing because she desperately wanted to have even a tiny piece of evidence she could present to Robert Hendricks whenever he next made contact. Delia had a feeling he probably wouldn't reach out until Monday at the earliest, though, just because he hadn't seemed like the kind of guy who would bug her over the weekend.

She supposed that was a good thing. The more time she had to dig into this, the better the chance she might have something to actually give him.

Although there really wasn't anything to see, she went ahead and pulled her iPhone out of her purse so she could take a few pictures of the section of the structure where she stood. If nothing else, she could show them to Pru when they met tomorrow evening for drinks. Her friend was a trained private detective, after all, and Delia thought it was possible she might be able to see something that a mere real estate agent couldn't.

Another car was coming up the ramp, so she took its appearance as a signal that she was done here and needed to head out. As she got into her SUV and pressed the button to start the engine, she couldn't help wondering if her mind had manufactured those odd sensations out of pure frustration at not being able to find anything when she was wandering through the casinos.

No, that was silly. While she wanted to do a good job for Robert the same way she wanted to make sure all her clients were happy, she still shouldn't be desperate enough to make up some kind of story about demonic residue. For one thing, if her brain really had conjured the whole thing, why do it here in the parking garage rather than on a casino floor?

She had no idea.

Which meant she had felt something real…even if she had no idea what it could have been.

Frowning, she backed out of the parking space and headed down to street level.

On the drive home, her phone pinged from inside her purse, and when she was safely stopped at a light, she pulled it out and took a quick look.

A text from Paige Loomis, saying she'd be at Delia's office at eleven on Monday morning to sign the offer papers and collect Caleb's proof of funds.

Well, that was something, she supposed. Not that she'd really expected Paige or her client to back out of the deal, not when that lemon of a property had been sitting on the market for almost a year—and not when Delia had come up with a buyer who was willing to do a cash transaction—but still, it felt like progress, and it was a piece of validation she needed right then, especially after experiencing that whatever-it-was in the parking structure at the Bellagio.

She had to wait for another red light to reply, but once that was handled, she returned the phone to her purse and continued the rest of the drive home without incident. After checking on the fish, she decided to do a little research to see if anyone had ever reported any strange phenomena in that location.

It wasn't the easiest of internet searches, since she kept pulling up all sorts of random information about the casino rather than anything directly connected to the supernatural, and not for the first time, she admired the way her friend Prudence always seemed able to get right to the heart of the matter no matter how arcane the topic might be. For a moment or two, Delia wondered if she should send Pru a text to ask her to check into the Bellagio as well, then pushed the notion aside. Investigating Caleb was more important, especially since she still couldn't say for sure whether what she'd experienced in the Bellagio's parking garage had been nerves and nothing more.

After all, being tasked to investigate whether any demons were roaming around in Vegas casinos was probably sufficient to put you on edge.

Annoyed, she closed her laptop and vowed to focus on the mundane for the rest of the weekend. Grocery shopping, housework—she had someone come in to clean into the corners once a month, but she took care of the in-between stuff—maybe going to the Sherwin-Williams store to pick up some paint samples for the continually delayed repainting of her home office.

Anything to keep her mind off demons and casinos...and Caleb Lowe.

By the time Sunday evening rolled around, Delia thought she was feeling a lot more grounded. The house was clean, she'd decided on a gorgeous color for the office—a pale, hazy blue-green named Waterfall—and absolutely nothing weird had happened, much to her relief. She'd chatted with her mother and promised to go over for dinner sometime this coming week, had made appointments for two new home listings, and was glad that life in general seemed pretty normal.

Even in Las Vegas, January evenings were too chilly to sit outside—a lot of places had those big outdoor heaters, but unless you were sitting right next to one, they didn't seem to help all that much —so Delia and Pru had already agreed to meet in the bar at Ghost Donkey and start there, then decide if they wanted to stay beyond drinks and nachos or move on to different restaurant if it turned out they wanted something other than Mexican food.

For a Sunday evening, the bar was pretty crowded. Luckily, though, it seemed as if Prudence had gotten there early, because she'd snagged them a high-top table off to one side rather than sitting at the counter.

Much better. Not that Delia was morally opposed to sitting at the bar, but it was a lot more difficult to have a private conversation that way.

Pru's dark eyes were dancing, telling Delia she must have dug up something. However, it seemed she was willing to wait until they'd ordered their drinks—a Cadillac margarita on the rocks for Delia and a frozen prickly pear for Prudence, after they'd decided a pitcher wouldn't be practical because they wanted different things—and also placed an order for a big platter of nachos before she was ready to launch into her findings.

"So, what've you got?" Delia asked after the waitress dropped off their margaritas and promised that their nachos would be out in a few minutes.

"Lots of stuff," Pru replied, then took a sip of her margarita. Unlike Delia, who'd let her natural hair color come back in after deepening it to shocking scarlet when she'd sung for Final Girl, Prudence still sported one brilliant color after another, depending on her mood that month. Right now, it was a bright turquoise, a shade that certainly stood out against her all-black clothes and pale skin. "For one thing, his name isn't really Caleb Lowe. It's Caleb Lockwood."

Delia stared at her friend. "How'd you find that out?"

Prudence grinned and sipped some more prickly pear margarita. "It wasn't that hard. I got his photo from his driver's license and then uploaded it to some other databases."

"So...he really is in the witness protection program?"

"Nope," Pru said, sounding cheerful. "If that had been the case, the stuff about his real identity probably would have been harder to dig up. But anyway, he's Caleb Lockwood from Greencastle, Indiana, he's thirty-one years old...and he's been missing for the past two-plus years."

"'Missing'?" Delia repeated. She supposed that was a precursor to starting over with a new identity, but in this day and age, completely erasing your existence wasn't as easy as it used to be.

The waitress showed up with their nachos right then, so they had to wait until she'd deposited the oversized plate on their table and asked if they wanted anything else before she took off and they had some much-needed privacy again.

Prudence grabbed a tortilla chip loaded with ground beef and tomatoes and cheese and popped it in her mouth. Once she was done chewing—and had washed the food down with another swallow of margarita—she said, "Yeah, it looks like Caleb and his father and a group of their friends went on some kind of chartered fishing trip in the Gulf two years ago in November, and the boat vanished without a trace. Had quite the impact on the community, since it wasn't just that they'd lost fourteen of their own. Sounds like all the older-generation guys were what you'd call pillars of the community—Caleb's father was president of the local bank, and the rest were doctors and lawyers and even the principal of the high school—so it was definitely a blow."

Delia could imagine. And although she certainly wasn't the type to keep up with news about a small town in Indiana, usually if there was that much loss of life occurring all at once, the national media would have picked up the story and run with it for a while until they came up with something else to distract their viewers.

As far as she could recall, she hadn't heard a damn thing about the tragedy.

"Why wasn't it on the news?"

Prudence shrugged. "I don't know. I mean, I found articles in the local paper about what happened, and in places like Indianapolis and even Chicago, but it didn't seem to have made the national news."

"But if Caleb drowned in a fishing boat accident, then what the hell is he doing in Las Vegas with a new name and a new life?"

"I have no idea," Pru said, still sounding way too cheerful, considering their topic of conversation. "I guess he was a better swimmer than the rest of them."

The comment had been made as a joke, but Delia wasn't sure if she wanted to dismiss it out of hand. Although she'd never been out on the ocean, she had to imagine that a boat sinking with a bunch of people on board must have been chaotic, to say the least. Maybe Caleb had survived longer than the rest and had been picked up by another fishing boat. Maybe he'd knocked his head against something and had amnesia, and had been hanging out in Mexico or something until his memories resurfaced.

Delia had to admit that particular scenario sounded like something right out of a *telenovela*, but what else would explain why he'd been missing for two years, only to reappear now with enough cash on hand to buy not one, but two properties?

She had no idea. Also, her theory had about a million holes in it. Even if Caleb really had forgotten who he was for months on end, why wouldn't he have gone home to Greencastle once his memories reemerged? What would have sent him to Las Vegas and made him think that buying up properties was the best use of his time and resources?

"And there was absolutely no trace of him after the boating accident?" she asked, and Pru shook her head.

"Nothing at all. There's a total gap between November ninth two years ago and now."

Which she supposed would make sense if he'd been out of the country, surviving on other people's generosity.

Or maybe he'd had an interim identity, something he'd used before he decided to become Caleb Lowe, for whatever reason.

She asked Pru if that was a possibility, and again her friend shook her head.

"I couldn't find any other I.D.s with photos that matched his. Just the one from Indiana and the one that was recently issued here in Nevada. Maybe it's possible he couch-surfed the whole time and only used cash and took Ubers everywhere, but I don't think it's very likely."

Especially since the ride-sharing services got cranky with you if you tried to avoid having a credit card or a PayPal or Venmo account on file with them.

No—even though Delia wasn't sure how he'd accomplished it—Caleb seemed to have been completely off the grid for the past two years, right up until the moment when he'd applied for his new driver's license.

"How could he even get a license without a birth certificate?" she asked, and Pru sent her a look that seemed to indicate she couldn't believe her friend could be so naïve.

"You think they do a deep dive on those at the DMV? If you hand over a birth certificate and a Social Security card, they're going to issue you a license. Judging by how recent his credit history is and yet so super-high at the same time, I have a feeling he paid someone for a package deal—you know, SS card, birth certificate, maybe a passport. Plenty of people here in Vegas who'll do that for you."

"Could you?" Delia said, genuinely curious. While she didn't think Prudence was involved in anything illegal, considering how good she was at getting into various databases and digging up all sorts of information, she supposed it was possible that her friend might be able to manage such a feat...and make a little extra money on the side.

"Nah," Pru said at once, allaying Delia's fears on that account. "I mean, I could probably point someone to a person who could actually help, but even if I was able to create a fake credit report for someone—which I'm not sure I can—they'd still need to find a person with the necessary kind of resources to create realistic-looking fake paperwork.

I have a feeling Caleb must have used false documentation to get his driver's license, because that's definitely real even if nothing else is."

"None of this makes much sense," Delia said slowly, then remembered there were nachos and the cheese was starting to congeal. She scooped up a mouthful, then drank some of her margarita, glad of the extra shot of Cuervo gold she'd poured on top.

Yes, that was much better.

Voicing the question that had surfaced earlier in her mind, she added, "Why Las Vegas? Why not go home and let any surviving family know he was still alive?"

"Have you been in Indiana in the winter?" Prudence asked, and Delia had to smile. While she was a native of Las Vegas—a rarity, she knew—Pru's family had moved here from Minneapolis when she was in eighth grade, which was when they'd first become friends.

Anyway, Prudence knew all about Midwestern winters, while one ski trip to Tahoe when she was in college had been enough to convince Delia that she wanted as little to do with snow as possible.

"No," she said in answer to Pru's question. "So, okay, maybe he just phoned home or something. But this all seems a little weird."

"It does," Prudence agreed. "I guess the question is, what do you plan to do about it?"

The smart thing would be to do nothing. It didn't seem as if her friend's investigation had turned up anything illegal, and it certainly wasn't Delia's place as Caleb's real estate agent to start asking him probing questions about his past.

And yet....

Something felt off here. She couldn't even say what exactly, since she'd never encountered a situation like this before. It wasn't just the faint drift of whatever it was that she'd first sensed in that one casino several days earlier, or the weird, smoky psychic residue she'd picked up in the parking structure at the Bellagio.

Or even the way she'd dealt with two overtly hostile ghosts in a row, something that had never happened to her before.

Individually, maybe it all could have been explained away.

But put together?

"I don't know yet," she replied.

Deep down, though, she thought she might. If Caleb Lowe...Lockwood...wanted to work with her to renovate the house on Pueblo Street, then he was going to have to tell her the truth first.

Afterward...well, after she heard what he had to say, then she'd decide what to do.

No matter what happened because of it.

Chapter Eleven

—·‹‹·۞·››·—

DELIA HAD SENT HIM A TEXT ON SATURDAY afternoon letting him know to come to her office at eleven on Monday morning so he could sign the offer papers and give the listing agent, a woman named Paige Loomis, proof of funds from his bank.

That was why Caleb was out and about earlier than he usually would have been, going to the bank to get the necessary paperwork, heading over to Delia's office in the Winchester area. Some of the weather reports had been predicting rain, but only a few clouds drifted lazily across the sky, telling him the forecasters' talk of storms had been mostly wishful thinking.

Delia greeted him with a smile, but something about her seemed almost tense. Was she worried the deal might fall through at the last minute?

He really didn't see how, not when he was offering cash and the house had been sitting on the market for so long.

But despite the taut set to her jaw, she sounded pleasant enough as she asked him if he'd like coffee or tea or some water, and she only smiled when he replied that a cup of coffee would be great.

While she was fetching him a cup, the listing agent—a brittle-looking woman in her early forties with highlighted hair and the kind of tight-looking forehead that told him her aesthetician had a heavy hand with the Botox—and her client appeared at the door to Delia's office.

Caleb stood at once and offered a friendly hand. "Hi," he said. "Caleb Lowe. Nice to meet you."

The agent and her client, a man a few years older than himself, with a perpetually worried expression and brown hair that could use a good haircut, both shook his hand. Right then, Delia appeared and gave Caleb the coffee he'd requested.

"Anyone else?" she asked, offering the newcomers another smile, although she still appeared a little too tense.

Both Paige Loomis and her client declined, with the real estate agent adding, "We'd just like to get this wrapped up as quickly as possible. Tim has a meeting with his general contractor at eleven-thirty."

"Oh, you're working on another house?" Delia said politely, and the man nodded.

"Two others. So it'll be a relief to get this one off my hands."

Paige gave him a sharp look, as though she wasn't too happy with her client for being so honest about his situation, but Delia only nodded.

"I can imagine. Caleb, you have the paperwork from your bank?"

"I do," he said, and gave it to her. He'd decided to bring statements from two different "Caleb Lowe" accounts, just to be sure—and to show Paige Loomis that paying cash for the house definitely wasn't going to drain all his assets. Even with pulling out the $475K for the property on Pueblo Street, he would still have almost two million on hand, thanks to the way he'd bulked up his coffers over the weekend.

Because he'd gone ahead and returned to the casinos yesterday, earning himself another hundred grand. No sign of any demons lurking nearby, so wherever that imp had come from, he didn't think it had any buddies hanging around and waiting to pounce.

Paige studied the documents he'd handed her and gave a brisk nod. "Everything appears in order. Tim, I think it's fine to go ahead and sign the offer."

Looking relieved, he took the pen Delia handed

him and placed his signature on the designated line. Once he was done, he handed over the pen, and Caleb signed his name with a flourish.

Good thing he'd been practicing so he wouldn't mistakenly write "Lockwood" instead of "Lowe."

With that done, Delia picked up the paper, saying, "Let me make a copy of this, and then I think we're good."

After she walked out of the office, Tim seemed to relax enough that he thought it was okay to open up a bit. "You're taking on quite a project."

"I am," Caleb said calmly. "But Delia and I already discussed some options for the renovation, and she's going to put me in touch with some general contractors she knows."

"It sounds like she's being very helpful," Paige said, in tones that seemed to hint there might be more to her "help" than merely offering some advice to a client.

Because he didn't want to get into it—and because he knew there was nothing going on between Delia and him, more's the pity—he only shrugged. "I guess that's just what she does. But I appreciate it."

Luckily, the subject of their exchange appeared a moment later, so he didn't need to say anything else. She handed the original offer agreement to Paige and one of the copies to Caleb.

"Since we're waiving the inspection, we'll just go ahead with the title search," she said. "I assume there won't be any issues with that?"

"No," Tim replied, even as Paige opened her mouth to answer. "Despite the house ending up in probate, the heirs were able to provide a clean title. So everything should go smoothly."

Once again, he wore the expression of someone who thought he was getting away with something. No one present at the meeting had mentioned anything about the home's resident ghost, and Caleb guessed it would stay that way. There was no reason for him or Delia to announce that the spirit had been sent to its just rewards, and now the only thing wrong with the house was that it was going to need six figures' worth of repairs and updates before it was habitable again.

"Excellent," Delia said. "Then, once the title search is complete, we'll arrange to have the funds wired to you, and that should be that."

"Sounds perfect," Paige responded, although something about the set of her mouth told Caleb that she still was a little annoyed—probably because her client had spoken up even though she'd most likely told him she should be the one to do most of the talking.

But at least the matter was handled, and soon enough, both Paige and Tim left, leaving Caleb and Delia alone in her office.

Should he try asking her to lunch? It was now almost noon, and —

"Can we talk for a minute?" she asked.

Something in her tone set off his inner alarms. Was she about to tell him that she didn't want to be involved in the remodel after all and that he'd need to do the legwork of finding a decent general contractor?

He supposed he could muddle his way through that if he had to...but he much preferred to have her around to offer her expert advice.

Among many other reasons.

"Sure," he said, making sure he sounded utterly casual.

The corners of her mouth lifted, although her expression couldn't be construed as exactly a smile. Without saying anything, she went over to her office door and closed it, then turned around and faced him, arms crossed.

"Do you want to tell me about Greencastle?" she said.

How in the hell had she found out about that?

Caleb didn't know. But with Delia standing there, grim-faced, everything about her posture signaling that she wasn't too happy to have found out that her latest client had been lying to her about almost everything, he knew he didn't have a lot of options, not if he wanted to keep working with her.

It surprised him a little to realize how much he didn't want her to give him the boot.

"What's to tell?" he said, and her dark russet brows drew together.

"Quite a bit, as far as I can see," she replied. She moved past him to sit down behind her desk, as if she wanted its bulk separating them in case he tried anything funny.

Not that he would. He wouldn't lie to himself and try to make it seem as if he'd never resorted to violence in the past, but he couldn't be his old self, not if he wanted to keep working with Delia Dunne.

"You survived the sinking of the fishing boat?" she asked next.

Because he'd already learned from his mother that the "fishing boat accident" was the explanation his father had decided to use in case something went sideways when the Greencastle demon gang went to California to face down Rosemary and company, the question wasn't a complete surprise.

No, the big problem was how he intended to respond.

To be honest, he was kind of impressed that Delia had been able to unearth his real identity, even while he was annoyed at himself for how flimsy his new persona had proved to be.

"There wasn't a fishing boat," he blurted, surprising himself—and apparently Delia as well, since her frown only deepened.

"Then what happened?"

He'd never had much use for truth in his life. Not growing up, when he'd had to pretend he was just a normal kid from Greencastle, Indiana...not when he'd manufactured an entirely new persona to try to get information about *Project Demon Hunters* out of Rosemary McGuire.

And definitely not when he'd come to Las Vegas and done everything he could to hide who he was and where he had come from.

Despite that history of prevarication, he instinctively knew that giving anything less than the truth to Delia Dunne would be a huge mistake. After all, what could she do—rat him out to the authorities? A single comment about her latest client being part demon would get her laughed out of any police station in the country.

Besides, last time he checked, not being entirely human wasn't a crime.

"I spent the last two years in Hell," he said, and her frown disappeared, replaced by an expression of mixed surprise and irritation.

"Is that supposed to be some kind of joke?"

"No joke," he replied, then sat down in one of

the client chairs that faced her desk, since he'd risen from his seat when they were saying goodbye to Paige Loomis and her client. "I was banished to Hell along with my father and all the other part demons from Greencastle."

For the longest moment, Delia only stared at him, face now so blank that Caleb had no idea what she might be thinking. Then she said, "You seriously expect me to believe that?"

"Why not?" he returned. "You believe in ghosts. Are demons so very different?"

Something shifted in her expression then, a flicker of...what? Understanding?

Recognition, as though she'd heard someone else say nearly the same thing not too long ago?

"I think a lot of people would say they're *very* different." She reached for the mug of tea that sat on her desk and sipped from it, as if hoping that doing so might help to get her thoughts in order. "Why in the world should I believe you? For all I know, you're just a guy who has some kind of strange delusions about his origins."

"Because of this," he said softly, and opened his palm. For a few seconds, bright fire danced on his hand before it winked out.

Her gaze met his, cool and singularly unimpressed. "That could be a trick."

Caleb supposed she had a point there. After all,

this was Las Vegas, where magicians were almost as thick on the ground as escort services.

"Want me to take my shirt off?" he asked with a grin. "That way, you'll be able to see that I don't have any tubes of lighter fluid up my sleeve."

A barely detectable flicker of her gaze toward his bicep, and then she shook her head. "I don't think that's necessary." She hesitated before adding, "At the house on Pueblo Street...that was you, wasn't it?"

He didn't bother to ask what she meant by the question. "Yes, I'm the one who got rid of the ghost. He was a pretty nasty customer."

Was that a trace of a smile that touched her lips?

"Obviously, or he wouldn't have tried to push me into the pool." Her gaze sharpened. "Did he do that because he didn't want to move on?"

It seemed she'd decided to set aside the whole part-demon thing for now...or at least wanted a few other matters cleared up first. "Considering he was a serial killer who was going straight to Hell the second he stopped haunting that house, yes."

Now Delia wore the expression of someone who thought she could use a drink, even if she would never be so unprofessional as to say such a thing out loud to him.

"A *serial killer?*" she repeated, her tone incredulous.

"Yep," Caleb said. "The bodies of five women are buried under the floor of the bonus room on the lower level."

Like most redheads, Delia was naturally fair-skinned. Right now, she'd turned so pale that she looked as if she was about to faint.

"Bodies? How can you know that?"

"Because the ghost passed through me on his way to get to you in that pantry," Caleb replied. "For a second, our consciousnesses were mingled, and I could see everything about him, could see how hard he was trying to avoid going to Hell. Since that's exactly where he was supposed to be, I sent him there myself."

"Well...thank you, I guess." She was quiet for a moment, then said, "I'm not sure how I'm supposed to deal with all this."

"You deal with ghosts all the time," he pointed out.

Her mouth twisted into a rueful smile. "Somehow, this feels different."

Caleb could see why she might view the situation that way. Leaning forward a little—although he knew better than to rest his elbows on her desk or do anything that might be construed as invading her personal space—he said, "It's not that complicated. Demons come and go from Earth all the time. A few of them in Greencastle hung around long enough to have offspring with humans, and then those half-demons had children as well. That's how you get someone like me."

"So...you're more human than you are demon."

A simple fact he'd tried to point out to Rosemary McGuire on more than one occasion. Right now, he could only be glad that Delia was being so sensible.

"Yes," he said. "So were all my friends who were sent to Hell along with me."

Her eyes widened a little in comprehension. "The ones who were supposedly on the fishing boat with you."

It was hard to think of all of them still trapped down there. When crunch time had arrived, though, none of his friends had been close enough to the portal back to this world to have a chance to escape the way he did.

"And their fathers," Caleb said, adding, "I'm not sure why, but at least in our group, none of the demons had anything more than a single son each."

"No girls?" Delia asked then, looking startled.

"None."

His father had never explained why demon blood only bred males, and Caleb still couldn't say for sure whether that was because he thought it was immaterial or because he simply didn't know. Considering the way Daniel Lockwood had wanted to maintain an aura of invincibility at all times, Caleb guessed it was the latter.

After absorbing that reply, Delia said, "Are there others like you?"

A valid enough question, one he'd certainly pondered himself more than once. "Not that I'm aware of," he said. "Or at least, I've never encountered anyone else who seems to have mixed human and demon blood. I'm not sure why, except that there were...special circumstances...surrounding our group in Greencastle."

Circumstances that had involved the demon prince Belial bringing his chosen lieutenants to this plane to carry out his dirty work, but Caleb didn't think he needed to go into all that now. It was ancient history as far as he was concerned.

Especially now that Belial was dead and could no longer inflict his terrible will upon this world.

Delia's lips parted as though she wanted to inquire further about Greencastle, but then she shut them again, clearly not sure how she should respond to his statement.

"But that doesn't mean demons don't still come to this plane from time to time, for various reasons," he added. "I just ran into a pretty ugly customer in the parking garage at the Bellagio."

Upon hearing that revelation, her hazel green eyes widened. "The third level?"

Now it was his turn to stare at her in astonishment. "You felt that?"

"I did," she said. "I was there on Saturday—I had some business I needed to handle," she added, obviously thinking she needed to clarify what in the world she'd been doing in the casino's parking structure that weekend. "The place was crowded, so I had to park up on the third floor, and when I got out of my car, I felt this weird...smokiness...for lack of a better term."

Probably she'd detected the residue of his fight with the demon, even though it had happened the night before. It seemed she was an even stronger psychic than he'd previously guessed.

Stronger than she probably had any reason to believe.

"You saw me produce fire just a minute ago," Caleb said. "Well, I had to summon a lot more of it to get rid of that imp. As demons go, it wasn't all that strong, but any of them can cause some serious damage if they get the drop on you."

"But it's been banished?" Delia asked then, the strain in her voice telling him that she didn't want to contemplate the consequences of having a bunch of Hell's denizens running around her hometown.

Well, he assumed Las Vegas was where she'd been born. Maybe a false assumption, considering how many people here came from somewhere else, but there was something about her familiarity with the town that spoke of the kind of knowledge someone would only possess after living in one location for their entire life.

"Oh, yeah, I sent that sucker straight back to Hell," he replied, and she relaxed visibly. Before she could respond, though, he went on, "The weird thing, though, is that a lower-level demon like that couldn't have come topside of its own volition. Someone must have summoned it."

Delia frowned again. "Why would anyone do something like that?"

For as cool and confident as she looked, she sure had a naïve streak running through her. "Because if you summon a demon and do it right, then it's basically your slave. You could sic it on your enemies, have it be your spy...rub its head for good luck before you headed out to the casinos."

He added that last bit as a joke more than anything else, although he'd be the first to admit that adding those demonic energies to your own would help to increase your luck...for a while. Sooner or later, though, everyone had to pay the piper.

Well, most people, anyway.

Her gaze grew shrewd. "Is that what you did? Because I assume when you told me you 'came into money,' what you were really saying is that you've been killing it at the gaming tables."

Caleb didn't see any need to deny his means of accumulating his current fortune. "I figured that was the easiest way to get the money I needed. But I don't need an imp for luck. I make my own."

Thanks to the demon blood he carried, which was from the highest order of Hell's nobility. Diluted as it was by his human heritage, it was still stronger than anything a slave demon like that imp he'd banished could boast.

"I suppose that's convenient," Delia remarked. She settled against the back of her chair and regarded him for a moment, her green-hued gaze cool. "And I suppose I should say thanks for being honest with me. The problem is, I have no idea what to do next."

"You don't have to do anything," he said, and her brows lifted.

"Come again?"

Essaying a smile he knew had served him well in the past, Caleb replied, "So what if I'm a quarter demon? Does it change anything about the business we're conducting together?"

She made a small sound of disbelief. "I'd say it changes everything."

"Not really," he said. He knew he wanted to sound confident and unruffled, knew he needed to persuade her that they could continue with their plans for the property on Pueblo Street without any alterations. "I've never used my powers around you—well, except grabbing that killer's soul and sending it to Hell where it belongs. But I look at that as a favor, you know?"

"I suppose it was," she responded. Now her tone was dry, almost amused, and the shift made him think they'd turned some sort of a corner. A pause, and then she added, "But what are you going to do about those poor bodies in the basement?"

Good question. "Well, I have a few ideas, but I suppose it depends on how much I can do when the property technically isn't mine yet."

"It's all right," Delia said, and her mouth curved into a half-smile tinged with mischief. "The house still has a lockbox."

And in that moment, Caleb knew he wouldn't have to worry about her bailing on him. In fact, it seemed she was willing to stay the course.

No matter what might happen.

Chapter Twelve

—·《《·☾·》》·—

SHE COULDN'T BELIEVE SHE'D COME BACK here...and with a quarter demon, of all things.

Not that Caleb Lowe...Lockwood...whatever... looked like someone who had demon blood in his veins. No, he was as handsome as ever as he stood a few feet away from her in the lower level of the house that would soon be his.

But it wasn't his yet.

Good thing Paige Loomis hadn't come by to take off the lockbox. Delia assumed the other realtor wasn't going to take that step before money had changed hands...and that wasn't going to happen until the title search was wrapped up. She also guessed that Paige had set the wheels in motion as soon as she left the office, so it might be fairly soon.

Not soon enough, though.

"They're not here," Caleb said. If he was at all worried about being free with the property when it wasn't even his yet, he didn't show any sign of it.

Then again, would a quarter-demon even care about a minor transgression like trespassing?

Delia had no idea. All this was completely out of her area of expertise, despite all the experience she'd had sending the spirits of the restless dead into the next life.

Somehow she guessed that wasn't quite the same as banishing a demon.

Could you even banish someone like Caleb, who was more human than not?

Obviously, you can, she told herself. *Or he wouldn't have been in Hell in the first place.*

"You don't sense anything?" she asked.

True, she hadn't felt anything here, either—well, except the serial killer's spectral hands trying to push her into the swimming pool—but Caleb obviously had, which meant his senses for this sort of thing might be even more attuned than hers.

She wasn't quite sure what to think about that.

"No," he said. "Those poor souls had every reason to hang around, considering what happened to them, but I think they're long gone. Maybe they were here once but moved on after they realized their killer's spirit was stuck here as well."

A shiver moved down Delia's spine. Sure, it was pretty chilly here on the home's lower level, since the new HVAC system hadn't even been installed yet and the day outside was gray and lowering, threatening some rare winter rain, but she didn't think the icy sensation that had just inched its way down her back had anything to do with the temperature.

It was beyond horrible to think of those poor women's souls being trapped here...and then being forced to flee when they realized their killer's spirit had also gotten caught on this plane.

She'd much rather believe that their souls had never become earthbound at all and that they had moved on to the next plane the moment they'd been killed.

"We need to report this to the authorities," she said, and at once, Caleb frowned.

"Who will do what, exactly? These women were murdered more than half a century ago. The man who killed them is dead. It's not as if we'll get any justice for them."

A pat argument, but one she refused to accept without at least some pushback. "It would give closure to their families. Even if their parents or husbands have passed on as well, there still must be people who have spent all those decades wondering what happened to their mother or their aunt or their sister. Don't you think they deserve a little peace?"

Caleb's mouth thinned, and Delia could tell he

wasn't too thrilled with her right then. "How are you going to explain that we even knew the bodies were here? It seems pretty obvious that the original owner of the house buried them on this level because the floors hadn't been installed yet and it was easy enough for him to hide the bodies and then pour the concrete on top. No one knew anything about it—and there's no reason for us to have found them, either, because the floor is still intact. You really think the cops would be willing to listen to a hunch?"

If I talked to them...maybe, Delia thought, but even she knew she was reaching there. Sure, she had a minor reputation around town as the woman who could clear any troublesome spirits from your new home, but that wasn't the same as being a full-blown psychic.

Especially when she wasn't even the one who'd known the bodies were here.

"It doesn't feel right to just let it go," she said doubtfully.

"That's not what I'm suggesting," Caleb replied. "Look, even a quarter demon doesn't want a bunch of skeletons in his basement. I can try to extract them, and then we can figure out what to do next."

"You can do that?" Delia knew she still sounded skeptical, but that was probably because this whole situation felt utterly surreal. She didn't have any clear idea of what Caleb could or couldn't do, and that had thrown her off-balance.

One thing was for sure, though—she'd never look at him as a regular guy again.

"I don't know," he said. He didn't look particularly embarrassed to admit he was unsure of his abilities, and Delia had to grudgingly respect that. It would have been a lot worse if he'd tried to blow a bunch of sunshine up her ass.

"Can I help?" she asked then, surprising herself a little. This whole thing was way outside the scope of her abilities, but still, she didn't like the idea of just standing there and watching while Caleb tried to somehow extract the remains from underneath the concrete slab.

Now he grinned. "I doubt it. But thanks for the offer."

He moved away from her, pacing back and forth across the floor, and she realized he was doing his best to determine where the bodies were hidden.

Some kind of demonic dousing, she supposed.

Or maybe X-rays.

"They're all lined up in the middle," he said after a minute. "I guess our killer was a tidy kind of guy. So that makes it a little easier."

"What's the plan?"

His lips parted, and for a second—probably because of the glint she glimpsed in his dark eyes—

she wondered if he was going to tell her there wasn't a plan at all.

But then he said, "One of my gifts is the ability to transport myself wherever I want."

"Must cut down on airfare," she remarked, and he flashed her a grin that really made her wish he wasn't part demon.

"It does help," he replied. "But what I was hoping to do now was use that same gift, except to have it raise the bodies of the women from under the floor rather than just sending myself down to Bali, or whatever." He paused there, and the glint was back in those cola-colored eyes. "Unless you're in the mood for some daiquiris on the beach."

That sounded heavenly. However, Delia sort of doubted she'd ever take Caleb up on that sort of offer. Getting involved with a quarter demon was a level of complication she didn't think she could handle.

"You can take another person along with you?" she asked, and he nodded.

"I've only done it once or twice, but yeah, I can manage it. Which makes me hope I can use that same sort of power to get those poor women out from under the floor."

Exactly what they'd do then, she had no idea. But with Caleb's ability to send people—and inanimate objects, she hoped—to wherever he wanted, she supposed he could send the remains to the medical examiner's office or a local funeral home. Someplace where those women's bodies would be treated with respect and given the final rest they deserved.

"Fingers crossed," she said lightly.

He walked the floor one more time, probably so he could get the positions of the skeletons firmly fixed in his mind. Then he stopped in the center of the room, eyes shut and arms held out with his palms flat toward the floor.

Flames rippled up and down his arms, and Delia sucked in a breath. Yes, he'd conjured that one small flame earlier to prove there was a little more to him than met the eye, but this display was much more spectacular...especially as she realized the fire didn't seem to harm either him or the black leather jacket he wore.

Was that what it looked like when his power manifested itself?

For just the briefest moment, she could have sworn she saw a pile of skeletons resting on the hideous bright blue indoor/outdoor carpet. But then they vanished, and Caleb's eyes opened.

"All taken care of," he said cheerfully.

"What did you do?"

He sent her a glance that was almost indulgent. "Shipped them off to the coroner's office. Whoever goes in that exam room next is in for quite a surprise."

That was what Delia had hoped he would do, but she was still startled to hear the task had been accomplished so easily. "Just like that."

"Yes," Caleb replied. He was smiling now, obviously proud of himself for coming up with such an elegant solution to the problem. "I assume they'll be able to I.D. them by dental records, that kind of thing."

Maybe. How long did those sorts of records even hang around, though? They were dealing with women who'd been murdered six decades ago, not victims who'd only disappeared a few years earlier.

Well, that was for the police and the medical examiner to figure out. Honestly, they wouldn't have had that much more to work with even if Caleb had called them here to tell them the bodies had been hidden in the lower level of his latest real estate acquisition.

Except for the part where they could have at least pinned the killings on the man who'd once lived here.

It seemed Caleb wasn't too worried about that, though.

"Maybe it'll always be a mystery," he said. "The important thing is that the killer is in Hell where he belongs and that the families of the victims will eventually get the closure they need."

"I suppose so," Delia replied, even as she couldn't ignore the nagging thought that it would be better if the murderer could be publicly identified and, if not brought to justice, at least connected to his terrible crimes.

Caleb came over and reached out, almost as if he intended to give her a reassuring pat on the shoulder. At the last minute, though, he seemed to realize that probably wasn't the best idea and awkwardly lowered his arm to his side.

"Maybe the situation isn't perfect," he said. "But if the cops had done their jobs, they would have found the guy decades ago. At least we're fixing things so the families of the victims will have a few answers."

A practical way of looking at the situation, she supposed. Had there been a connection between the five victims, something the police back in the 1960s had overlooked? Or had the killings been completely random, making it very difficult for the authorities to put all the pieces together?

She had no idea. Possibly Caleb had some idea, since he'd seen into the killer's soul as the ghost passed through him, but she realized that Monday morning quarterbacking some sixty years after the fact wasn't going to change anything.

"All right," she said. "But let's go back upstairs —it's freezing down here."

He didn't argue. The flames that had run up and down his arms had disappeared as soon as his little magic trick—or whatever you wanted to call it

—was over, and she found herself wondering if they'd warmed him at all or were only a physical manifestation of the powers he was employing.

Did he even feel heat and cold the way a normal person would?

She had no idea. He seemed to dress for the weather, or he wouldn't have bothered with the leather jacket, but....

They headed upstairs. Delia had never thought she'd be reassured by a gutted kitchen, but it felt so relentlessly normal after that icy lower level and the horrible secret it concealed that she was just fine with the exposed subfloor and the pipes for the island's plumbing sticking up out of nowhere like a strange clump of metal and plastic weeds.

"What's your plan for the kitchen, anyway?" she asked, and he shot her an amused glance that signaled he knew exactly why she'd brought up that subject.

"I think I want white oak floors everywhere," he said. "I suppose the terrazzo would be more fitting for the time when the house was built, but these days, most people would prefer wood. Black cabinets and black granite or some other stone for the countertops."

"That's a bold choice," she replied, happy to talk about something so relentlessly normal. "Most people wouldn't go with that much black."

"I'm not most people," he said with a grin.

No, he wasn't. And if he wanted to do an all-black kitchen here, then she supposed that was his prerogative. Somewhere in this town, there was someone who'd be thrilled with that kind of decorating scheme. It was Las Vegas, after all, not a place known for its subtle understatement.

And even though he hadn't admitted it yet, she had the sneaking suspicion that he'd grow more attached to the house as time wore on and the remodel really began to take shape, and that he might decide to make this his permanent residence and sell the home he was in now.

Would she want to represent him in that sale?

Best to get through the reno first, she supposed.

He stood in the middle of the kitchen, fists planted on his hips, gaze roving the space as though he was already measuring the cabinets.

Obviously, he wasn't too worried about the history of the house.

But then, he knew it wasn't haunted, so there wasn't anything to stop him from getting the place fixed up and either ready to go on the market...or moved into, depending on what he decided to do once the renovation was finished.

The words were out of her mouth before she could stop them.

"Have you ever killed anyone?"

Caleb turned toward her, eyebrows lifted slightly. "What a question."

That was no answer. Even though Delia realized how awful it was that she'd blurted out such a query, considering his background, she thought it was a valid concern.

"Have you?" she pressed.

His head tilted to one side. "If I say yes, will you fire me as a client?"

"No," she replied at once. "That is, I'll keep representing you until the sale is final, but after that, you're on your own."

He was quiet for a moment. At length, he said, "No, I've never killed anyone. Caused some mayhem, sure. But murder? No. It might surprise you, but I lived a pretty ordinary life."

That comment made her want to laugh outright, but she could tell he was being serious. Then again, what did she really know of his existence, except that he was from Greencastle, Indiana, and that he'd spent the past couple of years in Hell?

"How ordinary?"

The familiar grin pulled at his mouth. "Quarterback of the football team and prom king."

Now she allowed herself to chuckle. "Those of us who were outsiders in high school might not look at being the quarterback and the prom king as exactly being 'ordinary.'"

"You were an outsider?" he asked, then added, "You look like prom queen material to me."

Oh, boy. Maybe some people would have considered that a compliment, but....

"No prom queen here," she said. "Just the punk rock chick with screaming red hair and Doc Martens sitting in the back row of your English lit class."

"We didn't have too many punk rock chicks in Greencastle," he said, which she could well believe. She'd looked up the town the night before after she got home...after Pru had dropped all those bombshells at dinner. It looked like a picture-perfect small Midwest town, with its own private liberal arts college and lots of brick buildings and green lawns and big, shady trees. Maybe there had been a few rebels, but she had a feeling that mohawks and combat boots had been few and far between.

Not that she'd ever had a mohawk. Dyeing her hair was one thing, but shaving off huge chunks of it was an entirely different proposition.

"Anyway," he went on. "Everyone thought I— and the rest of the part demons—were ordinary, upstanding citizens, and we did our best to rein-force that image. The last thing we wanted was anyone paying too much attention to us."

Beyond being the prom king and quarterback, she supposed. But then, she doubted anyone would suspect the high school hero of being anything more than what he appeared to be on the surface.

"Wise plan," she said, then decided to let it go. She'd had enough revelations today. The important thing was that they'd done what they could for the victims whose bodies had been hidden in the basement, and now it was just a waiting game until the title on the house cleared and the funds transferred.

Especially since they were technically trespassing right now. True, Paige hadn't taken down the lockbox, but still, etiquette generally suggested that Delia should have cleared this visit with the listing agent before she and Caleb came over here.

Well, what Paige didn't know wouldn't hurt her.

"Anyway," Delia added, "I have a client coming to the office at one-thirty, so I should probably get going."

And thank God they'd come in separate cars. After what Caleb had shown her, she guessed he could just blip himself wherever he needed to go, although it seemed as if he mostly drove around like a regular person.

Just another part of that whole not-attracting-attention thing.

For a second or two, he hesitated, and she wondered if he was going to ask if she wanted to go to lunch, and how she would reply. Yes, they'd had dinner the other night, but that was before she knew about the whole demon thing.

It was obviously going to take quite a while for her brain to adequately wrap itself around that unexpected piece of news.

Then he said, sounding casual, "Sure. I guess just let me know when the title search is done and what I need to do next."

That part was easy. "Absolutely."

They headed to the front door, where she returned the key to the lockbox and made sure it was secured before they both went down the front walk to the curb where their cars were parked. Still looking as if he didn't have a care in the world, he waved at her before he climbed into his shiny black Range Rover—a vehicle she guessed he'd also paid for with his winnings—and drove off down the street.

No concern of hers where he'd gotten the money, she thought as she got into her little hybrid SUV and fastened the seatbelt.

Except....

Robert Hendricks' face flashed into her mind.

What do you know about demons?

A lot more than she had a half-hour ago. But that wasn't the point.

No, the real point was that—she realized with a sinking sensation in her stomach—Caleb Lockwood was probably the very demon Mr. Hendricks and his buddies at the various casinos had been looking for all along.

Chapter Thirteen

—·(((+◎+)))·—

HAD HE REALLY JUST CONFESSED ALL TO Delia Dunne?

It sure looked that way.

Why he'd done such a crazy-ass thing, Caleb wasn't even sure. Maybe he'd decided to take a chance because she was someone who already had plenty of experience with the supernatural...or maybe he'd gotten tired of pretending to be something he wasn't.

Whatever the reason for unburdening himself, he thought she'd taken it pretty well. She hadn't freaked out or run away or tried to throw holy water on him—something he knew she could have easily done, since she always seemed to carry some in that little banishing kit she kept in her purse—and instead had asked some fairly sensible questions.

And even though he knew a real estate agent wasn't the same thing as a lawyer and they didn't have anything close to a confidentiality clause, he still thought he could trust her to keep his secret.

Probably because no one would believe her if she decided to spill the beans.

But at least he'd done one good thing today by removing the skeletons of those dead women and sending them to a place where someone could properly handle them. No doubt there would be a million questions and some finger-pointing, because a batch of remains from people who'd been dead for decades generally didn't show up out of nowhere, but he had to believe they'd still be taken care of and hopefully identified.

Just as he was turning onto his street, rain began to fall, spattering his freshly washed Range Rover, but he told himself it wasn't that big a deal. He'd take it to the car wash tomorrow or whenever it was obvious that they wouldn't get any more rain for a while.

All the same, he couldn't help feeling a little melancholy as he picked up his phone and ordered some DoorDash for lunch—a sub sandwich from a deli that wasn't too far away, along with a tub of potato salad. What he really would have liked was to take Delia out instead, but the expression she'd worn while they were wrapping things up at the house on Pueblo Street told him it would be a long time—if ever—before she was okay with sharing a meal with him again.

Damn it.

Despite that reaction, he was still glad he'd told her the truth. While she'd been shocked, she hadn't looked at him as if he was some kind of horrible mutant and had even talked about totally normal things afterward, like his plans for the kitchen and some snippets about their high school life.

He would have loved to see her with hair dyed an even brighter red than its normal copper hue, dressed all in black with Doc Martens to finish off the look.

Man, his mother would have freaked out if he'd ever brought a girl like that home.

Smiling in spite of himself, he sat down in the living room and watched raindrops hit the water in the swimming pool, sending up little splashes as they fell. It was a nice pool, surrounded by a carefully landscaped backyard, but he couldn't stop himself from thinking about the yard at the formerly haunted house on Pueblo Street, which was much bigger and gave the impression of being even larger than it actually was because of the way it backed up to the golf course and all that open green space.

The house had so much potential...potential he was fairly certain would now be realized, since it didn't seem as if Delia was going to back away from helping him with the renovations despite what she'd learned about him earlier today.

That had to count for something, didn't it?

And he knew it had been a novel experience to stand there and talk to a woman who'd learned the worst about him but was still willing to be matter-of-fact about the whole thing.

Although she hadn't stopped herself from asking whether he was a murderer, too, just like the man who'd once owned that house.

He'd answered honestly because he had nothing to hide on that front. He didn't think his father could have responded the same way and still been telling the truth, but their lives had been very different. By the time Caleb's generation had come along, it was much more about maintaining the illusion that they had nothing to hide and continuing to build their wealth and position in society, rather than merely biding their time in the hope that Belial might call on them to come to his aid.

Which he had...and the results hadn't been very pretty.

But he, Caleb, had escaped, and that was the important thing.

The doorbell rang, so he went to get his lunch from the DoorDash driver and then tip a little extra because the weather was so shitty. Now the rain was coming down almost in sheets, and he found himself wishing he'd ordered something warm instead of a cold sub and some potato salad.

Well, it couldn't be helped now.

He returned to the living room and switched on the TV and made himself eat, all the while wondering if Delia really had a client at one-thirty or whether she'd made up the story so she could get away from him.

No, she didn't seem like the type of person to lie about that kind of thing.

At least, he hoped she wasn't.

And although he'd had the passing thought that he might hit the casinos later today, he knew he didn't much feel like going out. Drivers around here went absolutely nuts when it rained, probably because it happened so rarely.

No, he'd sit tight, maybe watch some home reno shows for inspiration. He already had a few ideas as to what he wanted to do with the Pueblo Street house—Delia's obvious disapproval of his all-black kitchen notwithstanding—and he couldn't think of a better use of his time than sitting here with his feet up and letting the afternoon go by.

And the evening, and....

And as long as it takes, he told himself. Right now, he knew he was kind of in limbo, just waiting for the clear title on the house before he could finalize the transaction. Even once that was done, he and Delia would have to focus on finding a general contractor to oversee the renovations, and that would probably take a while, too. Although he certainly hadn't moved here with the idea of building a house-flipping empire, he thought that might not be a bad way to end up. If nothing else, it would keep him occupied for a while.

He went into the kitchen to get a beer and then, because he thought that was a whole lot of cold on a gloomy afternoon, switched on the fireplace before he sat down again. As he swallowed some beer, he pondered what Delia had told him about her experiences in the parking structure at the Bellagio.

Somehow, she'd sensed that he'd fought a demon there, which meant her strange abilities were attuned to a whole lot more than just ghosts and spirits. Good thing she was on his side—albeit marginally—or that could have caused some trouble.

The last thing he wanted was for anyone to know that a part-demon had been manipulating his winnings at the various casinos in order to plump up his wallet.

But she hadn't seemed too worried about that part of it. Maybe she figured that because everything was rigged by the casinos anyway, it wasn't too big a deal for him to indulge in his own form of cheating.

He appreciated that kind of morally gray thinking in a woman.

Delia Dunne wasn't morally gray, though. Or at least, while she seemed willing to keep his secrets, he doubted she would ever participate in any openly illegal dealings.

Too bad he wasn't on speaking terms with any of the *Project Demon Hunters* gang. Then he could have asked them if they'd ever encountered someone like Delia before, a woman who could whisper to ghosts but also somehow detect the residue of a day-old battle with a demon.

But they weren't speaking. In fact, all of them believed he was safely trapped in Hell, and he certainly wasn't going to do anything to disabuse them of that notion.

Well, except send a mysterious wedding gift to Rosemary, who might or might not have figured out that he wasn't quite as caught in the underworld as they believed.

He ate half his sandwich and some of the potato salad, then put the leftovers in the fridge so he could return to the couch and finish his beer.

That imp in the parking garage. Were there more of them hiding in various places around town, just waiting to attack?

Possibly. Or maybe he just had spectacularly bad luck.

If it wasn't bad luck...if someone had detected

his presence here and wasn't terribly thrilled by it... then he might be in for a whole world of hurt.

That didn't make much sense, though. While he knew the various casino owners probably weren't happy about losing several million bucks to him over the past few months, they were mortals. There was no way in the world—or in Hell— they'd be able to guess he was anything except an ordinary man.

Especially since he'd been so careful never to wear his real face—or the same face twice—when he went gambling. He was untraceable...unfindable.

He hoped.

The weather cleared the next day, and Caleb went out, determined to add a few extra hundred grand to his expanding bank accounts. Strictly speaking, that wasn't necessary, but with the purchase of the house looming—along with all its associated renovation costs—he thought it better to be safe.

That meant taking an Uber instead of driving; he was in no mood to have a repeat of the incident in the parking garage, and figured it would be safer to get dropped off and then call another car when he wanted to head for home.

And although he was careful, he still ended up

a hundred grand richer after visiting the first three stops—changing his face between each one, of course—and wondered if he should quit while he was ahead or try his luck one more time.

Since going home to an empty house in the middle of the afternoon didn't sound very appealing, he decided to go a little off the beaten track and head over to Treasure Island. He hadn't visited that casino for more than three weeks, and it seemed like working the tables there for a bit would be a good idea. After all, it had been almost a month since they'd suffered any big losses at his hands.

On that sunny Tuesday afternoon, the place wasn't very crowded. Caleb didn't like that as much, since big crowds gave him many more opportunities to hide. Still, he cleared about twenty-five grand at the blackjack tables before he went into the bathroom so he could switch his appearance once again.

Before, he'd been an older man in his sixties in a blue windbreaker and deck shoes. Now he wore the face of someone much younger, middle twenties at best, a good-looking Hispanic guy wearing a black long-sleeved T-shirt and faded jeans.

Most people probably would have thought his ability to shapeshift in such a way was downright miraculous. But because Caleb had always been able to change his appearance—well, since he was around seven, just old enough to understand his father when Daniel told him he could never do that in front of his mother or any other mortals—he didn't think it was that big a deal. The gift was one he'd been born with. It certainly wasn't anything he'd earned, unlike his position as quarterback on the football team, which had been the result of lots of coaching and summers spent working out and tossing a ball around with anyone who would humor him.

He'd wanted to have one thing he thought was truly his.

Unlike winning at poker or craps or roulette, which was accomplished purely by allowing his demonic talents to reach out and push the dice over so they showed a lucky seven, or to have the roulette ball fall on the correct color and number.

Or even subtly influencing a dealer's hands so they always gave Caleb the exact cards he needed.

Because the guy he was impersonating seemed like the type of man who would play craps, he headed over to that section of the casino floor, snagging a gin and tonic from a passing waitress who told him he could have it, that the person who'd ordered the drink had left the casino floor before she could deliver it.

His loss.

Gin and tonics weren't his favorite beverage, but he didn't care too much about the flavor right now. No, he only wanted some alcohol in his system—not too much, only enough to cushion reality a bit.

This time, he took it easy, losing almost as much as he won, but his winnings accumulated at a steady rate nonetheless. From time to time, the dealer shot him a considering look from under her false eyelashes, but she didn't say anything.

Why would she? His hands rested on the table in front of him, and it would have been clear to anyone watching that there was no way he could have been influencing the dice.

It would have been impossible to detect the mental nudges he gave them from time to time... well, unless you were another demon.

Only mortals around the craps table this afternoon, though, most of them tourists, mixed in with a few people of retirement age who probably came to hang out at the casinos because it was better than sitting at home and watching *Wheel of Fortune,* or whatever.

Even though Caleb was only about forty grand ahead, he decided to stop there. Something about the vibe here was getting to him, and he thought it might be better to call it a day and head home.

He thanked the dealer, tipped her generously, and collected his chips, then performed the familiar ritual of trading them in for cash, which went into his messenger bag. The bag was the only thing that might have given him away, but he changed its appearance as well—sometimes it was brown, sometimes black, and sometimes it wasn't a messenger bag at all, just a plain old backpack.

That was what it looked like today, dark green with worn straps. He hefted it over one shoulder as he pulled out his phone with his free hand, maneuvering so he could summon an Uber to take him home...or rather, to the strip mall not too far from his house that was his usual destination.

One gin and tonic definitely wasn't enough to make him forget all his precautions and have the driver go straight to his house.

And because it was Vegas and there were hundreds of rideshare cars roaming the city at any given time, one showed up less than five minutes after he made the request.

"Foursquare Plaza," he told the guy, even though the driver would have already known their destination from the app.

"Got it," the man said. He was probably around Caleb's age, with dark hair and a scruff of beard covering his chin. "Caleb Lowe, right?"

"That's me," Caleb replied, which seemed to be enough to satisfy the man that he had the correct person riding in his car.

After that brief exchange, though, the guy went quiet, and Caleb was fine with that. While in general he didn't mind chatting with his Uber and

Lyft drivers—he'd gotten some valuable local area knowledge through those exchanges—today he only wanted to be left alone to think.

Radio silence from Delia, and he didn't know why he should be so bothered by that. It had only been a few hours since he last saw her, and it wasn't as if the title check could have been completed that quickly. There was no reason for them to be in contact.

Except for the part where he'd hit her with some pretty earth-shattering information, and for some reason, he'd thought she might have more questions for him.

Apparently not.

Rain continued to fall, not as hard as an hour or so ago, but enough that all the streets were slick and people seemed to drive crazier than ever. Once or twice, the driver had to speed up or hit the brakes to avoid a collision, and Caleb found himself questioning his decision to Uber home. Yes, he knew it would look suspicious to go into a casino bathroom and teleport back to his house from there—the casinos had cameras everywhere, and they'd surely record a strange man heading into a restroom and never coming out, the whole reason why he took taxis and Ubers on the majority of these forays—but that still had to be better than getting creamed in a car accident.

Well, it couldn't be helped now. His fingers

tightened around the strap of the backpack that still hung from one shoulder, although he wasn't sure what that would do.

Up ahead, the light turned yellow, and the driver accelerated.

Goddamn it.

Approaching from the left was a big black truck, and Caleb knew they weren't going to make it. The Uber was a Mazda CX-5, a decent-sized vehicle, but that truck still massed a whole lot more.

His body clenched in advance of the impact. While he knew a car accident wouldn't kill him— even part demons were tougher than that—it didn't mean it still wouldn't hurt...a lot.

Wham!

The truck collided with the Mazda's front fender, and the SUV began to spin, gray skies and raindrops and the other vehicles in the intersection whirling all around him like some kind of horrible kaleidoscope.

And in the front seat, the driver turned to look over his shoulder, his mouth spreading in a horrible rictus of a grin.

A grin that kept widening, now showing yellow, jagged fangs.

Shit.

Even though the Mazda was still spinning, Caleb grabbed hold of the seatbelt and unlatched it. While he thought he might be able to teleport with the thing holding him in place, he didn't want to waste the time to find out.

Not with that disguised imp in the driver's seat, a demon who clearly wanted him out of commission for a while.

Still clutching the disguised messenger bag, he visualized the kitchen at his house, with its white quartz countertops and dark blue cabinets...cabinets that held some pretty fine tequila.

He was definitely going to need a drink after this.

And then he was out of the spinning vehicle and safely home. The world still revolved around him for a few seconds until his inner ear got caught up and realized he was now standing on solid ground.

Damn. That had been a close one.

He went to one of the cupboards and got out a shot glass, then headed into the pantry to pick up the bottle of Lalo he'd snagged at Total Wine a few weeks earlier. After pouring himself a half inch or so, he took one gulp, then another, and refilled the glass.

Outside, the rain began to pour down harder, so he went into the living room, turned on the fireplace, and sat on the couch.

A good day to stay home.

If only he'd done that very thing.

How the hell had that imp known he would be in that Uber?

He hoped the person driving the black truck was all right. Most likely, they would have survived the collision just fine, since their vehicle was much bigger and heavier than the Mazda.

Still, he wouldn't be surprised to learn that the truck had been totaled.

As for the Uber, well, he was sure the imp had fled the scene just as soon as it realized he'd flown the coop. The cops were going to have a hard time figuring that one out...not that it was so unusual for the person at fault in an accident to try to get away before the authorities arrived, but he doubted they had seen too many instances where any eyewitnesses on hand would swear they hadn't seen anyone leave the vehicle.

While he knew that demons could detect the presence of others of their kind, he'd done everything he could to shield himself and make his movements difficult to track.

Obviously, he hadn't done enough.

Another swallow of tequila. His phone was still in the messenger bag, which he'd set down on the kitchen counter as soon as he got here. Maybe he should call Delia and tell her what had happened, let her know she needed to be on her guard.

As soon as that thought went through his mind, however, he guessed that she shouldn't be in any danger—why would the demons who were after him be interested in harassing an ordinary human?—and that he only wanted to call her because he needed to hear a half-friendly voice. His own fault for not working very hard to develop any kind of a social circle here, he supposed, although at the time, he'd told himself it just wasn't safe to make connections until he was absolutely sure that no one had discovered where he'd gone to ground.

Well, those imps sure knew he was here...and that meant someone much higher up the food chain was the one pulling the strings. Lower-level demons like that simply didn't come topside on their own.

However, he got the feeling they hadn't yet discovered where he lived, or surely they would have already laid siege to the house. So maybe all his subterfuges hadn't been completely useless.

With that not entirely cheerful thought to buoy him, he headed back into the kitchen to get more tequila.

Whatever else happened, he didn't plan on going out again unless he had a damn good reason.

Chapter Fourteen

—·‹‹‹·◌·›››·—

THE REST OF THE AFTERNOON TICKED BY, and Delia realized she still hadn't come to any decision as to whether she should let Robert Hendricks know that she'd found the demon who'd been winning so much of the casinos' cash.

Well, part demon, anyway.

From what she'd been able to tell, Caleb possessed a lot of demon powers but otherwise was just as regular flesh and blood as she was. What she was supposed to think about that, she wasn't sure.

But her one-thirty appointment stretched into two hours as she showed the couple—who were around her age—house after house, driving through the rain only to learn this place was too small, or this one didn't have an open enough floorplan, or that one didn't have a yard big enough to put in a pool.

By the time they were done...still without having made a decision, or course...Delia had been all too ready to hide in her office and catch up on some paperwork. But even though she kept herself busy, her brain continued to poke at her, making her go over that conversation with Caleb just one more time as she tried to determine who she owed more loyalty to —the part demon who was going to give her a big, fat commission once the deal on the Pueblo Street house closed, or the man who'd hired her to see if demonic activity was behind the casinos' recent losses.

Technically, Robert had hired her first. However, they didn't have any kind of formal agreement—at least, not one backed up with a written contract—whereas Caleb was her official client, with the paperwork to prove it.

Jesus Christ, what a mess.

She'd halfway expected to hear from Robert sometime that day, but it seemed as if he was content to let her do her work for a while before he felt it necessary to check in.

Thank God for that. She needed as much time as possible to think.

The drive home wasn't much fun, thanks to the rain—and a traffic accident that had choked the intersection at McLeod and Vegas Valley Drive. By the time she got there, the wreckage had been moved off to the side...it looked as if a white Mazda

SUV and a big Ford F-250 had gotten into a wrestling contest, with the Mazda losing...but there were still lots of cop cars and officers standing around, more than she would have expected from a simple fender-bender.

Well, not her circus, not her monkeys.

By the time she got home, her nerves were a jangled mess, so she poured herself a stemless glass of cab and then stuck her head in the refrigerator, trying to figure out what she should have to eat that night. Nothing looked all that appealing, although she supposed she could put something together with the leftover rotisserie chicken she'd gotten at the grocery store over the weekend, maybe with some pasta to make it feel a little more filling.

So, dinner was settled, but she still hadn't decided what to do about Robert Hendricks.

What if she told him she'd detected something but hadn't been able to get any real details on what it was or where it had gone after it left the casino? That might be better than not saying anything at all, although she didn't much like the idea of having to lie to him.

And Caleb was her client in every legal sense of the word, meaning there was a good argument for keeping her mouth shut.

Damn it.

There didn't seem to be an easy solution to the problem...except the most obvious one.

She could call Robert, tell him she hadn't been able to find anything helpful, and offer to return the money. Yes, giving up ten grand wasn't the most appealing scenario in the world, but at least if she gave the deposit back to him, they wouldn't have a business relationship anymore, and she wouldn't feel obligated to tell him anything.

Besides, she was going to receive more than four times that amount when the deal on the Pueblo Street house closed. It wasn't as if walking away from her agreement with Robert Hendricks was going to stress her financially. She hadn't been expecting that money, so she wouldn't miss it when it was gone.

Yes, backing away from the whole thing definitely seemed to be the best solution.

Still, she wished she could call Prudence and talk over the situation with her, but although Pru was on board with all the ghost stuff, Delia had a feeling her friend might have a few issues when it came to demons.

Even ones who had only a quarter demonic blood.

Also, while Caleb hadn't sworn her to secrecy, she knew she would never betray his confidence by blabbing his secrets to her best friend unless he explicitly told her it was okay.

She had a feeling that wasn't going to happen. For whatever reason, he'd decided to trust her, but she doubted he'd be all right with her circle of friends knowing her latest client had a little more under the hood than most people might have expected.

By that point, it was around five-thirty. Delia supposed it would have been okay to call Robert now, since, while it wasn't strictly business hours, the time wasn't so late that doing so would have been rude.

However, because she was a chickenshit, she decided to wait until morning.

———

"It's only been a couple of days," came Robert Hendricks' startled voice through the phone's speaker. "I hope you didn't get the impression that I was expecting results right away."

"Oh, no," Delia replied at once. Again following the chickenshit principle, she'd told herself it would be better to call him after she got to the office and could reach out well after nine o'clock that morning. "That's not why I think it's better not to pursue this anymore. I visited several casinos over the weekend, but I never sensed anything that felt like the presence of a demon...or even a ghost."

Well, except the imp-thing that Caleb had told her attacked him in the Bellagio's parking structure. But, strictly speaking, she hadn't known what it was when she sensed the smoky residue on the third level of the garage, only that something weird had gone down there.

"I still don't think you should give up," Robert said. "We had some big winners over the weekend, but nothing that stood out as anything out of the ordinary. It's entirely possible that our demon stayed home...wherever that is."

Delia knew that wasn't true because Caleb had mentioned going to the casino on Saturday. Maybe he'd dialed down the winning to avoid arousing suspicion.

"I suppose so," she replied, knowing how dubious she sounded. "But even if that's the case, there's no way to know for sure whether I'd even be able to help you. Like I told you when we first met, I've only dealt with ghosts, and I don't know if I'd recognize a demon's energy on the off chance that I did somehow manage to bump into one."

That part wasn't even a lie. When she'd first met Caleb, she hadn't detected anything out of the ordinary about him...except maybe to admit to herself that he was the best-looking man she'd seen in a long, long time.

True, when he'd grabbed her arm to prevent her from getting pushed into the pool, she'd felt that odd tingle, but she'd only chalked the sensation up to a rush of adrenaline. She hadn't sensed anything strange when they shook hands the first time they'd met, back at her office.

"There's no one else in Las Vegas who can do what you do," Robert Hendricks pressed, and she had to smile.

"There are plenty of psychics and mediums in this town."

"Ninety percent of whom are fakes," he countered. "You're the real deal, though. That's why I came to you in the first place."

"And I appreciate the vote of confidence," she said. "But I don't think I'm going to come up with anything useful."

She almost added that she'd just taken on a new client with a challenging project and didn't think she'd have any room in her schedule for demon hunting. However, Robert spoke first, forestalling any comments on that topic.

"I still think you only need more time," he told her. "And I'm willing to be patient."

"What if your demon swoops in and wins a million bucks at Caesar's Palace or something?"

"Then possibly we'll have to revisit our agreement," Robert said without missing a beat. "In the meantime, do what you can. If the situation at the casinos remains as low-level as it was over the weekend, then things aren't as urgent as you seem to believe they are."

It sounded as if whatever argument she wanted to present, he'd just find a different rationale to counter it. And if he really wanted to let things run their course for a while to see what happened, then she supposed she'd have to go with his preferences for now. The ten grand was just sitting in her savings account, earning an extremely modest amount of interest, so it wasn't as if she'd have to worry about what might happen if she spent some of it and then decided to back out of their deal after all.

"Okay," she said, a little annoyed with herself for capitulating, even though she guessed there wasn't any way to get rid of the guy without being downright rude. "How about we give it another week? I really think at that point if I haven't found anything, then it's just not there...or at least, I'm not able to sense it."

"That would be fine," Robert replied. "I can see why you wouldn't want this hanging over you indefinitely, but another week will give you a chance to visit more casinos and figure out if you simply weren't looking in the right place."

Delia knew there was a lot more to the situation than that, but she didn't argue. Let Robert Hendricks think she was diligently inspecting every casino within a half-mile radius of the Strip. She planned to let the time slip by, and then at the end of that additional week, she'd go back to him and say she was sorry, but she still hadn't found anything, and here's a cashier's check for the ten grand.

No harm, no foul.

Maybe she'd even go to a couple of casinos, just to have it seem as if she was making some effort. That was probably the last thing she felt like doing on a weeknight when all she wanted to do was go straight home and feed her fish, but in case the personnel in the casinos were on the lookout for a woman with long red hair wandering around the premises while she carried out some kind of secret mission, it just felt better to cover her bases.

"It's a plan," she said. "I'll call you next Monday to let you know how things went."

"Or sooner, if you find something."

Delia knew that wasn't going to happen, but she made a sound of agreement anyway. "Of course. You have a good day, Robert."

"You too, Delia."

They ended the call there, and she set the phone down on her desk. Good to have gotten that over with, even though she wished she'd had the spine to tell Mr. Hendricks that no, she hadn't gotten a single ping, so it was time to call the whole thing off.

Almost as soon as it hit the desktop, her phone

rang again. She glanced down at the screen, wondering what she would do if it was Robert calling back to request that she extend their agreement for an additional week.

Lie again, she supposed.

But it wasn't Robert Hendricks. No, the number on the screen was Paige Loomis's.

"The title search is done," she said crisply when Delia picked up the phone. "My client wanted to know if Mr. Lowe is available this afternoon to sign off on the final paperwork and to bring the cashier's check or arrange a wire transfer."

Wow, that was faster than she'd expected. Yes, the house had been purchased by the current owner only three years ago, so she supposed any problems with the title would have been ironed out then, but still, she hadn't thought they'd make any real progress on the transaction until closer to the end of the week.

"Let me give Caleb a call and get back to you," Delia said. She didn't have any reason to think he wouldn't be available, but she wasn't about to make any promises when she had no idea what his schedule today looked like.

"Of course," Paige replied. "I'll be waiting."

No doubt about that. January generally wasn't a busy time in the real estate industry, so the other agent was probably salivating at the thought of getting a nice, juicy payout when she hadn't been expecting one.

Delia said goodbye and ended the call, then touched the screen again so she could go to her contacts list and reach out to Caleb. With any luck, he'd be at home and not back at the casinos...or grocery shopping or golfing or whatever it was he did with his spare time.

To be fair, she couldn't really imagine Caleb Lockwood on a golf course. Tennis...maybe.

But he picked up on the second ring, so it didn't seem as if he'd been too busy, whatever it was he'd been doing before she called.

"That was fast," he said, an echo of her own words from just a bit earlier.

"It was," she agreed, glad she sounded so normal. Although she'd known she would have to interact with him again at some point, she honestly hadn't thought it would be the very next day after he'd made all those revelations. "But it sounds as if everything went smoothly, so the seller would like to get this wrapped up."

"Not a problem," Caleb responded at once. "I just need some time to go by the bank. Does ten-thirty work for me to come by the office?"

"That should be fine," Delia said, fairly certain that Paige would have kept the rest of her morning open so they could finish their business. "I'll see you then."

"See you."

He ended the call there, so Delia sent a quick text to Paige letting her know to come to the office at ten-thirty.

Now it was just a waiting game. Not too long a wait, just about forty-five minutes, but Delia still knew it was probably going to feel interminable.

She used it up as best she could, fielding a couple of calls from prospective buyers, checking the new listings that had popped up on the MLS overnight. Her mother handled the majority of that sort of thing because it seemed as if sometimes she could sniff out a property before it even hit the database, but still, it never hurt to be familiar with the inventory.

Especially since Delia still hadn't found anything that would work with her one picky couple, who wanted the moon but wouldn't budge from their top range of around $350K.

Well, after they'd been looking for several months and still hadn't found anything they both liked, they might finally realize that either their expectations or their budget needed an adjustment.

At around 10:25, Caleb stuck his head in her office door. As usual, he wore jeans and boots and that same black leather jacket, although today the T-shirt underneath was a dark maroon color.

"I'm a little early," he said.

"That's all right," Delia told him, and made herself smile. Although it was still strange to look at him and know some part of his genetic makeup wasn't even human, she knew she had to act as normal as possible—especially with Paige Loomis and her client due to arrive at any moment. "Go ahead and take a seat."

He came into the office and sat down in the lefthand chair facing her desk. "You're doing a good job," he said, and Delia raised an eyebrow.

"A good job of what?"

"Pretending I'm a normal guy."

Before she could respond, Paige and her client appeared, and Delia uttered a silent thank-you to the universe for allowing her to dodge that particular comment.

She really hadn't wanted to get into it with Caleb Lockwood. No, all she wanted to do was get the paperwork signed and the money handed over to the buyer, and then she could get on with her life.

Except she wouldn't be done with Caleb, not by a long shot...not when she'd already agreed to provide what advice she could about getting the reno back up and running.

"Hello, Paige, Mr. Mackie," she said. "Mr. Mackie, why don't you take a seat next to Caleb? There's a lot of paperwork to be signed."

Which Paige handed over, setting it on the desk in front of her client. "And the check?"

"Right here," Caleb said, then pulled an envelope out of the breast pocket of his leather jacket and set it down on the desktop. "Plus the additional ones for both your fees."

In a regular transaction involving a mortgage, that money would have come out of the disbursement from the mortgage company. Because this was a cash transaction, though, he'd had to keep those funds separate.

Paige looked over his shoulder as though to confirm that the amounts were correct, then nodded. "Everything looks in order. Tim, it's fine to go ahead and sign."

And even though they didn't have to sign a bunch of loan paperwork, there were still plenty of forms to sign—disclosures and amendments and all the other minutiae involved in any kind of property transaction.

Eventually, though, both Caleb and Tim Mackie had placed their signatures or initials on all the necessary papers.

Tim reached into his pocket and pulled out a set of keys before handing them over to Caleb.

"Here you go," he said. "Hope you have better luck with the place than I did."

"I'm sure it'll go smoothly," Caleb responded as he sent Delia a significant glance.

Of course it would—the spirit of the serial killer had been banished and all his victims had been removed from the basement, so there was no reason to think they'd encounter any more supernatural activity at the property.

Unless Caleb brought it with him, she supposed.

They exchanged congratulations, and then Paige and her client left, no doubt to have an early celebratory lunch.

Caleb slipped the house keys into his pocket as Delia placed the cashier's check for her agent fee in her purse. At some point, she'd need to go to the bank to deposit the thing; carrying around that much money, even if it wasn't cash, made her nervous.

"Do you have a client lined up after this?" he asked, something in his manner almost diffident.

She halfway wanted to lie and say she did, if only to give her a little breathing space while she tried to sort out her thoughts on the subject of Caleb Lockwood.

That wouldn't have been professional, though. She'd signed up to work with him, and had to hope that as the days and weeks wore on, she'd get so used to knowing he was part demon that it wouldn't even register with her anymore.

"No," she said, and forced another smile. "Let me guess—you want to go over to the property."

"I do," he replied, something about his expression telling her that he was amused by her obvious awkwardness. "I want to see if all that rain yesterday caused any problems."

It might have, considering the roof was one of the first projects that needed to be tackled at the Pueblo Street house. Now that he owned the place free and clear, Delia could see why he'd want to go straight over and make sure the weather hadn't caused another ten grand or so in damage.

"Then let's take a look," she said.

To Caleb's obvious relief, the roof didn't appear to have leaked at all. It still needed to be replaced, of course, but at least now they were assured it would hold until the new one could be installed.

They went back to the living room, where Delia pulled her phone out of her purse. "I've got the names of some G.C.s you can contact," she said. "They may already be working on other projects, but I guess I'm hoping at least one of them will be available. Even if you don't have the contractor nailed down, we can start putting together some mood boards and samples of the materials you want to use, since we can hit the ground running that way. And—"

"Delia," Caleb cut in, but almost gently. However, a belying twitch at the corner of his mouth seemed to signal that he knew she'd been talking so fast because she didn't know what else to do with herself.

"Was I that obvious?"

The twitch turned into a full-blown grin. "Kind of. I suppose I get it. You've never met anyone like me before, and your brain is still trying to wrap itself around what working with a part demon even means." He paused there before adding, "I'll let you in on a little secret. That demon blood doesn't matter as much as you think it does."

Delia planted her hands on her hips. "Well, except for the part where it allows you to teleport and banish souls to Hell and influence the roll of a die or the flip of a card. Am I missing anything?"

"Oh, maybe a couple of minor details." He glanced away from her so he could look past the sliding glass doors into the yard, which wasn't the waterlogged mess she'd feared it might be. Even when they got that much rain, the thirsty ground usually drank it down in a matter of hours. "But none of that is a big deal. Hell, I barely made enough at the gaming tables this weekend to pay for the kitchen remodel."

Which was still probably at least fifty or sixty

grand. She found herself smiling despite everything. The way he earned his money now was very different from the career he'd probably once envisioned for himself, but Pru's poking around had provided enough details to show that the Lockwoods had lots of money, and his casual attitude toward it told Delia that he probably had no idea what it was like to exist without a nice, fat cash cushion to protect him from some of life's harsh realities.

To be fair, she really didn't know what that was like, either. Her mother had been a successful real estate agent for going on thirty-five years, and her father had worked as a civil engineer for the city of Las Vegas for almost as long. They weren't super-rich, but they were definitely comfortable.

"Oh, is that all?" she responded with a grin that matched his.

She was a little surprised to see his smile fade. "I suppose I just wasn't feeling it."

They hadn't known each other long enough for her to be able to accurately read Caleb's emotions, but she couldn't shake the feeling that something had happened, something that seemed to have rattled his composure, if only a little.

He certainly wasn't coming across as cocky as he usually did.

"Anyway," he went on. "I can start looking at some materials, sure." He paused there, and now he looked a little more chipper, the familiar glint returning to his dark eyes. "Any chance you'd want to go slab shopping with me?"

Damn, he'd just found her hidden weakness. While she enjoyed looking at cabinet designs and roaming through tile and flooring showrooms, what she loved most was going to the warehouses where they kept all those huge, gorgeous pieces of stone, whether granite or marble or quartz, or more exotic materials like soapstone and Dolomite.

"Um, maybe," she hedged, and he flashed her another grin.

"You know you want to," he said. "And I'll buy you lunch as an extra inducement."

"You don't have to do that—" she began, but Caleb only shook his head.

"I don't have to, I want to," he cut in. "Besides, the house is mine now, and I feel like we should celebrate."

When he put it that way....

"All right," she said. "Slabs first, lunch afterward."

"I like a woman who has her priorities in order," Caleb responded, and although she knew he was mostly joking, she wasn't quite sure what to do when his gaze met hers and held there for a second or two.

That look told her he would be just fine if their

relationship became a little something more than merely professional.

Well, that wasn't going to happen. Life was complicated enough without throwing hook-ups with a demon in the mix.

"Let's go," she said.

Chapter Fifteen

—·«‹‹·◎·››»·—

Overall, Caleb thought Delia was adapting to the situation fairly well. True, in that moment when their eyes had met, he'd seen her doubt and awkwardness, and understood she was in no way ready for their relationship to be anything other than professional, but that was okay.

The thrill of the chase was half the fun.

She took him to a warehouse that had what seemed to be thousands of slabs on display, both inside the showroom itself and out in the back lot as well. Getting his first look at all that stone, he wondered if maybe he should ease up on his all-black vision and instead get something that would contrast with the black cabinets he wanted. There was such a bewildering variety of colors and patterns, he didn't quite know where to look first.

But Delia seemed to understand what he wanted more than he himself did, guiding him to a slab of black soapstone whose veining was a soft beige color rather than white, an unusual combination that he thought would work well with the white oak floors he already had planned.

"One slab will be enough?" he asked, mostly because he hadn't seen another like it and wanted to be certain he wouldn't have to worry about running out.

"Oh, sure," she said, looking unconcerned. "This stuff goes farther than you might think. You'll need something different for the bathrooms, though."

Well, he wasn't worried about that, mostly because he'd already decided that he wanted each one to have a distinct personality, even if he intended to maintain the same color scheme of black and neutrals throughout the house. He wanted something sleek and modern and hip, a design that would pay homage to the mid-century inspiration of the house without being too slavish about trying to copy any original styles too closely.

"Then I think we can slap a 'sold' sticker on it," he told her. "But maybe keep looking so I can see what I might be able to use for the bathrooms."

In the end, they found pretty much everything he needed, including some dark gray Dolomite with off-white veining for the fireplace surround.

The manager at the warehouse said it wouldn't be a problem to store everything until it was needed, and once they were done, Caleb guided Delia back to his SUV, both his heart and his wallet feeling a lot lighter.

Because after the traffic accident, he hadn't left the house, and instead had ordered DoorDash when he didn't feel like making something to eat. He supposed one of the imps could have disguised itself as a delivery driver, except it still didn't seem as if the demons had figured out where he lived, thanks to the way he made sure he was picked up or dropped off in other locations around town. That didn't explain how the demon had known he was the one to summon that particular Uber, but he hoped he'd figure it out soon.

This was the first time he'd ventured out of the house since the accident, and on the drive over to Delia's office, he'd kept looking from side to side, wondering if some random vehicle was suddenly going to ram him or maybe one of those annoying little imp demons was going to pop up from the back seat and try to snap his neck.

None of those things had happened, though, and he had to wonder exactly what was going on here. Was it simply that he was in the company of a regular human being, and whoever was controlling those imps knew that sending them to attack him when there were mortal witnesses around wasn't a very good idea?

That didn't explain why they hadn't come after him at his house, the place where he was most vulnerable. He might have been part demon, but he had to sleep like everybody else.

"Now can I buy you lunch?" he asked after he'd slid the receipts into his wallet and he and Delia were walking away from the sales counter. "Because I think this time we really have something to celebrate."

He'd expected her to come up with some sort of excuse to avoid the meal, even though she'd half agreed to it already. Instead, she surprised him by saying, "Sure. I don't need to be back at the office until two."

They headed out to the parking lot and got into his Range Rover. He'd offered to drive, mostly because his vehicle was bigger and more luxurious, and Delia had gone along with the plan without argument.

So they drove to a nearby restaurant that served vaguely California-inspired fare, where they were seated quickly enough since they were coming in at the tail end of lunch. Before Delia could protest, Caleb ordered a bottle of pinot grigio, although she sent him a sideways look after the waiter headed off to fetch the wine.

"Hey," he said with a grin, "at least I didn't order champagne."

"True," she replied. Her mouth quirked at the corner, telling him she was trying to hold back a smile of her own. "I just have to hope my two o'clock won't mind if I'm the slightest bit tipsy."

He knew he wouldn't mind. Although she'd been friendly and professional this whole time, he still hadn't seen much slippage in her public veneer, and he wished she would let her guard down with him, if only a little bit.

After spending his entire life in Greencastle, surrounded by people he'd known since pretty much the day he was born, he had to admit there was something fascinating about being around someone who was a mystery to him.

"I'll drink most of the bottle," he offered, and Delia smiled outright.

"I appreciate your sacrifice."

They both chuckled, then spent a minute or so studying the menu so they'd be ready to order once the waiter came back with their wine. Which he did soon enough, so Caleb was glad that he'd already settled on the chicken sandwich, while Delia ordered an Asian salad with grilled chicken.

Did she have to watch what she ate, or was she only being moderate because she didn't feel like eating a heavy meal in the middle of the day? He couldn't say for sure; she seemed naturally slender to him, willowy and tall, but maybe she really had to work at it to stay that slim.

"To Pueblo Street," he said, lifting his wine glass, and Delia clinked hers against it.

"To closing the sale," she responded. "And to the project ahead of us."

They'd made one small step in that direction today with the order of the stone for all the various countertops. "You really think it's going to take a whole six months?"

She sipped some pinot grigio. "Maybe a little less. It just depends on how quickly you can get a crew in there, and whether all the materials you want are in stock or whether they're on back order. I'm sure you'll want custom cabinets, and those take a while."

Right. He wanted the house to be a showplace when it was done, which meant he needed something a little fancier in the kitchen and bathrooms than a bunch of prefab cabinets from a big-box store. It wasn't so much that he planned to entertain a whole lot, but more that he'd grown up in a large, elegant home, and while this one would be utterly different in design and feel, he thought it should still reflect a certain level of taste.

"Well, it'll be an adventure," he remarked, and helped himself to a swallow from his glass of wine.

Another smile. "That's one way of looking at it."

The waiter came over with their food, and they were quiet for a moment as they both attended to their meals. And although Delia had seemed cheerful enough at the stone warehouse and as they drove over to the restaurant, now Caleb couldn't help thinking something about her seemed almost subdued, as if she had some sort of problem weighing on her mind, one that didn't seem to have any connection to the house on Pueblo Street or its looming remodel.

If he'd known her better, he might have asked her what was wrong. As it was, he tried to keep the conversation going by talking about the various design choices for the home, and what she thought would be the best way to handle the ragged, over-grown front and back yards.

The last thing he could do was talk about the way an imp demon had attacked him in his Uber the day before, not when the hostess seated a couple of noisy men next to them, two guys who seemed to have the need to discuss their picks for the playoffs at the top of their lungs.

Although Delia's expression remained neutral enough, Caleb thought he saw her wince when the bros let out a loud shout of laughter. She might have spent some of her formative years playing in an all-girl punk band, but he could tell she had a low tolerance for idiots.

Yet another thing he liked about her.

Any chance at a real conversation had been effectively thwarted, so they ate the rest of their meals as quickly as they could without looking like they were trying to bolt their food. Not much respect was paid to the wine, either, but sometimes that was just how things shook out.

As they approached his Range Rover, Delia said, "It's a shame some people never learned to use their inside voices."

"That's for sure," Caleb replied, then opened the passenger door for her. "I promise I'm not that obnoxious after a couple of beers with the guys."

Her cool, green-hued eyes surveyed him for a moment. "Do you have guys to hang out with? It seems to me like you kind of keep to yourself."

Well, that was true. In Greencastle, he'd had plenty of people to socialize with, some of them part demon like him, a whole lot more just regular humans he'd gone to high school and college with. Here in Vegas, it seemed his closest relationships were with the DoorDash guys...and possibly Delia herself, even though Caleb guessed she might not appreciate that view of her very much.

"I'm working on the social network," he said, then headed around to his side of the vehicle so he could get in the driver's seat. "It's always hard to establish yourself in a new town."

"Especially when you have so many secrets to keep."

Although he'd been about to back out of their parking space, he allowed himself a quick sideways glance at Delia before he did so. Her expression was more thoughtful than anything else, so he guessed she hadn't made the comment as a dig at him.

No, it was more an expression of fact than anything else.

"It doesn't help," he allowed as he guided the Range Rover onto Desert Inn Road. "But I suppose you haven't had to deal with that sort of thing much, right?"

She had been staring ahead, her gaze apparently fixed on the cars in front of them. Now she looked over at him, waiting a beat or two before she responded.

"Not really," she said. "I mean, I grew up here. We moved a couple of times because my mother liked to find bigger and better houses for us, but my parents always made sure to stay in the same general area so I wouldn't have to start over in a new school and have to make a whole new set of friends."

Well, that answered that question. "Do you keep in touch with any of your high school friends?"

Again, she paused for a few seconds. Then she said, "A couple. But people are busy with their own lives, so it's not like I get together with them every

Friday to work on my fantasy football league or anything."

He supposed real estate agents could have crazy work hours, too, since they had to maneuver around people's schedules and would probably have to see their clients after work during the week and whatever time was convenient on the weekend.

That was one thing that made him easy to work with, he supposed—he didn't have anything like a real job, so he could come and go according to times that worked for both of them.

But since it seemed as if Delia was willing to share at least a little personal information, he thought he might try to ask another question.

"Do you come from a big family?"

He halfway hoped she would say yes. His family had been just his mother and father and him, and the Lockwoods weren't exactly the most loving, nurturing family in the world. He'd often thought that if he'd had a brother or sister, someone who could be a friend or at least an ally, then maybe his childhood would have been a little more bearable.

However, Delia shook her head. "No, it was just me and my parents. They tried to have more kids after me, but it never worked out." She smiled then, a little crookedly. "At least I never had to fight with someone over the bathroom or who was hogging the remote when I wanted to watch TV after school."

Caleb supposed that was one way of looking at the situation.

But she must be close with her mother, or he doubted Delia would have ever agreed to share an office and a business with Linda Dunne. He hadn't seen the other woman very much, only a couple of times in passing as he was coming and going from Dunne & Dunne, but she'd always seemed friendly, smiling at him in acknowledgment as she headed out to meet a client or host an open house.

She definitely seemed like a much more pleasant person than Brooke Lockwood.

"Being an only child does have its benefits," he agreed.

By that point, they'd almost reached the parking lot for the building where her office was located, so he turned on his signal and moved into the right lane.

"So...what now?" he asked, glad to spy a parking place almost immediately in front of the main entrance.

"Now," Delia said as she hefted her purse on her shoulder, "I'll make a few phone calls to my favorite G.C.s and see who's available. After that, I'll pass their names on to you so you can meet them at the property and have them give you a firmer quote on the scope of work. But in the meantime, the house is yours, so I think you should go back and really walk the property and get an idea of what you want to do. I always get much more of a feel for a house once I'm able to be alone there for a while and get into all the nooks and crannies."

At least he wouldn't have to worry about being attacked by a vengeful ghost while poking around in the linen closet. Then again, Caleb wasn't sure whether that had ever been a real risk. The spirit of the serial killer seemed to have known he wasn't exactly human and therefore not viable prey.

But Delia's suggestion sounded like a good one. While he'd certainly liked having her company as they walked the property and talked over possibilities for the design, there was something to be said for evaluating a place on your own without any outside input.

"All right," he said. "In fact, I think I'll head over there after this."

"Good plan." She opened the passenger-side door, then added, "And I'll call you as soon as I have some info about the G.C.s."

Caleb nodded, and she got out. For a moment, he remained where he was, watching as she headed into the building, coppery hair swishing with every movement, bright and shimmering against the teal blue jacket she wore.

Damn, she was gorgeous.

But she also wasn't interested, which meant there wasn't much point in sitting there and gawking at her.

He backed out of the parking space and pointed the Range Rover toward the house on Pueblo Street.

Because the garage hadn't been updated yet and didn't have a working opener, Caleb parked in the driveway. However, leaving his SUV there rather than on the street still seemed to send a subtle message that this place really was his.

Despite all the exposed two-by-fours and supplies stacked everywhere, the house felt a little more cheerful than it had the last time he was here. Sunlight streamed through the big windows, and a couple of birds—plain old finches and sparrows, from what he could tell—had settled on the back wall and were cheeping away.

And he could tell no more ghosts lingered here. The worry had floated around in the back of his mind that maybe he hadn't located all the victims and maybe a spirit or two would emerge from the woodwork now that their murderer was gone, but that didn't seem to be the case.

No, his was the only presence here.

As he was poking around the master bedroom,

trying to decide whether he should leave the closet as-is or whether he should have the contractors steal a little space from the bathroom to expand it, he saw that Delia had been right. It was good to get familiar with the house and have a clearer idea of what he wanted to do with it.

During the process, though, he realized that he truly did want to make this place his—not as an income property, but as the place where he lived. The remodel would allow him to put his personal stamp on the house, something he hadn't been able to do with his current home, which had been completely updated—and furnished—before he moved in. Sure, this property wouldn't be ready for months and months, but whenever the reno was complete, he would live here, not in the house he'd thought would be a good place to set down roots.

Some people probably would have thought he was crazy for wanting to move into a murder house like this, but the ghosts were long gone. Whatever residue of sorrow and pain might have lingered after their deaths, it certainly wasn't around anymore.

He went back into the living room and peeked outside. The Range Rover sat unmolested in the driveway, telling him that whoever was directing those imp demons, they didn't seem to know he was here.

Unless....

Now that he thought about it, the answer seemed ridiculously simple. The attacks had occurred when he was either on-site at a casino—or at least its parking structure—or while he was en route to one. Nothing at all had happened when he was only driving to Delia's office or the grocery store or the bank.

Which meant that whoever was in charge, they seemed a lot more interested in keeping him away from the casinos rather than making sure he was permanently removed from the equation.

Contrary to popular belief, demons weren't that invested in killing people. They liked to torment them, relished their pain, but outright murder raised a lot of questions, even if there was no chance of actually finding the killer, not when demons didn't leave any real evidence behind and could pop back to Hell and escape detection.

And killing him now that he'd woven himself a little more tightly into the fabric of the city by buying property and interacting with people like Delia—or even Paige Loomis—on a professional level made such a proposition even more problematic. Maybe if the other demons had figured out who he was and what he was doing much earlier in the process, when he was still moving from hotel room to hotel room while deciding which house to buy, they would have had an easier time making sure his gambling activities were stopped permanently.

Now, though....

Well, if they had a bug up their ass because he'd won too much money at their damn casinos, it would be easy enough for him to stop gambling. He already had a decent chunk of change in the bank, and maybe now was the time to think about investing some of it rather than relying on the gaming tables to provide him with his income. Delia must know a financial advisor she could recommend.

After arriving at that solution, Caleb almost wanted to laugh out loud. Could it really be so easy?

He sure as hell hoped so.

Chapter Sixteen

—‹‹‹‹·◎·›››·—

AFTER MEETING WITH HER TWO O'CLOCK client—who didn't seem to notice that Delia had had two glasses of wine with lunch—she dutifully got out her phone and texted the two general contractors she'd been thinking of for Caleb's renovation project. Bruce Mills was already booked up, but Raul Martinez told her he'd just had a cancellation after the second mortgage his clients had been relying on to fund their remodel fell through.

"So I hope this one isn't on shaky ground," he said, and Delia had to smile.

"No, this client is paying cash for everything," she replied. "No bank involvement at all. And the wiring and the plumbing are mostly done, so you won't have to worry about that. There's still the HVAC system and the roof and all the cosmetic stuff, but—"

"You had me at 'paying cash,'" Raul cut in, and she could practically see him grinning at the prospect. "When did you want to get started?"

"As soon as possible," she said. "But you'll need to talk to Caleb and confirm that with him. Let me give you his number."

After that piece of business was handled, Delia set down her phone and opened her laptop. She didn't have another client meeting until four, so she thought this would give her a chance to get caught up on what was happening in Las Vegas and the world—and possibly distract her from the way she'd decided to go all in with helping a part demon remodel his dream house.

Or his income property, or whatever. She still wasn't entirely sure what he planned to do with the place.

But when she went to the website of one of the local news stations, she wondered if maybe it had been such a great idea to get caught up on what was happening in the world around her.

Mystery Bodies at Morgue Stump Authorities, the headline read, and Delia let out a breath. While she'd known intellectually that you couldn't just have a bunch of skeletons appear at the medical examiner's facility and not send up a forest of red flags, she supposed she'd hoped that maybe they wouldn't broadcast those details to the press until they'd had a little more time to investigate.

Apparently not.

But the article made it clear that neither the police nor the workers at the medical examiner's office had any idea where the remains had come from, so she supposed that piece of information made her feel a little better. There really wasn't anything to tie those skeletons to her and Caleb, since the two of them were the only people who even knew their true history. Maybe at some point, the medical examiner and his or her staff would be able to determine a cause of death, but she didn't think they'd be able to extract much more information than that, not when the remains had been removed from the crime scene and so much time had elapsed since those women's murders.

She and Caleb sure wouldn't be talking...not because they'd done anything wrong, but because she knew there was no way they could explain how they'd gotten the skeletons out from under the floor of his home's lower level without jackhammering the thing into oblivion.

And that didn't even take into account the little detail of getting them from Pueblo Street into the coroner's office without anyone noticing.

No, it was one of those crazy mysteries that would occupy the local media for a day or two until something just as sensational came along.

Even as she was about to navigate away from the news station's website and over to the Weather

Channel's site so she could check to see whether any more rain threatened in the forecast, her phone rang.

Robert Hendricks' number.

Delia hadn't expected to hear from him again so soon, not when they'd both agreed that they would give things until the end of the week before she decided whether to continue with their demon search.

Well, she already knew she didn't want to do this anymore and was only humoring Robert because he'd made it clear that he thought she needed more time, but still.

"Hi, Robert," she said. "What's up?"

"I have something you need to see," he replied. "Can you meet me at the business offices at the Dunes?"

She'd wondered where his office was located...if he even had one at all. He'd been sort of hazy about exactly where he worked, although it seemed clear enough that he was just the spokesman for a group of concerned casino owners and managers.

"I have a client coming to the office in less than an hour," she replied. "Can we do it after that, maybe around five-thirty?"

A pause, and she wondered if he was going to tell her no, that wouldn't work, that the matter was urgent and he needed to see her right away.

But then he said, "Five-thirty should be fine.

Just tell one of the security guards at the Dunes that you're there to see Robert Hendricks, and they'll take you up to my office."

"Sounds good," she responded. "Sorry I can't meet you sooner than that."

"It's fine," he assured her. "I understand that you have other clients you need to attend to. I'll see you at five-thirty."

They ended the call there, and she returned her phone to her purse, a little mystified.

Just what was so important that Robert needed to see her today after work, rather than waiting until tomorrow morning?

Well, she supposed she'd find out soon enough.

Her four o'clock meeting—to help an older couple put the family home on the market and find them a condo for their new, downsized lifestyle—went faster than Delia had expected, so she probably could have met Robert at closer to five than five-thirty. However, they'd already agreed upon the time, so she decided to roll with it and show up as scheduled.

She'd known the traffic would probably suck, and she gave herself a little cushion for the drive over to the casino. Good thing, because even though she didn't see any accidents like the one from a few days ago between the big black truck and the white Mazda SUV, enough cars still choked the streets downtown that she barely made it to the Dunes on time.

Once there, she followed Robert's instructions and went over to a security guard, telling him she had a meeting with Mr. Hendricks. At once, the guard—a friendly Black man who looked like he was probably around ten or fifteen years older than she—guided her over to the elevator and took them up to the tenth floor.

Not the penthouse, which of course would need to be a luxurious suite designed to cater to the casino's high rollers. Still, the tenth floor offered some breathtaking views, especially as the wintry dusk shifted into full dark and the lights on the Strip really came to life.

"Here you are," the security guard told her, and pressed the button on an intercom set into the wall next to the office suite's door. "Mr. Hendricks? I have a Ms. Dunne here to see you."

"Send her in," came Robert's voice, and the security guard nodded at her even as a faint buzzing sound told her the door had probably just been unlocked.

"You can go inside now."

She thanked him, then put her fingers on the door handle and pushed down. Immediately, the door swung inward, letting her into an office that showcased more of those dramatic views, with a big glass and steel desk at the far end of the space.

"Thanks for coming by," Robert said as he rose from behind the desk. He looked a little less casual than he had the last time they'd met, today wearing a black dress shirt and gray dress pants.

She went over to him and smiled. "It's no problem. What did you want to show me?"

"One of my colleagues found something on the security cameras at Treasure Island," Robert replied. "I thought you might want to take a look."

"Sure," she said, hoping she didn't sound too reluctant. While she knew the chances of him or one of his associates finding anything truly incriminating were fairly low, she knew she also had to understand that she was in uncharted territory now...and all bets were off.

Robert had one of those insanely expensive Mac Pros and a matching cinema display, a setup she knew must have cost him upwards of three or four grand...mostly because she'd thought about getting one for herself and had decided she couldn't really justify the expenditure no matter how much she wanted a shiny new toy.

Now he shifted the display just enough so it was facing more toward her. "One of the security cameras—the one near the men's restrooms—picked this up. At first, I thought it must be some kind of degradation of the signal, a sort of glitch.

But now I'm not sure, so I thought I should get your expert opinion."

She wanted to argue that she wasn't an expert at analyzing security footage and then decided to keep silent. Better to see what Robert thought he had found before she started getting too defensive.

He clicked the wireless mouse, and the screen-saver that had displayed a series of desert scenes abruptly flicked off, instead showing what looked like every single hallway leading to the casino bath-rooms that she'd ever seen. Yes, the pattern of the carpet and the color on the walls and the light fixtures might change, but they all felt slightly cramped and in person tended to smell of desperation.

The door to the men's restroom opened, and a dark-haired man who looked like he might be around thirty, wearing jeans and a henley-style shirt, stepped out. He was very good-looking, but Delia doubted that was why Robert wanted her to see this footage.

No, it was the way that handsome face slipped for a split-second, instead showing the features of a much older Hispanic man, before the model-pretty visage returned.

"I...don't understand," she said, knowing she sounded a little shaken...although probably not for the reason Robert Hendricks might believe.

Neither of those faces had belonged to Caleb

Lockwood, but she knew that it had to be him. She'd never watched him shift, and yet, who else could it be?

Another demon, she thought, but for some reason, that didn't feel right. Caleb was the one who'd gone around changing his appearance so he could gamble and win money all over town without anyone being able to find a connection among all those winners, so it only made sense that it would be his slip-up that the security cameras caught.

Why it had happened, she didn't know, but even with all his powers, she doubted he was infallible. Most likely, he hadn't realized there were security cameras trained on him in that moment, and since the hallway had been otherwise empty, he probably wouldn't have thought a little glitch like that was a big deal.

"So," she said, glad her voice sounded steady enough, "you think that person is a demon?"

"Yes," Robert replied. He didn't seem too shaken by what he'd just shown here, but she guessed he'd already watched the footage multiple times and had had enough time to come to terms with its implications. "We're fairly certain it's the same one who's been going around town and helping himself to some unearned winnings. Now that we know what he looks like, it'll be easier to keep an eye out for him."

Unfortunately for Robert Hendricks and his associates, the face they'd caught on camera wasn't Caleb's real one. Delia decided it was better to keep quiet about that particular point, though. She'd already decided that if she was forced to pick sides, she would be on Caleb's...as unlikely as that scenario might have felt to her only a few days ago.

"I can see that," she said, her tone neutral. "And if you know who to look for, I'm not sure you need my services anymore."

Robert raised an eyebrow. "You thought I had you come all the way over here just so I could tell you that you were off the case?"

She shrugged. "Well, and to show me the footage, I suppose. But since all of the casinos have security personnel who can be given a screenshot of the guy, I don't think my ghost-sleuthing abilities —or whatever you want to call them—are what you need right now."

"Actually, they're exactly what we need," he countered. "Just because we caught a glimpse of the man doesn't mean that he won't keep changing his appearance whenever he wants to visit a new casino and bilk us out of more money. Our security guards obviously wouldn't be able to detect when this demon shapeshifts...but you could."

"I don't know about that," Delia said. "I've wandered around a number of casinos over the past week and never felt anything except the very slightest whiff that could have been something else entirely. Like I told you on the phone yesterday, I don't think my talents—or whatever you want to call them—are what's needed here."

Robert Hendricks didn't reply at first, only stood behind his desk and watched her with eyes that had narrowed ever so slightly. "I respectfully disagree. And you already told me that you'd be willing to keep working on this for another week."

Yes, she had...a promise she now wished she'd never made. But because she couldn't go back in time and tell her past self to just end it and walk away, there wasn't much she could do about that now.

"I did," she said steadily. "And I'll keep trying. I just don't want to exaggerate what I'm able to accomplish."

"You haven't exaggerated," he replied. "If anything, you've underplayed your abilities. It's unclear to us whether this demon has an unlimited repertoire of borrowed faces or whether he has a set number that he likes to cycle through. If it's the latter case, then seeing these two appearances might help you spot him when you're out in a casino."

Maybe that would have been helpful...if she didn't already know exactly who Caleb was and exactly what he looked like.

"Yes, it might," she said. At this point, since she was still stuck spying for Robert Hendricks and his cohorts, she figured she'd just go along with whatever he said and then get the hell out of there as quickly as she could. "And it's definitely something I'll keep in mind. Was there anything else?"

That last question might have bordered on rude. Then again, this wasn't a social call. They were handling a piece of business, and since it seemed as if he'd passed the relevant information on to her, she didn't see the point in lingering.

Especially since she knew she needed to let Caleb know about this latest development.

A faint smile touched Robert Hendricks' lips. "No, that was all. Thank you for coming over here at what I know must be the end of a long day."

It had been long. Unfortunately, it wasn't over yet.

She made a polite demurral, and after that, he walked her over to the door and thanked her again for coming. When she rode down the elevator, she realized she shouldn't leave immediately, should make a show of wandering the casino floor and looking for their elusive demon gambler.

Who of course wasn't even there.

But she still walked past the blackjack tables and the craps tables with their usual throngs of people hanging around and watching the moment's latest high roller, wasting a good twenty minutes or so until she thought she'd spent enough time there that any report the security staff sent up to Robert Hendricks would show she'd done her due diligence.

Afterward, she went out to the parking lot and drove away. Once she figured she'd put some safe distance between her car and the Dunes—and after she'd nervously checked all her rearview mirrors, wondering if maybe he would have sent someone to tail her, ridiculous as that sounded—she waited for a convenient red light and then got her phone out of her purse.

Caleb picked up almost right away. "Hey, Delia. Did something come up?"

A fitting question, she supposed, since he probably would have assumed that after she gave him Raul Martinez's contact information, she wouldn't need to reach out for a while.

"Yes," she said. "But I'd rather talk in person. Are you home?"

To her relief, he didn't ask her why, only replied, "I am. Do you need the address?"

She did, because although she'd seen it on his paperwork, she hadn't committed it to memory.

"That would help."

He gave her the information, and she hurriedly programmed it into her nav.

"It'll be about fifteen minutes," she said.

"No worries. I'm not going anywhere."

After she ended the call, she hoped she wasn't interrupting his dinner. True, it was still a little early for that, but she had no idea what his schedule was like.

If he even had one. He seemed like one of those people who went where the wind took him—something that was a lot easier to do when you didn't have a real job.

The streets were crammed, and she found herself drumming her fingers impatiently on the steering wheel whenever a red light took too long. Yes, Caleb had told her he wasn't going anywhere, and he probably knew as well as anyone else that you couldn't control Las Vegas traffic, only do your best to coexist with it.

Eventually, though, she found herself winding through a neighborhood of older homes, most of which had been recently updated and restored. They were possibly a few years newer than the home he'd bought on Pueblo Street, but still very much mid-century in vintage and design.

In fact, the house she pulled up to felt oddly familiar, although she couldn't say why, precisely. Maybe she'd seen it on the MLS or a sales flyer.

When he opened the door and let her in, however, and she took note of the boldly painted shelves in the living room and the fixture of sculpted LED lights that hung over the dining room table, it suddenly hit her.

"You bought one of the *Flip or Flop Vegas* houses?"

"I did," Caleb said with a grin, ushering her into the living room so she could take a seat. "It was fully furnished and move-in ready, and I needed a home base, so I went for it. Drink? You look like you could use one."

Drinking here alone with Caleb Lockwood didn't seem like the best idea in the world.

On the other hand, it had been kind of a day.

"What've you got?"

"Pretty much anything," he replied, still smiling. "Just don't ask me to make a pousse café."

Delia had no idea what that even was and figured it must be some kind of a private joke for him. "Some wine would be great."

"Coming right up."

She waited on the couch while he went into the kitchen. A few clinks that she guessed were the sounds of Caleb getting a pair of glasses out of the cupboard, and then the sound of a cork getting pulled out of a bottle.

He came back into the living room, a glass of red wine in each hand. After giving her one, he sat down in one of the club chairs that faced the sofa.

Well, thank God for that. She wasn't sure how she would have handled him sitting right next to her. At least this way, their meeting could feel halfway formal, even if they were drinking wine.

No offer of a toast, which told her he was pretty good at reading the room.

Then again, she kind of already knew that.

"So...what's up?" he asked, and sipped some wine.

A swallow of wine sounded like a great idea. She drank some down and guessed it was probably pinot noir or a blend, since it wasn't heavy enough to be a cab.

"I just had a meeting with Robert Hendricks."

Caleb didn't appear overly worried by that revelation. "And?"

"He had some security footage of you."

At once, Caleb sat up a little straighter, his straight brown brows pulling together. "What?"

All right, now it looked as if he was paying attention. "You were coming out of the men's restroom at Treasure Island, and the cameras in that hallway caught a little blip as your appearance shifted."

"Well, shit," he said, although he still looked more annoyed than concerned, as if he was irritated with himself for being so careless.

"It could be worse," Delia told him, then sipped some more of her wine. "Luckily, the cameras caught you when you were wearing a different face, so Robert still doesn't know what you look like. He thinks your real appearance is some Hispanic guy who's around your same age." She stopped there and gave Caleb an inquisitive glance. "So...where do you get all these faces you wear, anyway? Are they people you've seen on the street or something?"

"Some of them," he replied. "Some I have an AI generate for me, so they don't look like anyone in particular. Sometimes that seems safer to me."

She supposed it would. If he was borrowing a real person's face, there was always the odd chance that someone might recognize him, whereas if the visage he decided to wear only existed in the mind of an AI, that wouldn't be an issue.

"Still," she said, "now they have solid proof that you exist...and that you can shapeshift. It's probably better if you lie low for a while."

A quick flash of a grin, the one Caleb seemed to employ whenever he needed to reassure her that everything was cool.

"Already on it," he replied. "After getting attacked by imp demons twice—imps I realized were trying to keep me from going to the casinos— I decided I'd focus on the remodel and get my money working for me a different way. Speaking of which, do you have any financial advisor recs you can give me?"

He sounded so blithe. And wait...*two* attacks? Delia only knew of the one from the parking structure at the Bellagio.

"What was the second attack?" she asked, ignoring the comment about the financial advisor. She had a few people she could recommend, but that didn't seem like the most pressing matter at the moment.

"Oh, I hired an Uber where the driver turned out to be an imp. He intentionally ran a red light, but I teleported myself out of there right after we got T-boned."

Once again, she had a hard time understanding how he could be so chill about the whole thing. "So...they already know who you are?"

"I don't think they know it's me, me," Caleb replied calmly, and drank some of his wine. "I think they just detected the presence of someone of demon-kind. They probably don't know where I live, or otherwise, they would have come after me here. But they obviously figured out I use Uber a lot to get around. So my plan is to keep a low profile until things calm down a little. Luckily, I've got plenty of earnings to live on, so it's not as if I need to worry about heading out to the gambling tables any time soon."

She supposed that was something.

"And I doubt they're going to try to kill me," he went on, sounding way too blithe, considering the situation. "I think they wanted to send a clear warning that they're not happy with me taking millions of their money."

Although she'd already done the unpleasant math in her head, she said, "So...the casino owners are working in concert with the demons?"

"Or some of them might be demons them-selves," Caleb said. He still wore a half-smile, making her think he still wasn't taking this too seri-ously. "It's hard to say without meeting them. Has this Robert Hendricks given you any weird vibes?"

Delia wanted to say no, he hadn't, but after meeting Caleb, she had to admit that she didn't quite trust her instincts the way she once had. There hadn't been a single sign, a single comment or word, that had made her think he was anyone except who he professed to be.

"Nothing I can think of," she replied. "Which unfortunately doesn't mean much, because it doesn't seem as if I'm as good at detecting demons as I am at working with ghosts. But he seems like a regular man to me."

"He could very well be," Caleb said. "Lots of instances of humans working with demons and having absolutely no idea who they were inter-acting with. But I don't see any reason why we can't peacefully coexist now that I've sworn off the casinos. Demons tend to be single-focus crea-tures, so once I'm off their radar, it should be fine."

Delia wished she could be that confident about the situation. Robert didn't seem like the type to give up easily, or he wouldn't have pressured her into working on the casino problem for another week.

Also, men who were pushovers generally didn't end up in a corner office with a panoramic view.

"If you think so," she said, and didn't bother to keep the skeptical tone from her voice. "But I figured it was better if you knew how much information they actually have."

"And I appreciate it," Caleb replied with a smile. "It's always good to know what your enemy is doing."

Before she'd heard about the attempted car accident, she might have commented on his use of the word "enemy." Now, though—even if she still wasn't entirely sure whether the demons who'd targeted him were the same group as those who were trying to figure out who'd been gaming the system at the casinos—it seemed pretty clear to her that at least one person wanted to scare him off...if not remove him from the chessboard altogether.

"Since you're over here," he continued, now sounding almost diffident, "do you want to stay and have something to eat? Just something from DoorDash, but I assure you that I'm expert at ordering from them."

A demurral rose to her lips, but then she took a good look at him. Most people would have said he still appeared casual enough, and yet there was something about the way he wouldn't quite meet her eyes that told her he was more invested in her staying for dinner than he wanted to admit.

In that moment, she realized how lonely he really was.

And she certainly didn't have anything on the docket except maybe sticking a quiche from Trader Joe's in the toaster oven. It would be okay to stay here and provide a little company...wouldn't it?

"Sure," she said, hoping he hadn't noticed her hesitation.

Maybe she was making a mistake.

She supposed she'd find out soon enough.

Chapter Seventeen

———— ‹‹‹⟐›››———

CALEB WAS A LITTLE STARTLED THAT DELIA had actually agreed to stay for dinner, but he told himself it was probably because she didn't have any other plans and figured she might as well get a free meal out of him.

No, that sounded like something he would do, not Delia. Whatever her reasons for hanging around, he wasn't going to question them too closely.

So they ordered Thai and adjourned to the dining room once it arrived, and had what he thought was a friendly enough meal. She mentioned a few people who could help him make his money do more than just sit around, and even added that she'd keep an eye out for any properties that might be ripe for flipping.

"They don't come up as often as they used to

because the market is so competitive now," she went on. "But still, every once in a while you can find a unicorn. And if it's all cosmetic stuff and nothing major, you can sometimes turn things around in a month. People used to do that all the time because they wanted to make sure a place was sold before they had to make a mortgage payment."

"But I'd be paying cash," he pointed out, and Delia only smiled.

"I figured," she said. "Still, you might be able to make fifty or sixty grand in only a month or so."

Whereas at the gaming tables, he could make that much in a day without breaking a sweat. However, that avenue appeared closed to him...at least for now...so he knew he might as well entertain the idea of flipping a property or two in addition to buying T-bills or starting a stock portfolio or whatever else a financial advisor might instruct him to do. He supposed if he'd paid more attention to what his father did at the bank, he might know more about this sort of stuff.

However, he'd never wanted to work at the bank. His father had been pushing him into it at the end there, after his business in Southern California was concluded, but then they'd all been banished to Hell and that was the end of that discussion.

Silver linings, he supposed.

At the end of their meal, Caleb didn't try to

put a move on Delia—he had a feeling it wouldn't be very well received—and instead just walked her out to her car and stood on the sidewalk for a moment, watching as she pulled away and then turned the corner, moving out to Pecos Road so she could head for home. Although she'd never told him, he knew exactly where that was, a neighborhood of larger homes that had been built in the late '90s and which a lot of people were currently in the process of updating. The only photos he'd seen online of her house were the ones from when it had been up for sale, so he guessed it looked quite different now.

Somehow, he didn't think she would have been too keen on keeping the wall-to-wall carpet or the white tile in the kitchen.

Maybe someday, if he could get her to relax a little more, she might invite him over.

In the meantime, he picked up the leftovers from their meal and put them in the fridge, then cleared away the empty plates and glasses and the bottle of wine. There was still a little bit of pinot left, so he poured the remainder into his glass and headed back to the living room. Outside, the night was utterly clear, the swimming pool a glowing blue-green gem in the darkness, but he knew it was way too cold to go swimming.

No, he just sat down and turned on the TV mounted over the fireplace, feeling oddly deflated.

If he hadn't known that someone or something connected to the casinos was gunning for him, he might have headed out, thinking it would be a good idea to kill some time and refill his coffers at the gaming tables as well.

That particular avenue of amusement had been closed off to him, though.

And if it had been later in the week, he could have at least whiled away the rest of his evening by watching a football game, but that diversion had been denied him as well.

He drank the rest of the wine and went into the kitchen to rinse out his glass. True, he had pretty much every streaming channel known to man available on his Apple TV, and he'd also amassed a decent collection of Blu-Rays during his time in Las Vegas. It really shouldn't have been that difficult for him to find some way to fill up the next couple of hours.

Unfortunately, he didn't think he'd be able to concentrate very well, not when he couldn't make himself stop thinking about Delia Dunne. She was the only person who'd ever been over here to visit him—he couldn't really count the maid service or the gardeners, since they came to the house to perform work he paid them for—and something about the place felt somehow different now, as though the short amount of time she'd spent in his home had changed its energy in some way he couldn't quite define.

Well, she'd gone home for the night, and he knew he'd sound like a complete idiot if he tried to call her now. They'd had a good talk at dinner, and he needed to leave it there.

Easier said than done.

You're obsessing over her because she treats you like a human being, he told himself, although he knew it was probably a little more than that. And sure, she was beautiful, but there were tons of beautiful women in Las Vegas. He should know, since he'd sampled a few of them when he first got here, driven by a need to reaffirm the mortal side of his nature and reconnect with the real world.

Delia Dunne wasn't the sort of person you just "sampled," though. She hadn't made a single mention of a significant other, so he had a feeling she wasn't seeing anyone. For whatever reason, she seemed content to focus on her work.

Had she scared off any prospective partners with the ghost-whisperer adjunct to her real estate business?

If that was the case, then the men here in Vegas must be a bunch of cowards. Caleb knew it would take a lot more than a few supernatural gifts for him to hit the highway. Rosemary McGuire's psychic powers hadn't fazed him...just the opposite, in fact.

But that was never going to happen, and he had to deal with it. Maybe fate worked in mysterious ways. After all, if Rosemary had ignored his demon blood and decided to give things a go, he most likely would never have come to Las Vegas at all.

He would never have met Delia Dunne.

So okay, he should take a deep breath and remind himself that all good things come to those who wait.

That didn't mean the awkward in-between stages couldn't be a total pain in the ass.

He was contemplating whether he should open another bottle of wine when the first demon came down the chimney.

It happened so fast that Caleb barely had a chance to blink. One minute he was alone in the house, and the next, the anti-Santa Claus appeared.

Ugly bastard, too, maybe a foot taller than he was, with scaly black skin and glowing yellow eyes and a pair of curved horns that poked up through its oily black hair. The second it was upright, it flung itself across the living room at him, claws out and shredding the long-sleeved T-shirt he wore.

Fuck, that hurt. Demon claws always had some nasty stuff on them, and if he hadn't possessed demon blood himself, Caleb knew he would've had to worry about getting some kind of crappy-ass infection from those slashes.

No real thought, just pure instinct as he kicked out, catching the thing in the gut so it released a shocked *whoof* of air and staggered back a pace or two.

Unfortunately, Caleb didn't have a chance to relish that small moment of victory, because a second demon, slightly smaller than the first, also came out of the chimney and hit his legs in a flying tackle that would have done the Raiders' defensive line proud.

He went down like a ton of bricks, and the larger demon took advantage of his stumble to advance again, claws now reaching for his throat.

At the last second, he rolled, but two of its talons still caught him. Hot blood flowed down his neck. Because it wasn't spurting, though, he knew the demon had only caught a vein and not the artery that would have spelled almost instant doom.

Still, those fresh wounds hurt just as much as the ones that throbbed on his bicep. The smaller demon's jaws closed on his leg, but the heavy denim of his jeans protected him from the worst of the bite.

For now. He had a feeling another chomp like that would slash right through the fabric.

He should have borrowed some holy water from Delia. If he'd had even a little on hand, he could have sent these scaly bastards back to Hell where they belonged.

As it was....

Fire flowed down his arms to his hands, and he hurled it against both of them. Because they were higher orders of demons than the imp he'd dispatched in the Bellagio's parking structure, he knew it wouldn't be enough to get rid of them entirely.

No, he was just trying to buy some time.

The one that was trying to bite his leg recoiled with a hiss, while the larger of the two also stepped back a pace, its yellow eyes blazing with fury.

That was all the opening he needed.

After all, he who runs away lives to fight another day.

A single blink, and then he appeared on Delia's front doorstep. He'd wanted to transport himself directly into her house, but because he didn't know what the interior looked like now, there was too big a chance that he might have appeared in the middle of a wall or some other similarly uncomfortable location.

Whereas the front of her house appeared pretty much the same as the photos he'd seen on the Zillow website when he looked it up, although maybe the front door had been updated.

No biggie. It was still in the same position it

had always occupied, and that was the important thing.

Limping, he went over to the doorbell and leaned hard on it. A simple *ding-dong* sounded somewhere inside the house, and a moment later, the door opened, and a shocked Delia stared out at him.

"Oh, my God! What happened?"

"Demons," he said briefly.

She opened the door wider. "Hurry."

Because he had no desire to remain standing in the entrance any longer than necessary, he slipped inside, and she closed the door behind him.

"Kitchen," she said briefly. "I've got a first aid kit in the pantry."

He should have known she'd be the kind of woman who kept her cool in a crisis.

As best he could, he shuffled into the kitchen and leaned up against the island. Everything in here looked as though it had been replaced over the past couple of years, with white cabinets and black quartz countertops and wood floors in a neutral brown. He had a feeling a few walls had been knocked out as well, which was exactly why he hadn't tried to teleport directly in here.

Plus, that would have been kind of rude.

Delia pulled a couple of kitchen towels out of a drawer and handed them over. "For your neck. Those wounds seem to be the worst."

"Only because you can see them," he said with a weak grin.

Nonetheless, he took the towels—both of them were a cheerful red, probably chosen to contrast with the overall black-and-white color scheme of the kitchen—and pressed them against his throat while she hurried to the pantry and came back with a decent-sized first aid kit, which she set down on the island.

And although her eyes were full of questions, she got out gauze and antiseptic and a roll of first aid tape and a variety of bandages, and proceeded to get him cleaned up and all his wounds covered. To his relief, most of them appeared superficial, not much worse than he would have gotten if a neighbor's dog had attacked him.

Except the ones in his throat, but those should heal soon enough. He was mostly mortal, and yet he still recovered from injuries much faster than any regular human being could.

"Can you walk?" Delia asked after she was done. "You'll be more comfortable sitting down in the living room."

"I don't want to bleed all over your furniture."

"You won't," she said crisply. "You're all patched up now."

True enough, but....

"There's blood on my clothes."

Her mouth pursed. For the first time, he realized she'd changed out of her slim skirt and teal jacket, and now wore a pair of Uggs, black leggings, and an oversized black sweatshirt with a glittery "Las Vegas" logo on it. He'd never seen her this casual before, and he liked it.

Even though every inch of his body hurt like a son of a bitch.

"Let me get you something to change into," she said. "Can you make it to the powder room?"

"Sure," he replied, even though he didn't know for sure where it was located. Yes, he'd seen photos of the house from the time when it had been up for sale, but the listing hadn't included a floor plan.

But the powder room turned out to be just on the other side of the great room, so he leaned up against the vanity and waited while Delia disappeared down a hallway he assumed led to the bedrooms. A moment later, she reappeared holding some dark gray sweats, with the shirt bearing the UNLV logo.

"There were jeans, too, but I thought these would be more comfortable."

Yes, easing his battered body into some sweats seemed infinitely preferable to trying to squeeze into a pair of jeans that might or might not be his size.

"Thanks," he said, and managed to smile. "Just give me a minute, and I'll meet you in the living room."

Worried green eyes met his. "Okay."

She closed the door, and he commenced the laborious process of peeling himself out of his bloodstained clothing and into the sweats she'd provided. Both pieces were a size large and a little loose on him—and would have been much too big for Delia.

Whose were they?

A mystery he'd clear up later, he supposed. For now, it just felt good to get into something clean and soft, and which didn't press too hard on his battered body.

The one thing she hadn't provided was a pair of replacement socks or any kind of footwear, so after he'd rolled his socks up with the rest of his bloody clothes, he padded out to the living room in his bare feet. A fire danced in the gas hearth, and she'd set a bottle of cognac and a couple of shot glasses on the wood and glass coffee table.

A woman after his own heart.

"I figured you could use a drink," she said. "I don't have much hard stuff on hand, but someone left this behind after a Christmas party and—"

"It's perfect," he said. "Thank you."

She poured a shot glass nearly full of cognac for him, then gave herself about half that much. "So... what happened?"

"A couple of demons got the jump on me," he replied. "So much for my theory that they'd leave me alone if I just stayed away from the goddamn casinos."

Her mouth compressed, but she lifted her shot glass and said, "Here's to getting away."

"Yeah, I don't think they guessed I was going to jump...or maybe they weren't sure whether I could. A lot of demons still don't know all that much about part demons and their abilities."

And they also didn't always communicate with one another, often holding on to information they thought they could use for leverage later on.

That was something he could only be thankful for. Otherwise, he might be in much worse shape than he already was.

The cognac was a welcome warmth in his wounded throat, a comforting heat in his belly. He swallowed some more, glad that the throbbing pain from the wounds the demons had delivered was already beginning to retreat. A good night's sleep, and, while he wouldn't have completely recovered, he knew his injuries would be at least half healed when he woke up.

Of course, that begged the question of where exactly he planned to sleep. No way he was going back to his house tonight. He supposed he could blink himself into the parking lot of a hotel—one preferably not attached to a casino, no easy task in Las Vegas—get a room, and hole up there until he decided what he should do next.

"Is there a way to keep the demons out of your house?" Delia asked.

"Holy water," Caleb said briefly, and drank some more cognac. "Lots and lots of holy water."

Her brows creased. "And that won't bother you?"

She sounded genuinely worried...which cheered him up immensely.

"No," he replied. "It generally doesn't have any real effect on those of us with human blood. So it's a cheap and easy way to make sure I don't have any more of those bastards coming down the chimney."

"That's how they got in?"

Was that a hint of amusement in her expression?

Not at his expense, he guessed, but only at the absurdity of a bunch of demons playing Santa Claus.

"I suppose they thought it would be funny." He shrugged and sipped some more cognac. Now more than two-thirds of the glass was empty, although he had a feeling Delia would refill it without him even asking.

Sure enough, she murmured, "Let me get you some more of that," and lifted the bottle of cognac and poured another healthy measure into his glass.

Once she was done with that task, she sipped some of her own cognac before she spoke again.

"You're staying here."

Her tone was so firm that he could tell she didn't want any arguments.

Still, Caleb thought he should make at least a token protest.

"There are hundreds of hotels in this town."

"True," she replied. "But I've got a whole cabinet of holy water, since I use it to help spirits move on. Can you think of a safer place to be?"

Most likely not. His teleportation couldn't be tracked, so he knew there was no way for the demons to know he was here.

Or at least, he didn't think there was. If they'd been watching him for a while, they might have figured out his connection to Delia Dunne, but unless they were just as good at digging around on the internet as he was, they would have had a hard time discovering her home address.

"I don't want to impose—"

"You're not," she said. "I'm the one who offered, remember? Anyway, this house has four bedrooms, and one of them is already set up as a guest space. I'll be glad to have someone use it, actually."

A lot of room for a woman living on her own, but he supposed she'd bought a bigger house because it was a better investment.

Anyway, it wasn't any of his business... although he'd certainly like it to be.

"Then thank you," he replied. "Tomorrow I'll get the situation at my house straightened out."

"As long as it's safe," she said.

Was that her oblique way of hinting that she'd be just fine if he stayed here more than one night? Probably not; she'd already made it clear enough that their relationship was a professional one and nothing more.

"Oh, sure," he said easily. "No point in making the great escape, only to get clobbered the second I let my guard down."

Delia smiled then, but there was still something strained about her expression, as if she'd only done so because she thought he expected it and not because she was genuinely amused.

He finished the rest of his cognac, feeling the slightest bit swimmy when he set the glass down. In general, alcohol didn't affect him as strongly as it would a person who didn't have any demon DNA in their veins, but that had been a lot of cognac.

And he'd lost a lot of blood.

So he was just fine with having Delia lead him down the hallway and show him the guest room and its attached bathroom, both of which were nicely appointed and didn't appear to have been used much, if ever. She even had a spare toothbrush still in its package and an accompanying tube of toothpaste, along with some other toiletries.

"You never know when someone's going to

forget something," she explained as she shut the medicine cabinet after showing him all the supplies. "So I like to stock a few things."

"You have a lot of guests?" he asked.

Now her expression was genuinely amused. "Not as many as I'd thought when I got all this set up. My dad's family is still back in Chicago, and I suppose I figured they'd want to come out here to visit during the winter to get away from the snow. But the couple of times they've come, they wanted to stay in a hotel so they could use the swimming pool."

Caleb was a little surprised she didn't have one —a majority of the houses in Las Vegas seemed to have their own swimming pools—but possibly part of the reason she'd gotten a deal on the house was that she would have had to put one in herself.

"Your parents wouldn't host them at their place?"

She grinned. "My dad is one of four brothers. There are a lot of relatives, so I was trying to be the overflow. I guess I underestimated the draw of a resort pool in February."

Her expression was so infectious, he just had to smile back. It was good to hear about normal families doing normal things, so unlike his own experiences. Because his mother was also an only child, he didn't have any aunts or uncles.

No, all he'd had were the other part demons in

his father's circle, and they weren't exactly known for being cuddly and "Kumbaya."

"Well, I appreciate the guest room, so thanks."

Delia's smile faded a bit. "You're welcome. I suppose I'll leave you to it."

The words ended with an upward inflection, indicating that she wasn't quite sure whether he was ready to go to bed.

On most nights, he wouldn't have been, since he rarely hit the sack before midnight. However, after that demon attack—and all that cognac—he thought he'd probably pass out the minute his head hit the pillow.

"Yeah, I'm going to try to sleep all this off. You have a good night."

"You, too."

He went into the bedroom and shut the door, glad that it was set up as a secondary main suite so he wouldn't have to wander down the hall to brush his teeth and splash some water on his face before he went to bed.

As he headed into the bathroom, though, he couldn't help wondering whether Delia intended to go to bed right away, too. It was kind of weird to think of her sleeping just down the hall.

No, it felt...intimate.

But it wasn't. She was offering him a helping hand, nothing more.

Still, he knew he needed to be grateful for it.

Chapter Eighteen

—·‹‹‹·☉·›››·—

Had she really invited Caleb Lockwood to stay the night?

Yes, she had. Temporary insanity, she supposed.

No, Delia knew it was more than that. Whatever her feelings about his demon blood, he definitely hadn't deserved to get attacked like that. Good thing he'd held off his assailants long enough to make a getaway.

Not before he'd suffered some pretty nasty injuries, though. He seemed fine with the quickie first aid she'd provided, but she couldn't help wondering if she should have insisted that he go to the closest urgent care and get himself patched up by a professional. Some of those gashes really looked like they needed stitches, not just a bunch of slapped-on Bandaids.

Unfortunately, she doubted he would have

gone along with such a plan. After all, how would he have even explained away those wounds? An attack by someone's pet tiger?

Siegfried and Roy had been out of the game for years.

Even though it sounded as though Caleb planned to go right to bed—which he should, after losing all that blood and drinking all that cognac— Delia knew she was way too keyed up to go to sleep. Although her days of staying out until all hours were long behind her, she still rarely went to bed before eleven, something that wasn't too hard to manage when she hardly ever needed to be in the office before nine o'clock.

So instead of heading into her own bedroom, she went into her home office and shut the door. The hour was inching a little past ten, but she knew it wouldn't be a problem to reach out to Prudence, not when her friend still maintained some habits from their girl band days and generally didn't go to sleep until at least two or three in the morning.

They usually texted, but Delia went to her computer instead of using her phone, figuring that using the messaging app on her Mac would be easier than trying to handle all this on a cell phone. After opening the app, she went to the last conversation she and Prudence had exchanged, the one where they'd discussed maybe taking a girls' trip to

Cabo in May after most of the spring breakers were gone.

You up? I was hoping you could look into someone for me.

Pru's answer came back right away, telling Delia that her friend had been camped on her computer, just as she'd expected.

I'm here. Who do you want me to check on?

This was something she probably should have done earlier, but at the time, she'd had no reason to distrust Robert Hendricks. After this latest attack on Caleb, however, she couldn't stop the niggling thoughts rattling around in her mind, the ones that seemed to tell her the casino executive might be a bit more involved than merely as a concerned party who didn't want his place of business ripped off.

A guy named Robert Hendricks. He's the VP of operations at the Dunes. I suppose I wanted to know if there was anything about his bio that seemed weird, or if he has some business contacts that feel iffy to you.

On it. How long're you going to be up?

Probably at least another hour.

Luckily, she didn't have any early appointments tomorrow. In fact, she didn't have much on her docket at all. Her mother had messaged her earlier, letting her know she was going to show a new listing in Summerlin and checking to see if she wanted to come along, but Delia had declined. She had enough on her plate right now, and she didn't want to run even the slightest risk of encountering a new ghost, even though her mother hadn't said anything about the house being haunted.

Funny how she didn't feel the same way about Caleb's place on Pueblo Street, considering how haunted it had been until he'd taken care of the problem.

Maybe it was just all the plans he was making for the property. She'd always loved home makeover shows, and it would be fun to watch the process as he turned the house into a modern mid-century showplace.

Especially since she'd only be there in an advisory capacity and wouldn't have to deal with the more unpleasant aspects of a massive renovation like that one.

Pru's reply interrupted her musings.

Okay. Let me check into it. I'll try to have something within an hour. If not, you can always follow up in the morning.

Thanks so much!

You owe me a margarita.

I'll buy you a whole pitcher.

Pru responded with a grinning emoji, but that appeared to be the end of the convo for now.

Probably the smart thing would have been to go into her bedroom and get ready—wash her face, brush her teeth—but Delia wasn't sure she wanted to be wandering around the house with no makeup on when Caleb Lockwood might emerge from his room at any moment.

All right, not much chance of that when it seemed clear to her he'd been about to pass out on his feet, but still.

And he'd looked adorable in those sweats, despite the bandages on his throat. Much better than Bill ever had.

The thought of her ex-fiancé made her lips thin a bit, but she pushed the recollection aside as best she could. Bill was long out of her life, and if he hadn't cared enough about his precious UNLV sweats to take them with him after he decided she wasn't the one and dumped her, then at least they could do her unexpected guest some good.

What they'd do for clothes after tonight, she wasn't sure. Would it be safe for them to go back to his house in the morning to fetch a few things, assuming they were well-armed with holy water? Or should they just say screw it and go shopping?

After all, she had the morning free, and she doubted the demons would have canceled his credit cards.

She realized then that she was thinking Caleb might be here for some time, rather than merely overnight as he recovered from the attack and regrouped, which was silly. They'd figure out a plan tomorrow, and then they could both carry on with their lives.

Assuming they were able to get to the bottom of this mess.

A glance over at her computer told her Prudence hadn't gotten back to her yet. Of course not—it had only been a few minutes, and Pru had said it would be at least an hour, maybe more.

Delia went back over to her desk and sat down, thinking she could browse the MLS and see if anything new had popped up that looked interesting. While she didn't have a lot of clients right now, she still had that annoying couple who wanted the moon...if it was under $350K...and she'd also told Caleb that she'd keep an eye out for any possible flips.

Even if she kind of doubted he was up for that sort of thing right now. The guy definitely had his hands full.

But browsing the listings was enough to keep her occupied for a while, meaning that she was still sitting there when Pru reappeared.

I've got a couple of things.

Like what?

From what I can tell, Robert Hendricks seems to be a normal guy. No red flags like I found with Caleb. Hendricks grew up in Thousand Oaks and got his MBA at Pepperdine. Moved to Las Vegas about fifteen years ago when he was offered his first position as a manager in the finance department at the Dunes and gradually moved his way up the ladder. Got the promotion to his current position four years ago. Married, son and daughter, both of whom are going to school in California—one at UCLA, one at Stanford.

Delia had to agree that all sounded pretty normal. A prosperous kind of normal, true, but she had to believe Robert Hendricks was probably pulling in north of seven figures as VP of operations at the casino.

Could it be that her instincts had been so terribly off on this one?

So...nothing that makes you think he could be involved in anything underhanded?

Although she couldn't see her friend right then, Delia had to believe Pru let out a snort of derision at that question.

He works for a casino. I'm sure he's done all sorts of stuff that could be considered marginal. But in terms of ghosts and the supernatural? Not so much.

Great. Delia had really been hoping that whatever impulse had driven Robert Hendricks to reach out to her for help had been born of some sort of back-channel connection to the demon world, but it didn't sound that way. No, he was just a regular guy who had probably read an article about her or maybe had someone in his social circle comment how Las Vegas had its very own ghost whisperer, and when the strange pattern of winnings popped up, and he and some of the other casino brass started sharing their notes, he figured he'd give her services a try and see if anything came of it.

Even as she started typing, Delia knew her next question had just a whiff of desperation about it.

So, you didn't find anything even the teensiest bit weird?

There was one thing.

What's that?

A few months ago, Hendricks—and a lot of the other casinos—contracted with an outfit called The Styx Group. I looked into them, and on the surface, they seem like your typical security consulting company.

When Pru threw phrases like "on the surface" around, you knew there was a lot more to come.

They're dirty?

More like impenetrable. Their website lists some of their clients, but I can't see anything about who runs the company or even who some of their representatives are. If I were a hacker, maybe I could really dig into their files and get some decent information, but that's not what I do.

No, it wasn't. Pru was great about getting into databases that regular people without private detective licenses couldn't access, but it wasn't as if she could hack into the Pentagon or anything close to it.

But the slightly sinister name "The Styx Group" caused a lot of alarm bells to go off in Delia's head. Maybe the company's founder was a big fan of '70s rock bands, but she had a feeling there was something else going on here.

Thanks, Pru. It's still helpful. And if you find anything else, just let me know.

I will...and drop me a note when you're ready to buy me that pitcher of margaritas.

Delia responded with a tongue-out emoji, and they ended the conversation there.

After she shut down her computer, she got up from her chair and went out into the hall. The door to Caleb's room was shut, and she couldn't hear anything from inside, not even a snore.

She told herself he would be fine. None of his injuries had been life-threatening, and what he needed more than anything else was a decent night's sleep.

The same could have been said for her, so she headed into her bedroom and also made sure the door was firmly closed. Normally, she left it open, but considering she had a part demon sleeping just down the hallway from her, discretion seemed the better part of valor.

As to what they'd do when morning rolled around...well, she supposed she'd figure that out after she woke up.

Although Delia normally rolled out of bed and headed into the kitchen to make coffee first thing, today she thought it was probably a better idea to shower and put on some makeup first, just in case Caleb was already up and about.

Good thing she'd taken that precaution, because when she emerged from her bedroom, he was already sitting on the couch and drinking a cup of coffee, watching the morning news with the sound turned down so low, she hadn't even realized it was on.

"Morning," he said, his tone casual in the extreme. "I hope you don't mind that I made coffee. I needed some after that cognac last night."

"It's fine," she replied automatically...then paused and took a closer look at him. He wore a knit pullover, jeans, and sneakers—none of which she'd provided for him. "Please tell me you didn't go home to get all that," she added as she inclined her head toward his ensemble.

"This?" He looked down at himself and grinned. "Vegas is the city that never sleeps, right? I found a twenty-four-hour clothing store online when I checked my phone and teleported myself over there so I could grab a few things. The sweats were great last night, but I figured I needed some real clothes for today."

Delia blinked. While she knew some shops stayed open 'round the clock—usually the boutiques inside the casinos, and probably some along Fremont Street—she'd never had any need to visit them and hadn't realized you could outfit yourself pretty respectably at those stores.

"Well, I'm glad you got it figured out," she managed, then went into the kitchen so she could pour herself a much-needed coffee. Although part of her had been a little annoyed that Caleb had made himself at home and fetched some for himself without waiting for her to come out of her room, she had to admit that it was nice to have her morning brew ready to go.

Once she'd filled a mug and added her ritual teaspoon of sugar and dollop of milk, she headed back to the living room and sat down on one of the chairs. Now that she was facing him, she could see that he looked much better this morning—his color was good, and he didn't have any noticeable dark circles under his eyes.

And those horrid gashes across his throat had healed to a couple of pale red welts.

He must have noticed her staring, because he said, "Demon blood, remember? I heal fast."

"Apparently," she replied. "But that's good to hear. I suppose now we need to focus on getting you back into your house."

The familiar glint returned to his eyes, almost

the same color as the coffee they were drinking. "What, you don't want a permanent house guest?"

She decided it would be better not to dignify that comment with a response, and instead swallowed some more coffee.

He grinned. "Well, I figure your holy water can help with that. We'll splash it everywhere, utter a few blessings, and the demons shouldn't be able to come back."

Since he'd already told her that holy water didn't affect him, she wasn't too surprised by his plan. Luckily, she had a lot on hand and could always get more, thanks to the way she'd made friends with a Presbyterian minister and his wife, finding them a killer deal on a house in their parish, a place they otherwise would never have been able to afford. Because of that professional relationship, all she had to do was make a phone call, and Father Bryce would have a new case of the stuff waiting for her.

"But," Caleb went on, "I thought I should take you out to breakfast first."

Delia wanted to protest that he didn't need to take her out to eat. However, considering all she had in the house was some yogurt that should have been tossed a few days ago and a box of Kind bars, she guessed she should probably take him up on the offer.

"Deal," she said. "And after that, we'll go take a look at your house."

They ate at a place practically around the corner from her neighborhood, a fun little bistro that had amazing omelets and frittatas and all sorts of breakfast pastries. Delia decided to skip the sweet stuff, just in case whatever they ended up facing at Caleb's house might require a bit more effort than merely splashing holy water around. When fighting demons, she supposed, it was always a good idea to lay down a good base.

A second cup of coffee, too, although she generally only drank one in the morning so she wouldn't get too jittery. Pru always laughed and called her a lightweight, but she'd never been able to down unending cups the way her friend could.

Delia drove, of course, because Caleb's Range Rover presumably was still parked in the garage at his house. Neither of them said much, and she wondered if he was more wary about the upcoming confrontation than he wanted to admit.

After she parked in the driveway and he let them into the house, though, absolutely nothing happened. No onslaught of demons, no blood dripping from the wall, no pentacles chalked on the gleaming wood floors...absolutely nothing to show that he'd been attacked by unholy adversaries here the night before.

"Looks like they took off," he remarked as he led her into the living room. "I don't even see any blood anywhere, and I know I was bleeding all over the place."

True, the house looked immaculate. "Demon housekeepers?" she quipped feebly, and one of his dark, level brows quirked.

"More like making sure they didn't leave any evidence behind," he said. "Demons don't like anything that can be traced back to them."

Apparently not. "Well, at least they're gone."

"For now," Caleb said darkly. "Just because it looks as if nothing weird happened here, that doesn't mean I'm still not going to splash the hell out of this place with that holy water."

Which she'd brought along in the Trader Joe's bag that hung from one arm. "Well, we've got plenty of that. Do you want to work together, or should one of us take the upstairs and one the downstairs?"

"I'll do upstairs," he said at once. "You can get the downstairs. Let me do this first, though."

He reached into the TJ's bag and pulled out one of the little plastic vials of holy water, then marched over to the fireplace and sprinkled it liberally all over the hearth, then bent down so he could dab it on the stone surround as well.

"It's weird, though," he remarked, and Delia sent him a quizzical look.

"Weirder than demons coming down your chimney?"

White teeth flashed at her. "Yeah, weirder than that. Gas fireplace, right? So how the hell did they get past the glass? It should have been smashed all over the place."

She supposed she should have thought of that. There weren't many wood-burning fireplaces left in Las Vegas, and, like most—well, aside from those who'd gone to electric models—his was a gas setup with a handsome set of faux logs inside the firebox. Those logs were protected by glass, just like her own fireplace at home.

If demons really had come down the chimney and attacked him, wouldn't there be glass everywhere?

Maybe. She still didn't have a very good handle on demonic powers, but she supposed they might have somehow managed to blink their way past that glassy barrier without leaving any trace of their passing.

"I have no idea," she said. Some people might have thought the lack of any physical evidence left behind was a sure sign that Caleb had somehow set up all of this, but she didn't think so. She'd seen the way he was bleeding the night before.

Those hadn't been self-inflicted wounds.

"Anyway," he said, now sounding much more cheerful, "they'll probably think twice before they try coming in that way again. I'll just go take care of the upstairs."

A quick wave with the hand that held the bottle of holy water, and then he headed up the staircase. For a second or two, Delia wondered if he'd left her to do the lower level so she wouldn't find anything incriminating upstairs—for all she knew, he had a massive collection of vintage porn or something—but then she told herself it wasn't any of her business.

For now, she needed to focus on making sure the ground floor was safe from any further demon intrusions...and hope like hell that their counter-measures worked.

Chapter Nineteen

—∘⟨⟨⟨∘☽∘⟩⟩⟩∘—

It felt a little weird to be up here when he knew Delia was downstairs, diligently splashing holy water everywhere so the demons wouldn't be able to come back inside without inflicting a world of pain upon themselves.

Possibly, they'd think that was a decent trade-off for being able to really get their claws into him, but he didn't think so.

He just wasn't that important.

No, he focused on splashing the water on as many surfaces as possible, especially the window frames in all the upstairs rooms, being extra careful in the main suite so it would be the very last place in the house where they'd want to set foot. Right then, he was just thankful that he'd decided against having a second gas fireplace installed in his bedroom, since that would have given the demons an additional point of entry.

At least nothing seemed to have been disturbed up here, as if the demons had disappeared right after he did. With their prey gone, they probably wouldn't have had much reason to stick around. Also, while they were bigger than the imps that had attacked him at the Bellagio and in his Uber the other evening, they were still from the lower orders of demons and wouldn't have had the native intelligence to dig through his things to see if they could find any clues as to where he could have disappeared.

Satisfied that all the important surfaces upstairs had been rendered inimical to demon-kind, he went downstairs to find Delia finishing up with the windowsill in the living room.

"I think that's about it," she said. "Everything okay upstairs?"

"Looks like it," he replied. "I don't think they even went up there. So I suppose now we need to decide what to do next. Do you have any appointments today?"

He didn't think she did, or otherwise she wouldn't have been so leisurely about breakfast…or about coming over to his house to help. Also, unlike the other times he'd seen her during business hours, she wore skinny jeans and boots and a close-fitting sweater in a deep shade of green that only served to set off the lustrous copper of her long hair.

While he liked the understated sexiness of her business attire, he had to admit this was even better.

But the outfit also seemed to signal that she didn't have any real demands on her time today— at least, not from her clients or at the office, which he thought could only be a good thing. Although they'd done what they could to make sure his house was impervious to any further demon attacks, he'd never been in a situation like this before and wasn't sure what might be next.

He definitely didn't care for that feeling.

"No," Delia replied, confirming his suspicions about her schedule. "It's a pretty light week."

She didn't sound very concerned. But then, why should she? Thanks to the sale of the Pueblo Street house closing so quickly, she'd already banked a nice, plump commission. She could take the rest of the month off if she wanted to.

However, he doubted she would do anything so indulgent. Maybe once upon a time she'd been a punk chick—or possibly, more post-punk—but she'd definitely morphed into a brisk, no-nonsense professional woman.

He didn't say "good," because he thought that

might have sounded dismissive. "Okay. Then I suppose our next step is trying to figure out who's sending these demons after me."

Delia nodded, her expression thoughtful. "I had a friend of mine who's a private detective look into Robert Hendricks, but she didn't find anything suspicious. He seems like a regular guy—a successful one, sure, but there's no crime in that."

"A P.I.?" Caleb responded, and couldn't help grinning. "You have all kinds of connections, don't you?"

"I do," she said serenely, although something flickered in her eyes as she made the reply. During that telltale moment, brief as it was, he realized this was how she must have discovered his real name and his past in Greencastle. He couldn't even be angry about that, not when telling her the truth about himself was the very reason why she'd stayed on as his agent. She added, "Pru was the bassist in my band, and we've stayed friends."

A helpful friend to have. "Did she find anything else?"

"No." A pause, and Delia added, "Well, except that Robert Hendricks' casino and a bunch of others signed a consulting contract with some sort of private security firm called The Styx Group. Ever heard of them?"

He hadn't, so he shook his head. But that name....

"They sound kind of dodgy."

"My thought exactly," she replied. "Pru tried digging into them, but she couldn't find much. She's not a hacker, though, so maybe someone else might be able to get more information on the company." Delia's green eyes took on a mischievous glint. "Don't suppose you know anyone like that."

Unfortunately, no. One of Michael Covenant's associates had been some kind of computer hacker, but Caleb sort of doubted the man would be too enthusiastic about lending his services to someone he could only view as the enemy.

"Nope," he said, not too bothered by their lack of resources on the hacking front. "It looks like we're on our own with this one."

Which was about what he'd expected. He'd only been in town for a couple of months and hadn't formed any real connections during his time here, so he didn't think Delia would find it too strange that he didn't have any acquaintances or associates who could help out.

And since she was a native of Las Vegas and still didn't have any computer hacker friends, he wasn't going to beat himself up too badly about not being able to call in the digital cavalry.

"Does The Styx Group have offices here?" he asked, thinking they could at least try sniffing around in person if there wasn't much to be found online.

She shook her head. "The website only lists an office in L.A.—on the Westside, I think, judging by the address."

Caleb supposed that was slightly better than downtown, which was uncomfortably close to Pasadena, the city where Michael Covenant and Audrey Barrett...and Rosemary McGuire and Will Gordon...lived.

Still, he didn't want to go anywhere near their orbit, which meant a reconnaissance of The Styx Group's corporate offices probably wasn't in the cards.

"Well, we won't worry about that for now," he said. "We don't have any reason to believe they're connected to this mess anyway."

He went over to the couch and sat down, and Delia, who'd been hovering near the window this whole time, took the hint and seated herself on one of the chairs that faced the sofa.

"But who *is* connected to it?" she said softly. "You said these demons had to have been summoned, so who's doing the summoning?"

A very good question. "Someone who knows what they're doing," he replied. "Contrary to what all those horror movies like to show, it's not as easy to summon a demon as you might think. Especially when you consider this person started with imps and only ramped up to more destructive demons when they figured out they'd need to get some bigger guns if they wanted to take me down."

Had that sounded too much like bragging? He hadn't meant his comments to come across that way, but he supposed Delia might still interpret them in a negative light.

However, she only looked thoughtful, so it seemed she was too engaged in trying to get to the bottom of the problem to worry about his delivery.

"Someone who's good at summoning demons," she said in musing tones, then shook her head. "Las Vegas is full of palm readers and psychics, but I don't think demon summoning is the sort of thing most people want to put on their shop window."

Probably not. Her remark got him thinking, though. While he knew the vast majority of those psychics were complete fakes, there had to be one or two who were the real deal.

And demon summoning left its own traces behind. It was the very darkest kind of magic, something that should show up as toxic sludge against the overall psychic energy of the city.

"Can you reach out to your friend Pru again?" he asked, and Delia blinked.

"I doubt she's awake yet," she replied. "But I can send her a text anyway, and she'll see it when she gets up. What did you have in mind?"

Maybe it was a crazy idea. On the other hand, a psychic—a real one—might be their only hope of tracking down the person who'd summoned those demons.

"I need her to find us a psychic," he said.

———

Delia, to his relief, didn't find his suggestion quite as crazy as he'd feared. In fact, she immediately said, "To find our demon summoner? Isn't that the kind of thing you should be able to do?"

Should he be annoyed with her for thinking he possessed a whole lot more talents than he actually did…or a little flattered that she believed he was so powerful?

Caleb decided to go with the latter. "No," he replied. "I have demon blood, but I'm not psychic. And while I can sometimes sense when they're nearby, there's no way I can trace those demons back to their source. Summoning them takes a lot of psychic energy, though, so I'm hoping someone who really is talented and isn't just trying to bilk tourists out of a few bucks might be able to help us."

Delia absorbed that comment, then nodded. "Okay, I guess I can understand that. Too bad my own talents seem to be mostly restricted to ghosts."

Since he'd already thought pretty much the

same thing, he only lifted his shoulders. "I think you might eventually get there, since you've already picked up hints of the wrongness our demon friends have left behind. But in this case, we don't really have the time to sit around and wait for that to happen. I don't want to have to keep looking over my shoulder for the rest of my life."

All right, he'd partially resigned himself to such a prospect, just because he'd come here with an assumed identity and had done his best to leave his former life behind. Even so, he'd been expecting some kind of ordinary trouble, like the DMV suddenly deciding his birth certificate wasn't valid, or his bank discovering that his credit history was a total house of cards.

With Belial dead and the rest of the Greencastle gang trapped in Hell, he honestly hadn't thought he'd be dealing with demons again.

"Of course not," Delia said at once. "We'll get this figured out one way or another."

She looked utterly determined, like a warrior queen about to head into battle.

Not for the first time, Caleb found himself very glad he'd spotted her in that casino last week. What would have happened if he didn't have her to help him through this?

He supposed he would have muddled through somehow. There was also the possibility...even though he didn't want to admit it to himself...that he might not have gotten dragged into this at all if their paths hadn't crossed.

Impossible to say. The only thing he could do now was make sure they found a way to make it out to the other side.

Delia got out her phone, unlocked it, and then sent off a quick text, her fingers flying across the screen. "Okay, that's done," she said, then returned the phone to her hip pocket. "Pru's a serious night owl, so we probably won't hear back until at least eleven, maybe later. What's the plan until then?"

Even though they'd thoroughly doused his home with holy water and it was probably fine, Caleb still didn't like the idea of hanging around here. Besides, he thought they'd better check on his other property, just to make sure the demons hadn't decided to go over there and wreak havoc.

If they even knew he owned the place. He was still a little hazy on how much information they'd gathered on him, or whether they'd mostly paid attention to his comings and goings from the casinos and didn't give a rat's ass what he did with the rest of his time.

Also, it had only been a couple of days since the property had changed hands, so there was no way it had hit the county recorder's database yet.

"Let's go over to the Pueblo Street house," he said.

Delia didn't ask why, only replied, "All right. Let me get my purse."

When they got there, everything seemed to be in order. Or rather, the place was just as much of a wreck as the last time he'd swung by. Although he'd gotten things set up with Raul Martinez, the general contractor, work wasn't scheduled to start until next Monday, and the house was utterly deserted.

"Well, at least the demons didn't come over here and trash the place," Caleb remarked as they walked through the living room, where pallets of drywall still sat everywhere.

Delia grinned. "How would you be able to tell?"

About all he could do was return the smile, since she definitely had a point there. "This is why I don't think they've been tracking my every movement, or they would have learned I've been coming and going from here even if they wouldn't have been able to tell I bought it."

"How much *do* demons know, anyway?" she asked, pausing by the pantry after they'd crossed into the kitchen.

"Depends on the demon," Caleb said. "The ones who've been attacking me—they're lower orders of the creatures, powerful enough to do some damage, but they're nowhere close to omniscient. The farther up the rung you go, the stronger demons get...and they get smarter and wiser, too. The princes of Hell were once the highest order of angels, so they pretty much know everything going back to the dawn of time."

Or at least, that was the general impression he'd gotten from his time in Hell. Before they'd all been banished, he probably wouldn't have even known that much. His father hadn't wanted to talk about their demon heritage, except to explain some of the powers that had come down to his son along with his demon blood, and Caleb had sometimes wondered if that was because his father hadn't known everything, either. Yes, Daniel Lockwood was half demon, but he'd been born on this plane to a mortal woman and didn't have any firsthand experience of the underworld.

Well, he was getting it now. Caleb didn't think he could even bring himself to care about that, not when it was his father's fault that they'd all ended up getting sent there in the first place. The original demons who had been Belial's lieutenants had returned to the underworld once they thought they'd established a good beachhead on this plane, and with them gone, there really hadn't been anything to keep Daniel Lockwood and the rest of the cambions—half demons—to settle into their ordinary lives and act as if they weren't anything except normal, everyday humans.

But no, Daniel had to go after that goddamn *Project Demon Hunters* footage...and everything went in the toilet soon afterward.

"Then I guess it's a good thing we're only dealing with the minions right now," Delia said lightly.

"True. It could be worse."

On the other hand, it could be a lot better, too.

Her phone pinged from inside her purse, and she pulled it out and glanced down at the screen. "Pru thinks I've lost my marbles...but she also has two suggestions for me, along with their contact information. So I guess I should call and see if I can make an appointment?"

Thank God they hadn't been forced to wait until noon or later. Delia's P.I. friend must have decided to get up early today.

"That would be great," Caleb said. "Unless you want me to do it?"

She sent him a slightly indulgent smile. "I call people all the time. If I had phone anxiety, I'd be out of business pretty fast."

He supposed she had a point there, so he only inclined his head while she touched the screen again, presumably so she could call one of the numbers Pru had given her.

For a moment, Delia stood there, phone

pressed to her ear, but then she lowered it, looking annoyed. "It just went to voicemail," she explained. "I'll try the next one."

"Okay."

She touched the screen again and then lifted the phone to her ear. This time, though, she spoke soon enough, telling him that someone had picked up on the other end.

"Hi," she said brightly. "I know this is last minute, but I was wondering if you had any appointments available now, or maybe in the early afternoon today? A friend and I would like to come in."

A pause, and Caleb felt himself tense. What if the psychic didn't have any open appointments today?

Then maybe you'll crash at Delia's house again, he thought, a not entirely unwelcome prospect. No, it wasn't as if anything had happened between them, but there had been something almost cozy about hanging out there together, even when they were just standing around in the kitchen and drinking coffee.

"Oh, perfect," she said next, "we can be there in about fifteen minutes. Okay—good. See you then."

She returned her phone to her purse and sent Caleb a brilliant smile.

"We're in," she told him. "Her place is over in Angel Park, so we need to hurry."

While relief didn't exactly sweep over him, he had to admit he felt a lot better. Maybe the psychic wouldn't be able to help them, but at least now they had a plan of action.

"All right," he replied. "Let's go see this psychic."

Chapter Twenty

— ·(((· ◎ ·))). —

ONCE MORE BEHIND THE WHEEL, MOSTLY because they'd both decided that Caleb's Range Rover, while much bigger and sturdier than her little Hyundai Kona, might also be known to the demons who'd been set on his trail. It just seemed smarter to take a vehicle that was a lot less conspicuous.

However, Delia could tell he wasn't entirely thrilled to be relegated to the passenger seat once more, because he fidgeted with his seatbelt and tapped his fingers against the knees of his jeans every time they had to stop at a red light.

Or maybe he was just worried that they'd be late for their appointment with the psychic.

At least their route kept them far away from downtown and the Strip. It was an area she generally tried to avoid, just because it was almost always choked with traffic no matter what the time of day, but now she had an extra incentive to give that part of the city a wide berth.

According to Caleb, the demons had particularly focused on his movements whenever he was coming or going from one of the casinos there.

His attention seemed to be held by the cars around them and the strip malls and housing developments they drove past, so she was a little startled when he said, "Why Delia?"

"Excuse me?" she responded, not sure what he'd meant by the question.

"Your name," he explained. "It's not very common."

No, it wasn't. She couldn't say the same thing about his given name, not when she'd known several Calebs in high school and college.

"My parents met in line at the first *Beetlejuice* movie," she said. "They were huge fans. So after they got married and I was coming along, they decided they were going to call me Lydia after the goth girl in the movie. Except when I appeared, I had bright red hair, so they thought Delia would be a better fit."

Caleb nodded, so either he was familiar with the film and didn't see the need to ask any other questions, or he'd decided she'd already given him more than enough information.

Apparently the former, because then he said, "Does your father have red hair?"

"No," she replied. "Just regular brown. But there are redheads on both sides of the family, so my hair wasn't as huge a surprise as it might otherwise have been."

And she'd always liked her red hair, liked how it made her stand out in a crowd. True, she'd used Overtone on it to brighten the natural copper to something more approaching Woody Woodpecker red when she was singing with Final Girl, but she'd never wanted to dye it blue or purple or any of the other rainbow shades Pru had gone through over the years.

Definitely not black, either. She'd talked to her hairstylist about it once, and had been warned that putting black dye on her hair pretty much guaranteed that it would take years—and a lot of lost length—to get her tresses back to their natural color.

"I think that's the place up on the right," Caleb said, then grimaced. "I can't believe we're going to see someone who calls herself Marvelous Marva."

"Hey, Pru said she was one of the best," Delia returned, although she was forced to admit that she'd experienced much the same misgivings as Caleb when she'd first read her friend's text.

He sent her a side-eyed look but didn't say

anything, probably because he was thinking the same thing she was.

Beggars couldn't be choosers...especially when they were in a hurry.

At least the small, one-story house Marvelous Marva used for her office looked well kept, with the only indication of her profession a small sign out front that said "Readings."

Delia guided her SUV around the corner and turned off the engine, thinking it would be rude to pull into the driveway since it wasn't specifically marked as client parking. "Here we go," she said. "You ready for this?"

"I guess I have to be," Caleb replied as he unfastened his seatbelt.

She did the same, and soon enough, they were standing at the front door. He reached over to press the doorbell, and the sound of a soft flute echoed somewhere inside the house.

Well, she had to admit that was much nicer than those annoying Westminster chimes.

The door opened a moment later, revealing a woman Delia guessed was probably around her mother's age...even if Linda Dunne would never have been caught dead dressed like that unless she was going to a Halloween party or something. Most of the woman's salt-and-pepper hair was concealed with a colorful silk scarf in shades of red and purple and green, and she wore a flowing red silk kimono embroidered with fanciful dragons, with an equally flowing black silk skirt and blouse underneath.

"Come in, come in," she said, stepping out of the way so they could enter the house. Almost at once, the scent of patchouli incense hit Delia's nostrils, and she had to work hard not to cough.

Next to her, Caleb was wrinkling his nose as well, so it didn't seem as if he was too happy with the olfactory assault, either.

"This way," Marva told them, and led them through the living room—which had been set up as a library, with bookcases placed against all the walls, their shelves so stacked with books and crystals and figurines that you could barely see what kind of wood they were made of—and into the dining room.

Or really, the reading room, since there was a round table in the center of the space with a silk cloth covering it and several Chinese screens that could be positioned to offer more privacy.

Since it was only the three of them right now, Marva ignored the screens and pointed at the two antique chairs that faced the table.

"Go ahead and have a seat," she said.

At least she sounded ordinary and friendly enough, and wasn't trying to put on some kind of fake Eastern European accent or something to make herself sound more mystical. Delia took that as a plus—and did her best to ignore the dubious look Caleb sent her just before he sat down on one of the chairs.

Well, he could think what he wanted. They were here to get some information, and she really didn't care how the conduit for that knowledge looked or dressed as long as they got the intel they needed.

Delia sat down as well—the chair was just as hard as it looked, a carved piece with a flat cushion that felt as though it needed some serious reupholstering—and did her best to arrange a pleasant expression on her face while Marva took the seat on the other side of the table.

"Do I have your permission to take your hands for a moment?" she asked. "It always helps me to have that contact with my querents, although I understand some people may be uncomfortable with the practice."

"It's fine," Delia replied, even as she glanced over at Caleb. He still didn't look entirely thrilled, but he went ahead and laid a hand on the tabletop.

"Do what you need to," he said.

Marva nodded, then reached over to wrap her fingers around both their hands. Although she wore gold dangly earrings and a gold necklace set with what looked like a big cabochon of either carnelian or some kind of agate, her fingers and wrists were completely bare of jewelry.

Did the metal and precious stones interfere with her psychic connection with her clients?

Not being in the habit of visiting psychics, Delia couldn't begin to guess. Marva's fingers were cool but not cold, and she held their hands lightly for a moment before letting go again.

"Something has been weighing on both of you," she said, and then she sent them both a smile that was almost wicked, her dark eyes dancing. "But I suppose you would tell me that much is obvious, or else you wouldn't have come to see a psychic."

Delia couldn't quite prevent her own mouth from quirking. "Yes, we've had an...eventful... couple of days."

Marva looked over at Caleb. "There's something about you, though...something I can't quite place."

Expression completely neutral, he said, "That a fact?"

The psychic didn't even blink. "Yes, it is a fact, I think. As to what it means, I suppose I'll let the cards help me figure it out."

She reached for a black velvet bag that had been lying on the tabletop, then pulled out a set of Tarot cards. Although Delia had played around with Tarot a bit in high school, all she'd had was your garden-variety Rider-Waite deck, and not the gorgeously illustrated cards that Marva began to shuffle, her long fingers displaying the sort of dexterity usually not seen outside a dealer in a casino or a magician who specialized in up-close tricks.

"We'll try the downward pyramid," Marva told them as she kept shuffling. "It's a good spread for getting a quick and easy answer to your problem. If it's not conclusive, or if you feel as if it doesn't apply to your current situation, then we'll move on to a Celtic cross."

"Um...sure," Delia replied after a quick sideways glance at Caleb, who didn't seem to have an opinion one way or another. Back when she was in high school and playing around with the cards, she'd only done simple three-card spreads, so she didn't know much about any of the other kinds.

If Marva had noticed the dubious tone in her voice, she didn't show any sign of it. Then again, she'd probably encountered plenty of skeptics over the years.

"The first three cards describe the current situation," she explained. "The two beneath that represent what surrounds the current problem or any problems that may surface because of it. The single card at the bottom signifies the outcome."

That seemed simple enough. Next to Delia, Caleb nodded, signaling that he also understood what they would be looking at.

One final shuffle, and then the psychic laid down the first card.

"The Moon," she intoned. "Secrets...illusions... that which is hidden."

Well, a whole lot felt as if it had been hidden from them, so that particular card seemed pretty on the nose.

Marva set the second card next to the first. This one depicted a handsome older man with a raven perched above him, although it was in the reversed position, which Delia vaguely remembered meant something negative.

"The King of Swords, reversed," the psychic said. "A person of intelligence and cunning, someone who is at cross purposes to you."

Lately, the whole world felt as if it had been at cross purposes with her—and with Caleb—so Delia wasn't sure how much illumination that particular card provided.

The third card was placed next to the stern-looking king with his raven companion. It showed a woman sitting in the lotus position with a group of wands placed around her, but it, too, was reversed.

"The Seven of Wands reversed," Marva said. "This could signify some sort of attack—and of course, it doesn't need to be a physical attack. Mental and spiritual assaults leave their own wounds."

While that made sense, Delia didn't think she and Caleb needed to dig into the deeper meaning of the card, not when he'd quite literally been attacked by demons just the night before.

As she finished speaking, Marva pulled another card from the deck and set it below and slightly offset from the Moon card. On it, a dark-haired woman was being attacked by a pair of crows or ravens.

"The Two of Swords," she said. "Stalemate...or a difficult choice needs to be made."

Delia hoped the psychic was wrong about that. Stalemate meant they'd have to find a way to live with the current situation...and that was something she knew Caleb didn't want. He didn't move, his dark eyes intent on the cards that lay on the table before them, and she really wished right then that she was the kind of psychic who could read someone's mind.

Or maybe not. She didn't know for sure whether she wanted to go tromping around in a part-demon's brain.

But although her memories of the Tarot's meanings were hazy at best, even she recognized the card Marva set down next.

The Tower.

"It's not always a negative card," Marva said quietly. "In this case, where I'm working to get a sense of the energy surrounding your current circumstances, it could mean more a change of some sort, a shift. Something is about to break loose."

Well, that could be good or bad, depending on who was doing the breaking. Caleb rubbed his chin, looking thoughtful; he hadn't shaved that morning, and a faint haze of dark scruff covered his jaw.

If possible, it made him even more good-looking.

Not what you should be thinking about right now, she scolded herself.

"And the outcome," Marva continued as she pulled the final card from the deck.

Not much doubt about that one, either.

A dark crimson hood with a night forest scene contained within. Written at the bottom was *Death ∞ Rebirth.*

Caleb let out a rusty chuckle. "So...we're going to die?"

"The Death card usually shouldn't be taken so literally," Marva replied, looking unruffled. "In general, it usually means the end of a cycle and a new beginning. Often, it can be a hopeful card."

Judging by the way one corner of Caleb's mouth turned down, Delia got the feeling that he thought the psychic was blowing a bunch of sunshine up their collective asses.

"So, the outcome is a change of some sort," she said, doing her best to be politic.

"Yes," Marva replied. She closed her eyes and placed her hands on the tabletop, outstretched fingers covering most of the spread she'd just laid there.

Delia looked over at Caleb, and his shoulders hitched slightly. It seemed he didn't have any more idea of what the psychic was doing than she did.

Before the moment could get too uncomfortable, though, Marva opened her eyes and gave them both a thoughtful look, even as she lifted her hands from the spread and folded them in her lap.

"There is a difficult energy here," she said. "It comes from dark places and works in darkness. Whatever it is that you're currently dealing with, you need to be cautious...and you need to rely upon one another."

Since Delia thought she and Caleb were already doing that, she wasn't sure whether the psychic's advice had contributed much to the conversation.

Then again, they were certainly working together, but were they really relying on one another...trusting each other?

Delia had a feeling that Caleb had much more faith in her than vice versa. So far, it didn't seem as if he'd done anything terribly underhanded, but could she allow herself to implicitly trust someone who was part demon?

She didn't think she could answer that question. Not yet, anyway.

Caleb didn't seem to have the same reservations, though. "We are working together," he said. "She's already saved my ass several times. But do you have any words of advice for defeating this 'difficult energy'?"

The psychic's mouth curved into a smile. She wore deep red lipstick almost the same color as her silk kimono, and although her expression was amused, something in her dark eyes told Delia that Marva understood this was serious business.

Instead of replying right away, she selected a card from the center of the deck and laid it down on the table, covering the Death card.

The Lovers.

Almost at once, heat rose to Delia's cheeks, and she prayed the other two were too involved with looking down at the cards on the table to notice the way she'd blushed.

"Again, it's not always the literal meaning that's the true one," Marva said. "This card can also signal friendship or a partnership of some kind. But I feel that once you get past this chaotic energy"—she waved a hand over the inverse pyramid of cards that had constituted the main part of the reading—"then something good will come of it." She paused there, dark eyes keen as she took in her two clients and the expressions they wore. "Does that help to clarify the situation for you, or would you like me to do another reading?"

"Not a whole reading," Caleb responded before Delia could say anything. "But maybe a little more detail about the King of Swords there?"

Frankly, after seeing the Lovers card, she was ready to quit while she was ahead, but clearly her companion didn't have the same view of the situation.

Looking unruffled, Marva pulled another card out of the deck and laid it down on the table, a little separate from the others.

The Ten of Swords. Not exactly the most cheerful card, although in this deck, the image was still beautiful, showing a woman with her back to the viewer, standing in the middle of a bleak landscape while ten crows flew overhead.

"Painful endings," the psychic said, and Caleb lifted an eyebrow.

"For the King of Swords, or for us?"

Marva didn't blink. "I can't say for sure. All I know is that particular energy is connected to this person, whoever they are."

Typical. Although the cards the psychic had laid out did seem as though they had some relevance to her and Caleb's situation, Delia still couldn't help thinking it all felt like a bunch of double-speak. No absolutes, just a bunch of statements that were entirely up for interpretation.

This was one of the best psychics Las Vegas had to offer?

But then, even though Delia had only played around with Tarot and had never gotten serious about interpreting the cards, even she knew that it wasn't the sort of thing that would come right out and state an absolute fact. It was all about knowing the meaning of the cards and doing your best to see how they applied to your situation. Maybe Marva actually had told them everything they needed to know, but they were just too dense to figure it out.

"Well, thanks," Caleb said, and although he didn't add, *I guess,* Delia could tell he'd wanted to.

"I'm sorry I couldn't give you something more concrete," Marva replied. "But I know in my heart that this is an accurate reading. It's up to you to see how it fits your current situation."

Somehow, Delia managed to slap on one of her cheery real estate agent smiles, saying, "Oh, it's been very helpful. I think Caleb and I have a lot we need to discuss."

At least that much was true. She could tell he was fairly bursting to sit down and talk over what Marva had told them.

The psychic seemed to realize they were done, because she shuffled the cards from the spread back into her deck and returned it to its velvet pouch.

"Yes," she said, "I think you do."

Chapter Twenty-One

—‹‹‹‹·☾·›››—

WELL, THAT HAD BEEN A WASTE OF A hundred bucks. Sure, he'd barely miss it, but still, he'd kind of been hoping that Marva the Marvelous could have offered a bit more in the way of concrete advice.

About the only thing he could agree with was the Lovers card. Although Delia hadn't given him the slightest hint of encouragement, he had to hope he'd still be able to get her thawed out one of these days.

Or, as the psychic had pointed out, maybe that card really had meant only a partnership. Considering how Delia had agreed to lend advice and moral support for the reno at the Pueblo Street house, you could say they'd already become partners of a sort.

At least it was a nice day, the temperature way

above average for January, just kissing seventy. That meant he might be able to coax her into getting an outside table for lunch, preferably one that was off in a corner so they could talk about what they'd just heard at Marva's without having to worry about anyone eavesdropping.

"Buy you lunch?" he said, and Delia, who'd just pulled away from the curb, lifted an eyebrow.

"We only had breakfast a couple of hours ago."

"It'll be almost one by the time we find someplace to eat and sit down and get served," he responded, and she let out a small breath, as though she knew she might as well capitulate.

"All right," she said. "See what you can find that's near here."

He got out his phone and had Google pull up all the restaurants within a ten-minute drive of the route they were currently traveling.

"There's a kind of farm-to-table place about five minutes away," he said. "Turn left at the next light."

Delia obliged, following his directions until they pulled into the restaurant's parking lot. Since it was just past twelve-thirty by that point, the place looked packed, but luckily, someone was backing out just as they arrived, so they were able to snag a prime spot near the entrance.

"Do you have reservations?" the pretty blonde girl at the hostess station asked as they approached.

"Um, no," he said, then sent her a smile he knew generally made most of the female half of the population a little weak in the knees. "We were in the area and hoped you might have a table."

Next to him, Delia shifted her weight, and he wondered if she was going to say it was okay and that they'd just go somewhere else.

But then the hostess replied, "I think we might have something on the patio, if that's all right."

Since it was exactly what he wanted, Caleb knew it was much more than "all right." "That would be great," he said. "Thank you."

She led them out to the patio, where a wall fountain burbled quietly away on one side and a latticed pergola provided some shade. However, she took them to a table that was mostly in the sun, probably figuring that on a mild day like this, there was no reason to hide from its rays, which in the summer could be absolutely scorching.

After she handed them their menus and said a server would be out to see them shortly, she went back inside, leaving him and Delia alone. Her gaze was already fixed on the contents of the menu, but he guessed that wasn't what she was actually focused on.

"What do you think?" he asked.

Her mouth pursed. Without looking up, she said, "I think we should wait until we've ordered our food."

It turned out she was right, because their server appeared right then, a guy with extremely bleached hair who looked like he was probably a student at UNLV or one of the other local colleges.

They both ordered iced tea, although Caleb would have rather had a beer. Still, he took his lead from Delia—and was glad she'd already decided on something, because then he could do a quick survey of the menu and choose something for himself while she was still talking to their waiter.

A beef dip sounded good and he asked for that, along with extra French fries. He had no idea what awaited them in the next couple of hours, so he figured a little carb loading couldn't hurt.

Once the waiter had left, Delia said, "I'm still trying to unpack what Marva told us."

Caleb, on the other hand, thought it had all been fairly straightforward, now that he'd had a little time to ponder the reading the psychic had done for them. "I thought it was pretty obvious."

One russet eyebrow lifted slightly. "How so?"

"Well, the King of Pentacles totally must be Robert Hendricks."

She crossed her arms, settling against the back of her chair. "I doubt it's that simple."

"Why not?" he argued, then had to pause because their server returned with their iced teas and told them their sandwiches should be out in about ten minutes or so. After he'd gone, though,

Caleb thought it safe to resume the conversation. "It makes total sense that he's the King of Pentacles —'a person of intelligence and cunning.'"

"He doesn't seem that cunning to me," Delia returned, then reached for her iced tea so she could take a sip. "Successful, sure, but it's not like he's some kind of criminal mastermind."

Now it was Caleb's turn to lift an eyebrow. "Do you really think criminal masterminds go around advertising that they're criminals?"

She chuckled and sipped some more iced tea. "All right, you have a point there. But even if Robert Hendricks has engaged in some kind of underhanded behavior that we don't know about, do you really think he's the type to be summoning demons? He's a casino exec, for God's sake."

"Okay, on the surface, it might seem crazy," Caleb said. "But not every person who dabbles in that kind of stuff goes around dressed in all black with pentacles around their neck or whatever. I'm sure most of them do what they can to pretend they're good little Christians like their friends and neighbors."

Or at least, that was what he assumed. It wasn't as if he hung out with Satanists—they'd been pretty thin on the ground in Greencastle, Indiana —but he had the example of Jeffrey Whitcomb, the man whose identity Belial had subsumed, to prove that someone could dabble in the very darkest magic...and get possessed for his efforts...without anyone around them knowing what that person was involved with.

And all right, Whitcomb hadn't come to a very good end, but he'd lived a life of wealth and success before then, all fueled by the dark forces he'd summoned.

"Why would Mr. Hendricks even take such a huge risk, anyway? I mean, isn't there always a chance that any demon you call will eventually turn on you?"

"Oh, it's more than a chance," Caleb replied with a grin. "Demons are always out for themselves, and harder to control than a classroom full of kindergartners. Anyone who summons a demon and doesn't think there's going to be some blowback doesn't know what they're doing."

Delia seemed satisfied with that response, because she inclined her head toward him before saying, "Then I can't see how Robert Hendricks would be mixed up in something like that. You don't get to his position in life by taking those sorts of dangerous risks."

"I'm not so sure about that," Caleb said. "Usually when you have someone that successful, it's because they stepped on a few heads along the way."

Her lips curved in a wry smile. "Speaking from personal experience?"

"No," he replied easily. "I was going to inherit all my money, so I didn't need to waste my time stepping on heads."

"Why didn't you?" she asked, then went on, "I mean, with your father in Hell these past two years, wouldn't your mother have had him declared dead?"

"I'm sure she did," Caleb said. "But when I dropped in back home before coming here, we didn't go into a lot of details. She just gave me some seed money and sent me on my way."

Delia's expression shifted to one of equal parts sympathy and shock. "After thinking you were dead all that time? She didn't try to get you to stay in Greencastle?"

He really didn't want to reflect on that brittle little convo. Brooke Lockwood had had two years to come to terms with her new existence, and he'd been an interruption, nothing more. While she'd certainly passed on some good genes to him, she'd never been much of a mother.

"We weren't exactly your Hallmark holiday special kind of happy family," he replied. "So no, she didn't ask me to stick around. It's fine. I wouldn't have stayed even if she'd wanted me to."

Definitely not. One thing he'd enjoyed about the time he'd spent in California—even though he'd gone there at his father's behest—was the freedom the experience had given him. Sure, he was there looking for the *Project Demon Hunters* footage, but at least Daniel Lockwood had stayed back in Indiana, and therefore couldn't supervise every moment of his son's day.

It had been a welcome change of pace.

And when he escaped from Hell, he'd known there was no way in the goddamn world he'd go back to that same life, even with his father gone. He'd wanted something different.

Las Vegas was about as different from Greencastle, Indiana, as you could possibly get and still remain on the same continent.

Delia's mouth opened, but then she stopped herself. Had she been about to offer him some words of sympathy?

He didn't want that. No, all he wanted was to get to the bottom of this thing with Robert Hendricks and the demons.

If they were even connected. Delia seemed dubious, and Caleb supposed he couldn't blame her, not when all they really had to go on was a Tarot reading that could have been interpreted in a variety of ways.

"Well, you seem to have settled into the Las Vegas lifestyle pretty well," she remarked.

With that comment, he knew she wouldn't bring up the sore subject of his mother again unless he was the one to initiate the conversation.

It was the sort of thing a friend would do.

Were he and Delia friends?

He honestly couldn't say for sure. Some kind of business associates, he supposed, but he still couldn't get a clear read on how she felt about him.

Maybe that was for the best.

"Working on it," he said.

The waiter arrived with their food then, so they thanked him and were quiet for a bit while they picked up their sandwiches and had a few bites. Even though Caleb probably could have gone another hour or so before eating again, he had to admit that it felt good to take this break and replenish his stores of energy.

Being on edge all the time could take a lot out of you.

But once they paused to have some iced tea, he ventured, "We really need to pin Hendricks down. Maybe you're right and he really doesn't have anything to do with any of this. If we could get some kind of confession out of him, though, we'd have a better idea of what we're dealing with."

Delia wiped her fingers on her napkin and sent him a level stare. "Get him to confess how? We're not the police. We don't have any kind of leverage over him."

All right, she had a point. On the other hand, Caleb could think of a few ways to put the screws to the guy if necessary.

"Threaten to expose him," he said easily. "If

he's been summoning demons to do his dirty work, I kind of doubt that's the sort of thing he wants spread around town."

"I don't do blackmail, Caleb," Delia said, her tone flat.

"It's not blackmail," he countered, even as he realized there were obvious limits to how morally gray Delia was willing to be. "We're not trying to extort anything from him. We just want the truth —and to get him to back off from sending his imps after me."

"If they're even his imps at all."

Since Caleb didn't have any definitive proof that Hendricks had been controlling all those demon attackers, he knew he didn't have much of an argument to provide on that particular point. Instead, he dunked his beef dip in its *au jus* and took a bite first so he could collect his thoughts.

"Right," he said. "There's a whole lot we don't know. But the only way we're going to get anywhere is to go to the guy directly."

Delia didn't look too impressed by that line of thinking. "And risk offending someone who's technically a client of mine."

"Whatever he's paying you, I'll double it," Caleb said. After all, it was only money...and he could always get more.

"It's not about what he's paying me," she responded. "It's about offending someone who has a lot of connections in this town. If it turns out we're wrong, he's going to tell everyone that I'm a crackpot who believes demons are real."

Even though Hendricks was the person who'd first brought up the subject of demons to Delia. However, since Caleb was forced to admit her concerns were valid, he only said, "Well, you do get rid of ghosts."

"Not the same thing, and you know it."

They lapsed into an uneasy silence then, each of them returning to their food because they weren't quite sure what they should say to each other.

But after he'd eaten one half of his beef dip, he sipped some iced tea to wash it down, then said, "I know I'm asking a lot of you."

Her cool green eyes met his. "You are."

"If I'm right—if he really is the one who summoned those demons—then this is the only way to stop him. People who dabble in this kind of stuff don't want to be found out."

For a second or two, she didn't say anything. Her fingers tapped against the side of her plate, and she looked off toward the fountain as though hoping she would find some kind of insight from watching the way the water splashed in the cool January sun.

"Maybe you have a point there. But there's still so much that could go wrong."

She hadn't said she wouldn't do it, which meant she must be backing down just a little.

Good. Now all he had to do was reassure her that she wouldn't be going in to beard the lion in his den all on her own.

"Not as much as you think," he said. "You can have your phone in your purse and have a call connected to me so I can hear everything—and record it, just to be safe. The first hint of trouble, and I'll teleport into his office and get you out of there."

"Just like that," she said, now looking almost amused.

"Just like that," he echoed. "One of the perks of being part demon, you know? I've done it before—carrying another person isn't a big deal. And since Robert Hendricks is supposedly just a normal guy, there won't be much he can do to stop me."

Delia's lips pressed together. He wasn't sure whether their soft, rosy hue was natural or whether she used some sort of lip stain. If it was makeup, then it was pretty sturdy, since she didn't seem to have eaten off any of it.

"And you don't think he's going to be a little startled by the two of us just disappearing into thin air like that?"

"Why would he be? If things go sideways, it'll be because he definitely was the person behind summoning those demons, and that means seeing us vanish isn't going to throw him off very much."

Once again, she went quiet as she seemed to weigh all the various arguments he'd presented.

"Besides," Caleb went on, "I'll disguise myself, just like I always do. He won't even know who I am."

"He'll sure as hell know who I am," she returned without missing a beat.

"Yes," he said. "But he already knows you're not the person who's been winning big at his casino...and others. What he won't know is who you've been working with, and we need to keep it that way."

She picked up a French fry and dipped it in some ketchup—not, he thought, because she was particularly hungry, but because she needed some cover while she pondered his proposal.

"He won't be able to retaliate," Caleb said, hoping this angle might make Delia a little more receptive to his plan. "Doing that would only prove he's been the bad guy all along."

"You sound very confident."

"It's because I am."

She popped the French fry in her mouth, then followed it with some iced tea. "All right," she said after a few more seconds. "I still don't like it, but you're right—things can't keep going on like this indefinitely."

Caleb wouldn't allow himself to smile...he didn't want her to think he was being too triumphant...but he nodded. "Thanks, Delia."

He didn't add, *You won't regret it,* because he knew if this all blew up in their faces, she might very much regret throwing in her lot with him rather than telling him it was his problem and that he needed to fix it on his own.

She wasn't that kind of person, though. In her mind, she'd probably already decided where her allegiance lay...and it wasn't with Robert Hendricks.

And that could only be a good thing.

Chapter Twenty-Two

———‹‹‹‹‹ ◎ ›››·——

Delia seriously couldn't believe she'd agreed to this. Did Caleb have some kind of demonic powers of persuasion in addition to all those other otherworldly abilities, like teleporting and shapeshifting?

Maybe so. At this point, it probably didn't matter so much, not when she'd already pulled the trigger.

After lunch, she'd called Robert Hendricks and told him she had some new information she needed to discuss, and was wondering if he could make some time for a short meeting?

He'd agreed at once, although he'd added that he had appointments all afternoon and hoped she wouldn't mind coming by around six.

No argument there. Or rather, although she

couldn't help being uneasy about meeting the man after dark, she knew that postponing their confrontation until the next day wasn't an option. Not when both she and Caleb wanted to get this over with.

They'd gone to her house to plot, partly because it was closer to the casino than Caleb's place in Winterwood and partly because they'd both agreed that, since nothing untoward had happened at her home, it just seemed safer to be there. Sure, they'd splashed what felt like gallons of holy water around his house, but still, it was on the demons' radar, and that meant it felt safer to be somewhere else entirely.

The plan was simple enough. Since Robert Hendricks was already expecting her, no one would think anything strange about her going up to his office on the tenth floor of the hotel. And because Caleb could travel anywhere in the blink of an eye, they decided he would be gambling a few blocks away at the Palace Station, a casino he rarely visited and one that never seemed to have any kind of demonic activity. At the same time, he'd have his Airpods in and would be listening to her conversation with Hendricks, ready to jump in the second something went wrong.

On the surface, that all seemed fine. At the same time, Delia couldn't help being uneasy at the idea of having Caleb in a different hotel entirely. Sure, he could travel in an instant...or at least, he said he could...but she still didn't like knowing her only backup wasn't there in the building with her.

But because they couldn't risk having any demons in the vicinity pick up on his presence, they didn't have a whole lot of options.

Going to her house also allowed her to change out of her jeans and sweater and into a skirt and blouse and jacket and heels. Robert Hendricks had always seen her in work clothes during the times they'd met, so she didn't see the point in arousing any suspicions by appearing casually attired at his office.

When she emerged from her bedroom, she thought she noticed a flicker of admiration in Caleb's dark eyes, although he sounded businesslike enough when he spoke.

"I don't think we should drive over there," he said. "Casinos have security cameras everywhere, and I don't want them to get any footage of us arriving in the same car. It's better if we teleport and appear in a spot without any surveillance."

She crossed her arms. Just in case things got messy, she'd worn one of her less favorite shirts, the stiff black one that always made her feel like an FBI agent or something. "You just said they have security cameras everywhere."

"All right, almost everywhere," he amended, then got up from the couch where he'd been waiting for her. "But there's a service hallway just off the kitchen that doesn't have any. It'll be the best place for us to appear."

A frown creased her brows, telling Caleb she wasn't too thrilled by that suggestion. "And have someone carrying a tray of wings and jalapeno poppers out to the casino floor stumble over us?"

"It's better than arriving in one of the restrooms and having the security cameras see us the second we walk out the door...and risking someone really looking at the footage and picking up on any discrepancies. The last thing we want is for someone to notice that we never went in."

Maybe he had a point there. And while Delia could see why he didn't want the cameras in the parking structure to get any images of them arriving in the same car, she knew he was relying on luck to make sure no one walked out of the casino kitchen at exactly the wrong time.

Then again, he must have a whole hell of a lot of luck in his back pocket. Otherwise, he wouldn't have been able to free himself from Hell in the first place.

However he'd managed it. He hadn't provided much detail on that point, and she hadn't pressed the issue, not when it was still somewhat unbelievable to her that he'd been trapped there at all.

Well, she'd worry about that later. She had much bigger claims on her brain space at the moment.

"All right," she said, and looked over at the clock that hung on the wall opposite the fireplace. "Five minutes until six. We should probably get going."

He nodded, then came over to where she stood a few feet away from the sofa. "You'll need to hold on tight," he said as he extended his hands.

This was the part she really wasn't looking forward to. Not touching him, *per se*—his fingers were warm and friendly as they closed on hers— but just the idea of somehow folding space to get them from here to there.

No other words. Just an odd little blink of darkness, and then they were standing in a corridor that looked very plain and industrial compared to the flashy, neon-lit casino floor just a few yards down the hall.

It was deserted, just as Caleb had predicted, and Delia began to let out a sigh of relief —

— only to have him press her against the wall in a faux embrace when a server wearing one of the Dunes' brightly colored uniforms emerged from the kitchen, a tray of appetizers in one hand.

"Just play along," he murmured in her ear.

As much as she wanted to push him away, she knew doing so would only alert the waitress that they were loitering in the hallway for some other purpose than grabbing a kiss in a location that had few observers.

So she allowed him to continue pressing his body to hers, although she noticed he didn't try to steal a kiss. This close, it was impossible to ignore the strong muscles in his chest, or the faint warm scent that must have been his alone, since he'd showered at her house that morning, and she knew she sure as hell didn't have any cologne or after-shave in her guest bathroom.

"All clear," he said a moment later, stepping away so she could regain her balance.

She ran her hands down her skirt and straightened her jacket, telling herself that the slight shaki-ness she detected in her fingers had everything to do with their close call and nothing at all to do with the way they'd practically been kissing just a moment earlier.

Before Delia could comment—not that she even knew exactly what she planned to say—he pulled his phone and a single Airpod out of his pocket. "You ready?" he asked as he inserted the earbud in his left ear.

A few moments earlier, she would have said yes. Now she knew she felt way too off-balance and wanted to scold herself for being so susceptible to his physical proximity.

Never in a million years would she confess such

weakness to him, though. Instead, she gave him what she hoped was a brisk nod. "I'm ready."

"I'm going to call you now," he told her, then touched his phone's screen.

A second later, her phone started ringing from inside her purse. "Okay, we're good," she told him as she accepted the call, and he nodded.

"Perfect. The coast is clear again, so I'm going to bip out of here. Just remember that I'll be listening the whole time. You've got nothing to worry about."

Delia thought she had plenty to worry about no matter what he said, but she didn't bother to contradict him. "Then I'll head upstairs."

He placed a hand on her shoulder and gave her an encouraging squeeze...and then promptly disappeared.

Whew. Maybe someday she'd get used to all this.

Doing her best to look unruffled, she reached up to smooth her hair and then headed out to the casino floor so she could make her way over to the elevators. Luckily, no one seemed to be paying much attention to her, but why should they? It wasn't as if Robert Hendricks' offices on the tenth floor were locked off in some restricted penthouse. Anyone could go up there...although she had a feeling that any interlopers who tried to go into his office without permission would soon find a security guard escorting them off the premises.

She'd been invited here, so Delia wasn't too worried about getting hauled away for trespassing. No, she was much, much more concerned about exactly what the hell she was supposed to say to Robert. Caleb seemed certain he was their villain, but she wasn't nearly so sure. Although she'd already decided that her part-demon client was the one who deserved her loyalty the most, she still didn't think it was the best idea in the world to napalm the bridges she'd built with Mr. Hendricks.

And yet, here she was.

Head up, she exited the elevator and made her way to his office. Today, the double glass doors that opened onto the space were unlocked, signaling that he was waiting for her, so she went on in.

He'd been standing by one of the windows, watching the ever-changing neon lights of the Strip, but he turned around almost at once and sent her a pleasant smile.

"Delia. Thank you again for accommodating my schedule and coming at the end of the day. I hope I haven't interfered with any of your plans."

Right then, the only plan she had in mind was the one she and Caleb had cooked up together... and maybe grabbing some takeout afterward if she somehow managed to survive this encounter with her dignity intact.

"No, not at all," she said, wishing Robert wasn't acting so nice. This would have been a lot easier if he was some arrogant asshole who thought everyone else on the planet had been put there to serve him. "I'm glad you could take the meeting—there are a couple of things I needed to talk to you about."

His expression revealed nothing except simple curiosity. "Have you learned something new?"

Oh, she'd learned a whole bunch of things. Whether any of them were particularly relevant to his activities was a whole other question.

"There's definitely been some detectable demon activity," she replied. "A couple of attacks."

At once, Robert Hendricks' brows drew together. "Not against you, I hope."

"No," Delia said quickly. "I'm fine. And it wasn't the sort of thing that would have sent anyone to the hospital."

Well, she hoped not. Caleb had mentioned a traffic accident, but he hadn't seemed too worried about the other parties involved. Was that because he'd seen them walk away, or was it simply that he was part demon and therefore didn't give a shit?

She didn't want to believe that of him. Also, she'd seen his face when he talked about his mother. Those fleeting expressions of guilt and worry...yes, and of sadness...didn't seem like the sort of looks a being who cared about no one other than himself would have worn.

"That's good to hear," Robert said. Then his head tilted slightly as he regarded her for a moment. "Do you have any idea who might have summoned the things?"

Talk about giving her an opening she could drive a tank right through.

She pulled in a breath.

"That's why I wanted to talk to you," she replied, glad that she sounded so steady, so brisk and unconcerned. "You see, I've uncovered some evidence that suggests you might have been the one to do the summoning."

For the longest moment, he only stared at her. Surely as soon as he opened his mouth, he'd tell her how ridiculous she was being.

But he didn't.

No, instead, he began to laugh.

His reaction was so surreal that for a second or two, Delia wondered if he'd somehow misheard her. After all, who in the world would break into cackles of almost hysterical laughter after being told they were a possible suspect in a series of demon attacks?

After a few seconds, though, he seemed to regain control of himself, although he still grinned at her like a shark who'd just swallowed a whole school of minnows.

"That's quite the imagination you have, Ms. Dunne," he said. "I'm sorry for the laughter just now, but I couldn't think of how else to respond."

A flat denial would have seemed much more appropriate, but she thought it better not to provoke him too much.

"It's not my imagination," she replied, mentally adding, *Although it could be the imagination of Marvelous Marva.* "Some of the clues just don't add up."

His expression abruptly sobered. "And your accusations don't add up, either. For one thing, why in the world would I hire a demon-finder if I was actually controlling a bunch of them?"

She'd already pondered that angle to the problem, so she didn't even hesitate as she said, "Because it wasn't your own demons you were worried about. No, you were much more concerned about the one who's been winning all that money off you and the other casino owners. Probably you were thinking that if I reported on any of your pet demons, you could just ignore my findings. I guess my question is, why would a guy like you be messing around with summoning demons in the first place? The corner office and the big salary weren't enough for you?"

"I'm afraid you have no idea what you're talking about," he said, his voice flat, all humor gone, and she crossed her arms.

"Maybe I don't. In that case, please enlighten me. Why were you the one to approach me and not some other casino exec? Were you trying to keep tabs on me so I couldn't figure out what you were really up to?"

His eyes narrowed, and in that moment, the first trickle of fear moved down Delia's back. If asked, she would have said that Robert Hendricks was a pleasant-looking guy, someone who took care of himself but didn't try to roll back the clock and use a bunch of treatments that only made him appear desperate rather than fifteen years younger.

Now, though...now she saw the cruelty in his gaze and the set of his mouth as though viewing them for the first time.

Maybe she was.

"What if I double what I'm paying you?" he asked, his words an echo of Caleb's offer during lunch. In Robert Hendricks' case, though, she doubted he'd upped the ante merely to make their arrangement even more appealing.

No, he wanted to see if he could buy her off.

"People are getting hurt," she said. "Someone's probably going to die if all this crap keeps up. There's no amount of money in the world that would let me stand by and watch that happen."

His lips thinned. "Then I'm afraid we're at an impasse. And that can mean only one thing."

She began to ask him exactly what he intended

by that comment...and then took a step back in horror.

Red glowed from his eyes, and his face began to shift and stretch, mouth widening and baring pointed yellow teeth, while his features sharpened and his skin grew scaly, morphing into the stuff of nightmares.

Into a demon, in fact.

Without thinking, she reached into her purse, fingers scrabbling for the little purification kit she always carried with her...and its accompanying bottle of holy water.

"Back off, demon!" she cried—more to warn a listening Caleb about what had just happened than because she thought Robert Hendricks...or whatever the hell that thing was...would actually heed her warning.

And she splashed about half the vial's contents onto the creature.

It screamed and recoiled, smoke bubbling up from its flesh everywhere the holy water had hit. A second later, Caleb appeared right in front of her, blocking the demon from physically retaliating. Even in the strain of that moment, he'd kept the borrowed face he wore when they'd appeared in the hallway outside the kitchen, and she couldn't ignore the stab of relief that went through her.

With any luck, the demon would have no idea of who he was dealing with.

"Get back!" Caleb yelled, and she did as she was told, knowing this was not the time to argue.

If he wanted to play macho demon slayer, he was welcome to do so. Besides, he presumably knew what he was doing, while Delia knew she sure as hell didn't. The holy water had worked, but she'd already used up half of it, and she had a feeling the bit that remained wasn't going to be enough to get rid of the creature that had possessed Robert Hendricks' body.

Or maybe he'd been a demon all along, and she'd been lulled into a false sense of security by the supposedly normal life and background Pru had dug up about him.

Well, they could figure all that out later...if she and Caleb survived this encounter, of course.

The demon hissed at him, baring yellow fangs that were the polar opposite of Robert's straight white teeth. "This is no concern of yours, demon," it said, and Caleb only grinned at the thing.

Delia could see why. If the demon had addressed him that way, then it probably had no idea who he really was and thought he was another full demon like it. Obviously, a regular mortal would never have been able to pop into existence out of nowhere the way Caleb had just done.

"Oh, you've made it my concern," he replied. "I don't know what kind of game you've been playing here, but it stops now."

He reached into his jacket pocket and pulled out a vial of holy water identical to the one Delia still held, then splashed some of the blessed liquid on the creature. It screamed in agony, so loudly that she thought it was a good thing Robert Hendricks' office was located down this corridor away from the guest rooms, or someone surely must have heard it and called security...or come to investigate for themselves.

What they would have found would require a level of explanation she didn't think she was capable of right now.

But the demon was also backing away. Clearly ready to finish the thing off, Caleb pursued, throwing more holy water at the creature, tossing the used-up bottle aside once it was empty before pulling another one from his jacket pocket.

Exactly how many of those things did he have? And where had he gotten them?

Well, that part was easy enough to answer. He'd probably gone poking around while she was in the shower this morning, somehow sensing it would be better to be armed with the only weapon that seemed to work against the things.

The whole time, the demon screamed and writhed...right until the minute when it reached the back wall of the office, one that was covered in glass and let in yet another jaw-dropping view of the Strip. Neon light silhouetted the demon's ugly form.

And then it disappeared.

"Coward," Caleb said, turning toward Delia and wearing what she could only describe as the ultimate in shit-eating grins.

She was about to return the smile—and stopped when a heavy arm snaked around her throat and dragged her backward.

"Never let your guard down, my dear," the thing growled into her ear, even as her heart pounded and the pits of her disliked black shirt grew damp with sweat. Then it looked across the room at Caleb. "Drop this whole thing, or your girlfriend here gets it."

Caleb's eyes met hers, and then he gave a very small nod.

What the hell was that supposed to mean?

"She's not my girlfriend," he said, his tone conversational. "Just a partner in crime, I suppose."

The demon made a hissing sound that might have been its version of a laugh. "Not a very good pair of criminals, I'm afraid."

"Maybe not," Delia remarked, a little surprised how calm she sounded, considering the way her body had reacted when the creature grabbed her. She was trying not to breathe in too deeply, because man, that thing stank worse than a port-a-potty at a music festival. "But we still have a few tricks up our sleeve."

With that, she dumped the rest of her bottle of holy water on the creature's arm, while at the same time ramming the spike of her stiletto heel right into the big, scaly foot that had busted its way out of "Robert's" nine-hundred-dollar Manolo Blahnik loafers.

Even though the shriek it let out was loud enough to rupture an eardrum, Delia couldn't help experiencing a surge of gratification...of power...at its reaction.

These things weren't invincible.

At the same moment, Caleb blinked over next to them and splashed more holy water on the demon, causing its flesh to smoke and bubble. Its grip on her throat loosened, and she took a step backward, gasping for air.

Another splash of holy water, and then Caleb intoned, "I banish you, Calach! I send you back to the unholy realms!"

It hissed again, even as it spat back, "You're no priest! You don't have the power!"

"I don't need the power," he said, looking remarkably calm. "I've got the holy water. More importantly, I know your name."

The demon snarled, but Caleb appeared unim-pressed.

"Go to Hell, Calach," he said, and splashed two more vials' worth of holy water right in its face.

Unearthly flesh began to melt like a candle left out in the sun. The demon screeched, clawing at the holy water glistening on its scaly skin, which only served to accelerate the ruin of its hideous visage.

And then it disappeared.

Delia looked around wildly, sure it must have just blinked to another corner of the office, but no, it really was gone.

"You banished it?" she asked. "I thought you needed an exorcist for that kind of thing."

"Nope," Caleb said cheerfully as he came over to her. "That demon wasn't possessing anyone."

"But it looked like Robert Hendricks—"

"It did," Caleb cut in, although in a friendly way, as if he was trying to keep her from tying herself up in knots over the situation. "And it probably started out by possessing him. But then it would have just...taken over."

A shudder worked its way down Delia's spine as she thought of Robert Hendricks' friends and family going along as if nothing had changed, and all the while, a demonic creature had usurped the face and body of the person they thought they knew.

"Anyway," Caleb went on, "once it was no longer possessing him and instead had only stolen his identity, the demon could get banished by anyone armed with a little holy water—and its name."

"Which you knew," she replied, knowing her voice sounded way too shaky.

"I did," he said, and his dark eyes practically danced with mischief. "You spend a couple of years in Hell, you learn a few things."

"Well, thank God for that," Delia said.

They looked at each other for a few seconds, and then they both burst out laughing.

Chapter Twenty-Three

—‹‹‹‹ ◐ ›››—

CALEB WAS GLAD TO SEE DELIA HADN'T been so rattled by their encounter with the demon that she wasn't willing to listen to his advice as to what they should do next.

"The security cameras would have seen you come in here," he said, and she flicked a worried glance toward the double doors that led into Hendricks' office. "So you need to go back out the same way."

"Isn't the Dunes' security team going to have a few questions when they discover I was the last person to see their main man alive?"

She'd looked calm enough as she made that query, but he could see the way her hand shook as she lifted it to push back a stray lock of coppery hair.

"Probably," he admitted. "But there's nothing

to show what actually went down in here, and I have a feeling it's going to be a little while before they even realize Hendricks is missing."

Her gaze moved past him to take in their surroundings. While there were a couple of wet blotches here and there on the floor from all the holy water that had been thrown around, that would dry soon enough, and because none of the furniture had gotten knocked over or even moved, you couldn't tell that they'd had an altercation with a demon in the office just a few minutes earlier.

There wasn't a body, either, making it that much harder to figure out exactly what had happened to the erstwhile Mr. Hendricks.

"All right," Delia said. "And then what...meet you in that same hallway where we first materialized?"

Caleb had already thought about that. Although there were cameras everywhere, they couldn't pick up on every single person who came and went in the casino. It had been important for them to not be seen arriving together, but he didn't think there would be a problem with her heading out the front door and grabbing a taxi.

When he explained this to her, though, she only frowned.

"You think someone isn't going to ask why I didn't take my own car?"

"They might," he replied. "But you can just say

it wouldn't start or something, and that you took a taxi here because you didn't want to miss your meeting. Unlike an Uber, you can't be tracked in a taxi as long as you pay cash."

"All right," Delia said. She still looked a little reluctant, but she didn't seem willing to argue the point any further. "And then what?"

"Then we have the post-mortem," he said, and smiled. "Your place or mine?"

In the end, they decided it was smarter to have the taxi drop Delia off at her house, just because that was the logical place she would have headed after she met with Robert Hendricks. To make everything look on the up and up, Caleb blinked himself home first so he could get his Range Rover and drive to her place.

Nothing in the house had been disturbed...and he had a feeling he wouldn't have to worry about that anymore, not with Calach banished. He'd been a higher order of demon than the ones he'd summoned to stick a crowbar into the safe existence Caleb had created for himself, so there wasn't much chance of any further demonic interference now that the lead guy had been sent back to Hell where he belonged.

Well, no more demonic interference for now, anyway.

When he arrived at Delia's house and knocked at the door, she answered wearing the same black leggings and big black sweatshirt she'd worn the night before, signaling that she'd been in a hurry to get out of the outfit she'd worn during the confrontation with the demon.

He couldn't really blame her for that. Most likely, it would take a couple of dry cleanings to get all the stink out of those clothes.

An open bottle of a red blend from Trader Joe's sat on the kitchen counter. "Want some?" she asked as he followed her inside.

"Hell, yeah."

She grinned, then went over to the cupboard to fetch another wine glass. After pouring him a healthy measure of the red, she said, "Let's go sit down."

As he'd done the other times he'd visited her house, Caleb made sure to seat himself in one of the club chairs rather than next to Delia on the couch. While she'd been much friendlier these past couple of days, he knew he couldn't push it...even if he also couldn't quite forget the way it had felt to embrace her in that corridor off the kitchens at the Dunes.

Too bad that embrace had been all pretend.

At least on her part.

"How're you doing?" he asked, and she grimaced.

"I'll probably have a stiff neck and nightmares for a couple of days, but I'll get over it."

Caleb had no doubt of that. For all her outward prettiness, she was tough as nails.

"Do you think they'll question me?" she said next.

"The cops?"

She nodded.

"At some point, probably. But there's nothing to connect you to Robert Hendricks' disappearance, and my being over here right now will only help you with your alibi."

One eyebrow arched as she sipped some wine. "How so?"

"Because we've already decided your story is that you had to take a taxi to the hotel because your car wouldn't start. You can tell them I came over to help you out with jump-starting it or whatever."

Apparently, she thought that particular detail was a decent addition to the alibi they'd already concocted, because she nodded and helped herself to another swallow of wine.

Caleb thought that looked like a good idea and sipped some of his red blend as well. It wasn't top-tier stuff by any stretch of the imagination, but he still thought it would do the trick.

"Okay, so hopefully we've got that part figured

out," she said. "But what about the demons? Are they going to keep attacking you?"

"I doubt it," Caleb replied, since he'd already pondered that question on the drive over here. "I think Robert Hendricks summoned Calach, for whatever reason, and then once it had taken over his appearance and his life, it was the one calling the lesser demons to try to kick my ass—or get rid of me permanently. I still haven't muddled my way through that part. But my gut instinct is that he was mostly trying to scare me off from visiting any casinos."

Delia's greenish eyes glinted with amusement. "Did he?"

"For now," he said, and thought he saw a flicker of approval cross her face. "Sure, Calach has been sent back to Hell...but I don't know for sure whether there are any other demons hanging around here and watching to make sure I toe the line. I haven't sensed them, although that doesn't necessarily mean anything. Now that they know I'm here—even if they haven't been able to puzzle out exactly who I am beyond not being completely human—they could be taking measures to disguise their demon natures."

It wasn't a prospect he much enjoyed contemplating, and since Delia frowned slightly before she sipped some more of her wine, Caleb could tell she wasn't exactly thrilled, either.

"Or it could be that Calach was the only demon here," he added, since he didn't want their conversation to turn into a shit spiral. After all, they'd gotten rid of the creature who'd usurped Robert Hendrick's existence, and that was a pretty big accomplishment. At some point, they'd need to figure out why Hendricks had summoned a demon in the first place...and probably try to do a little more digging about The Styx Group, because he couldn't shake the feeling that the mysterious company was involved in all this somehow. For now, though, Caleb was okay with resting on his laurels. "And if Calach was the only demon in Las Vegas, then I suppose I have carte blanche to do what I want. But it just seems smarter to me to do what we already talked about—invest my money in other ventures and stay away from the casinos for a while."

"But what will you do for fun?" she asked next, mouth quirking into a half-smile, and he couldn't help but shake his head.

"Maybe I'll get a boat or something. Then again, I have a feeling I'm going to be pretty occupied with the reno on Pueblo Street for the next few months. That should keep me out of trouble for a while."

"A little while," Delia commented, amused expression not budging in the slightest.

She probably had a point. Still, even though

winning at the casinos had both helped him fill his empty days and plump up his bank accounts quite nicely, he knew he was sitting on enough cash that he wouldn't need to replenish those funds for quite some time.

"Or maybe," he said, as a sudden idea occurred to him, "I should work on getting my real estate license. Then I would have more leverage when looking for investment properties."

"Seriously?" she responded. Judging by the way her mouth had pursed slightly, Caleb could tell she wasn't totally thrilled by the idea.

All the more reason to pursue it. He liked Delia...he probably didn't want to admit to himself exactly how much he liked her...but he also liked to mess with her head just the littlest bit.

Getting to do so on an ongoing basis seemed like a pleasing prospect.

"Maybe we'll even go into business together," he said, and now she actually chuckled.

"Isn't that kind of what we were doing already, considering you want me to basically design the Pueblo Street house for you?"

He supposed one could look at their arrangement that way.

"Sure," he said easily. "But this would be more like a real partnership...if you're interested. I just think we work pretty well together."

For a long moment, she didn't say anything,

and instead gazed down into her half-drunk glass of wine as though she was hoping to discover the mysteries of the ages in there.

Then she looked up and gave him a lopsided smile.

"Sure," she replied, then added, "I think this might be the beginning of a beautiful friendship."

In answer to that comment, he clinked his glass against hers.

They could start with friendship...and then see where things led from there.

He thought he might be all right with that.

———

Vegas Slayers continues with *Devil in the Details,* releasing in June 2025!

Also by Christine Pope

Unquiet Souls

Unbound Spirits

Unholy Ground

Unseen Voices

Unmarked Graves

Unbroken Vows

Unholy Night

THE DJINN WARS*

(Paranormal Romance)

Chosen

Taken

Fallen

Broken

Forsaken

Forbidden

Awoken

Illuminated

Stolen

Forgotten

Driven

Unspoken

Hidden

Written

Given

Mistaken

FAMILIAR SPIRITS*

(Cozy Mystery/Paranormal Romance)

Spells and Spaniels

Cauldrons and Cats

Hexes and Hedgehogs

Charms and Chihuahuas

Runes and Ravens

LATTES AND LEVITATION*

(Cozy Mystery/Paranormal Romance)

Caffeine Before Curses

Muffins After Magic

Pastries and Prophecies

Eclairs and Ectoplasm

Sugar Skulls and Specters

Wedding Cakes and Wishes

HEDGEWITCH FOR HIRE*

(Cozy Mystery/Paranormal Romance)

Grave Mistake

Social Medium

Household Demons

Perpetual Potion

Jingle Spells

Wandering Monsters

Uninvited Ghosts

Prophet Motive

Ballroom Bits

Spell Check

Brew Confessions

Charm School (July 2024)

UNEXPECTED MAGIC*

(Urban Fantasy/Paranormal Romance)

Found Objects

Finders, Keepers

Lost and Found

Finding Destiny

THE WITCHES OF WHEELER PARK*

(Paranormal Romance)

Storm Born

Thunder Road

Winds of Change

Mind Games

A Wheeler Park Christmas

Blood Ties

Healing Hands

Wishful Thinking

Smoke and Mirrors

MISS PRIMM'S ACADEMY FOR WAYWARD
WITCHES*

(Fantasy/Academy Romance)

Misspelled

Dispelled

Expelled

THE DEVIL YOU KNOW*

(Paranormal Romance)

Sympathy for the Devil

Charmed, I'm Sure

A Wing and a Prayer

Wish Upon a Star

THE WITCHES OF CANYON ROAD*

(Paranormal Romance)

Hidden Gifts

Darker Paths

Mysterious Ways

A Canyon Road Christmas

Demon Born

An Ill Wind

Higher Ground

Haunted Hearts

THE WITCHES OF CLEOPATRA HILL*

(Paranormal Romance)

Darkangel

Darknight

Darkmoon

Sympathetic Magic

Protector

Spellbound

A Cleopatra Hill Christmas

Impractical Magic

Strange Magic

The Arrangement

Defender

Bad Blood

Deep Magic

Darktide

Star Bright

THE WATCHERS TRILOGY*

(Paranormal Romance)

Falling Dark

Dead of Night

Rising Dawn

THE SEDONA FILES*

(Paranormal/Science Fiction Romance)

Bad Vibrations

Desert Hearts

Angel Fire

Star Crossed

Falling Angels

Enemy Mine

TALES OF THE LATTER KINGDOMS*

(Fantasy Romance)

All Fall Down

Dragon Rose

Binding Spell

Ashes of Roses

One Thousand Nights

Threads of Gold

The Wolf of Harrow Hall

Moon Dance

The Song of the Thrush

THE GAIAN CONSORTIUM SERIES*

(Science Fiction Romance)

Beast (free prequel novella)

Blood Will Tell

Breath of Life

The Gaia Gambit

The Mandala Maneuver

The Titan Trap

The Zhore Deception

The Refugee Ruse

STANDALONE TITLES

Hearts on Fire (Paranormal Romance)

Taking Dictation (Contemporary Romance)

Golden Heart (Gaslamp Fantasy Romance)

Night Music: A Modern Reimagining of The Phantom
of the Opera (Contemporary Romance)

Ghost Dance: A Sequel to Gaston Leroux's The
Phantom of the Opera (Historical Mystery/Romance)

Flight Before Christmas (Fantasy Romance)

* Indicates a completed series

About the Author

USA Today bestselling author Christine Pope has been writing stories ever since she commandeered her family's Smith-Corona typewriter back in grade school. Her work includes paranormal romance, cozy paranormal mystery, and urban fantasy, among others. She makes her home in Arizona.

Christine Pope on the Web:
www.christinepope.com

facebook.com/ChristinePopeAuthor
bsky.app/profile/christinepope.bsky.social
bookbub.com/authors/christine-pope

www.ingramcontent.com/pod-product-compliance
Lightning Source LLC
Chambersburg PA
CBHW021129260626
47169CB00005B/1525